Fedowar Press Presents

ALWAYS DARKER INSIDE

A Cursed Objects Anthology

www.FedowarPress.com

ISBN-13 (Digital): 978-1-956492-74-3
ISBN-13 (Paperback): 978-1-956492-75-0

Edited by D.W. Hitz & Heather Ann Larson
Cover Art by Matt Seff Barnes
Interior Design by D.W. Hitz

Collections from Fedowar Press

Contents

The Occurrence on Crantor 4
Patrick C. Harrison III

PLANET 871509Y—WHAT CAME TO be known as Philosopher Rock—was discovered just under 200 Earth years earlier by a deep-space drone searching the outer reaches of the Milky Way for life. Life, it had not found. No such discovery had yet been made beyond Earth, lest one considered the replicating vapor found beneath the ice of Europa *life*.

What the drone found and documented was Philosopher Rock, and that discovery birthed more mysteries than any alien life ever could. It was a waterless, airless, lifeless planet. Truth be told, it was like the planet Mercury in many ways, a relatively small planet made mostly of basaltic rock.

Only, on Philosopher Rock, much of the basalt was inexplicably *carved*, as if an army of stonemasons had been whisked away from Earth in secret, traveled 50,000 light years, and spent many centuries turning Planet 871509Y into the universe's largest and grandest art exhibition.

Why the connection to Earth? Couldn't an alien race have carved Philosopher Rock many millions of years ago, back when, perhaps, the planet was inhabitable?

Only if the aliens were time travelers with an intense fascination for humanity's greatest thinkers. Indeed, that was the theory of some.

If the Dutch explorers were shocked by the hundreds of moai upon their arrival at Easter Island in the 1700s, they would have fallen over dead with awe when laying their eyes upon Philosopher Rock. Every sculpture—of which there were many hundreds of thousands, as estimated by AI and scientists alike after reviewing photographs from the deep-space drone—was of a human head. Not a full bust—rarely a neck and never shoulders and chest—but just the heads of thousands and thousands of people, all different, ranging in sizes from a few meters tall to over a hundred meters tall.

They were carved into mountainsides and boulders all across the planet with expert precision, displaying deep knowledge of the anatomy of the human head and face. By some as yet unidentified mechanism of technology or mysticism, 431 of the stone heads floated through the air of Philosopher Rock, as if they were as weightless as hot air balloons. The largest one of these was over fifty-four meters tall and estimated to weigh several tons. Yet, there it floated, the stone head of Seneca the Stoic.

What gave Philosopher Rock its name was that every identifiable stone head represented an Earth-born philosopher. Aristotle, Plato, Epicurus, Nietzsche, and Locke, as well as all the other well-known philosophers were there. There were also lesser-known philosophers, like Beauvoir, Stirner, Butler, and Ennenbach.

Then there were many thousands of stone heads thus far unidentified. There was one presumed to be Jesus of Nazareth. Another was thought to be Buddha. And another, Moses. Yet, there were many more who could be *anyone*. Philosophers or theologians or prophets, perhaps, but their stone representations were not recognized as such by those who investigated the subject, nor by their AI assistants. They were mystery people, with pasts or presents or futures of unknown greatness. Some theorists suggested the unknown stones represented great thinkers, like the others, but thinkers who had never attained notoriety—not on Earth, anyway. For that's what Philosopher Rock appeared to celebrate—great thinkers of humanity.

It was the supercomputer Logos, the then-president of Eurasia Proper, who suggested Philosopher Rock was not created by aliens or some time-traveling wing of humanity, but by the universe itself. Like a traveler who collects jars of soil from all the places they ventured, the universe, too, collected mementos of its favorite humans—the thinkers.

And if Philosopher Rock was created by the universe itself, what then did that make the universe? *God?* If the universe was indeed God and there was any truth to Logos's suggestion, then one thing was clear: God was listening.

Thus, the Echo Initiative was born.

They were about three billion miles past the Kuiper Belt—not far, yet, for the crew of the Crantor 4, but far enough for Captain Hamilton to quiet the boosters for a time, to let them drift in the nothingness of space and send their words of wisdom to the stars, to whoever was listening.

They were broadcasting Descartes currently, using a language sonification of electromagnetic waves and pulsed light patterns. So far as the Crantor 4 was concerned, no response had yet been received from the void of space. None of the 3000-plus transentor-class broadcasting vessels launched from Earth or its bases on the moon and Mars had made what anyone could consider *contact* since the project began nearly two centuries ago. But the Echo Initiative was still in its early stages.

"Dinner's about ready, Cap."

The voice startled Captain Hamilton out of a brief slumber. He was seated in the captain's chair on the small bridge of Crantor 4, a series of monitors before him showing maps of the cosmos and the vessel's various mechanical and broadcasting statuses. The person who woke him was Ennis, the systems engineer.

"Dinner?" Captain Hamilton said, rubbing sleep from his eyes. "Didn't we have dinner earlier?" He turned in his chair to see Ennis, a burly redhead, standing just inside the bridge door with a smile on his face.

"No, sir," Ennis said, "we had breakfast and lunch. But who can really tell in space, though, right?"

"Right. What is Steely whipping up for us this evening? Not the meatloaf again, I hope."

"Chicken-fried chicken, black-eyed peas, and mustard greens," Ennis said, his smile expanding. "My favorite."

"Ah," Captain Hamilton said, rocking once before standing up from his chair, "my favorite too. If Steely has some sweet tea ready, I'll close my eyes and dream of sweet home Alabama."

"That old-timey song?"

"Not a chance, Ennis. The place where I was born and raised."

The bridge doors slid open and the two men crossed the adjoining corridor to the lift, dropping two floors to the mess hall. The other four crewmembers were already there, seated around the long white table and talking unimportant pleasantries.

Seated at the head of the table was Latz, of German-Japanese descent and the crew's philosophical archivist. While the Crantor 4 was Captain Hamilton's to manage, Latz was the mission lead. It was his job to select and prepare the various philosophical texts for transmission to the stars.

Seated next to Latz and currently talking about a baseball game from 400 years previous was Galloway, the transmissions officer. He was a sports guru, but mostly he was a linguistic and mathematics genius whose job it was to encode the various messages for long-range transmission across the cosmos.

At the middle of the table, scrolling through a holo-phone, was Lavender, the crew's only female, so-named because of her lavender hair and lavender lips, both of which were inscribed in her DNA prior to birth. She was the crew's cognitive anthropologist, and it was her job to anticipate how non-human minds might interpret and respond to human philosophy.

Lastly, sitting at the other end of the table, was Goggins, the risk assessment officer. He was tall, muscular, and bald and, in general, he lacked a sense of humor and offered a smile only on rare occasions. Goggins's job was to make sure no one got in over their head in any situation.

"Where's Steely?" Captain Hamilton said as he and Ennis entered the mess hall. "Where's the chicken-fried chicken?"

"No chicken for you tonight, Cap," Galloway said, pausing his speech about some guy named Babe. "Steely only materialized five chickens tonight. Ol' Goggins told him you'd rather have—what was it, Gogs?—meatloaf?"

Goggins raised an eyebrow at Galloway, then looked to Captain Hamilton and said, "I didn't say shit to that bag of bolts."

"I didn't figure you would," Hamilton said with a chuckle. Then, turning to Ennis: "I was catching a good nap on the bridge and you came and got me for an empty dining table."

"Hey, Steely said it was coming right up."

"He probably overcooked it," Latz said. "He burns dinner more than any bot I've ever seen. I'm glad you two are here, Ennis and Hamilton—I'm not sure I'd trust ol' Steely to be our engineer *or* our pilot."

"He's supposedly programed to do all our jobs and then some," Hamilton said with a shrug as he pulled out a chair and sat across from

Lavender.

"He's also programmed to be a flawless sex partner," Lavender said, and all the men's eyes turned to her, conversation falling silent. "Apparently his sex parts are interchangeable. So I've heard." Then, clearing her throat, she looked back at her holo-phone and scrolled through something unseen by the others.

Silence hung for a moment, then the men burst into laughter, even Goggins, and Lavender eyed them with a humored smirk. The laughter may have lasted for a while had Steely not interrupted them over the loudspeaker.

"I assure all of you I am the best cook on this vessel," said the voice in a crisp male tone, though it always somehow still sounded mechanical. "The cooking components provided for this mission, however, are less than optimal for my talents. And yes, I am capable of fulfilling any of your sexual needs. Frankly, I'm surprised only two of you have come to me for such services."

"Wait, what?" Latz started, his mouth dropping open with shock. "Who has been w—"

"Steely, I thought I told you to stop monitoring our conversations through Crantor 4's listening system," Hamilton said, leaning back in his chair and crossing his arms.

There was a pause. Then: "Quite right, Captain. I was listening through the door."

The door on the far side of the mess hall slid open and in stepped Steely, the Crantor 4's AI bot, balancing six plates of food, three on each hand. Steely's outer layer was not stainless steel—as his name suggested and as his appearance also suggested—but a high-tech blend of tungsten, platinum, and an advanced form of silicone that allowed for optimal maneuverability and even warmth when touched, like a living being. He was smooth and even soft, yet durable beyond belief. His face was nothing remarkable—designed to appear like a common human face, with the exception of the stainless-steel hue. Steely was dressed in his typical attire, a tan smock.

"Dinner is served, lady and gentlemen," he said, and began setting plates of chicken-fried chicken in front of the crew.

"It's about time," Ennis said. "I'm fucking starving."

"You're hardly starving, Mister Ennis," Steely said, pausing as he set the engineer's plate before him. "I believe you're the most well-fed member of the crew, in fact. At least that's what your last physical would suggest."

This caused another eruption of laughter around the table.

"And, Mister Goggins, I resent you calling me a bag of bolts. I am far more advanced than such mundane materials."

"My deepest apologies, Steely," Goggins said, putting a hand to his chest. "A soldier has a soldier's mouth. I'm sure you understand."

"Thank you for dinner, Steely," Captain Hamilton said before the bot had a chance to turn the mouths of soldiers into dinner's topic of conversation. He grasped his fork and knife and began sawing into his chicken. "How are the cosmos looking this evening?"

"Beautiful, as usual," Steely said. "There is an object floating in our vicinity, which is why I was late delivering your dinner. I was assessing the likelihood it could damage the Crantor 4. I found it to be a zero percent threat."

"An object?" Hamilton said, holding a soggy bite inches from his open maw.

"Pardon me, Steely," Goggins said, "but risk assessment is my domain. You're backup."

Then in unison, Hamilton, Goggins, and Latz all said, "What kind of object?"

"What the hell do you mean a chair?" Latz said, swallowing his first bite before he choked on it. He'd been listening to Galloway drone on about sports for the billionth time and was thinking about something Nietzsche said about eternal recurrence, feeling as if he were reliving the same experience over and over again. Then here was Steely telling them a chair was floating outside the spacecraft like a balloon in the sky. Well, that was not a repetitive occurrence. "We're a million miles from the nearest other vessel. Maybe more."

"Definitely more," Hamilton said. "Closer to five million. Closest vessel is the original Aristotle. Unless one of the Nightingales is this far out."

"A chair?" Latz said again.

"Just a common chair," Steely said, clasping his hands together pleasantly as he stood near the exit of the mess hall. "As I said, it poses no threat. Mister Goggins, you are, of course, welcome to ensure my assessment is accurate."

"No such thing as a common chair in space, Steely, my friend," Galloway said.

"We have visuals of this chair?" Lavender said, not having touched her dinner yet.

"Indeed," Steely said. "It's less than fifty yards off the port side as we speak."

"Dinner's over," Latz said, taking the napkin from his lap and tossing it onto the table. "A chair, Steely? You sure?"

"Positive, Mister Latz."

"Show us," Goggins said, already making his way to the exit.

The chamber's port-side protective shield slid up with a whir, revealing the viewing window and the billion-plus stars beyond. At first he didn't see it but then stepped forward and peered downward and there it was.

Goggins had fought in the Moon Wars around Saturn and witnessed the implementation of acoustic weapons that disabled entire battalions. He was stationed on Europa when the replicating vapor was discovered and had seen it himself in a lab setting. Because of his role contributing to galactic space exploration, he'd been one of the first to see images of Philosopher Rock, so long ago that he'd not yet been given Eternalize, the senescence prophylaxis—or the anti-aging serum, as it was more commonly known. During all that time, he'd never been as shocked or perplexed as he was looking at this chair floating outside of Crantor 4.

It didn't belong. Not just here, floating two billion miles from Earth, but in space at all. Steely was right—it was a common chair. An old classroom chair, in fact, if Goggins had to guess at its origin, like the types used in elementary school classrooms in the days before auto education intake. It had a wood back and a wood seat and a metal frame. There even appeared to be words scrawled on the wood portions, as if this chair had been plucked from some schoolhouse from yesteryear and dropped here.

But that was impossible. And, anyway, why would it be done?

"What the hell?" Captain Hamilton said, leaning against the window next to Goggins.

"Steely," Latz said, standing on the other side of Goggins, "where could this have come from?"

Goggins looked back at the bot. His silver face tilted and his vacant eyes blinked.

"Not from a spacecraft, most likely," Steely said. "A chair of this type would see little use on a spacecraft. Plus, there's the problem of how it ended up outside of the vessel. Not to mention this region beyond the solar system. Only six vessels, according to my database, have passed within a million miles of this location."

"Best guess," Goggins said, "where the hell did it come from?"

"Best guess, Mister Goggins—perhaps thrust into space from a nuclear blast. During the second or third world war, most likely."

"That's only a few hundred years ago," Lavender said, turning away from the window. "It couldn't have traveled over two billion miles—hell, nearly three—in that amount of time. Could it?"

Steely's head tilted curiously again. "No. Not to mention, the amount of thrust needed to get the chair this far would have destroyed it."

"Not a very good guess then, Steely," Galloway said, still looking down. "It's like something you read about from books, that kind of chair. Looks old."

"You are correct, Mister Galloway. Perhaps it *is* debris from an Earth-based craft. An unlogged mission, perhaps. Top secret."

"Unlogged?" Ennis said. "I thought your database had records on every space flight ever."

"That is my understanding, Mister Ennis."

"Quantum displacement, maybe," Lavender said. "A glitch in physical reality. One moment the chair is in Kentucky in 1989, the next," she snapped her fingers, "it's floating outside our window."

"Extremely improbable, Miss Lavender," Steely said. "There has never been any documentation of a quantum displacement event."

"The math exists, though," Galloway said, facing the bot. "Improbable but not impossible."

Steely nodded but did not respond to this.

"I don't think the Crantor's arms will reach far enough to grab it," Captain Hamilton said, looking out again. "And I don't want to turn on the boosters while we're broadcasting. Who wants to go out and get it? Goggins?"

Goggins sighed, knowing the question would be coming. "As the risk assessment officer, Captain, I have to say the risk outweighs the reward in this scenario. What exactly do you think the benefit of bringing that chair on board is?"

"I don't know, Goggins. But I think the perplexity of its existence is enough reason."

"I agree with the captain," Latz said. "The importance of that chair could be endless. Might be a simulation artifact, residual code from another layer of reality."

"Or it may not be a chair at all," Lavender said, sounding excited, "but a mimetic phenomenon. An alien intelligence taking the shape of something familiar as a means of communication."

"I'm not sure that quiets my reluctance, Lavender," Goggins said.

"Your reluctance is noted," Captain Hamilton. "But Latz and I agree. The mission demands we retrieve that chair. So, who is going? If not Goggins, then Ennis."

"I'll go, goddammit," Goggins said, pursing his lips and crossing his arms. "But I don't like it. Note that in your log, Captain."

Lavender watched alone from the same window as Goggins went out on a tether in his spacesuit to the chair. Ennis and Galloway waited for him at the airlock, in case assistance was needed. Captain Hamilton and Latz had gone to the monitor room where they could watch the task with better views from the multiple exterior cameras. Steely was somewhere but not on the viewing deck.

What the *hell* was that chair doing here? The more she thought about it, the more Lavender felt mimetic phenomenon was the logical explanation. But if it was alien life imitating something familiar...why did it choose a chair? Why that kind of chair? Where had it seen such a thing? What was it trying to say by taking the form of a chair?

Or, maybe it was projecting the chair. The alien entity could be somewhere else—perhaps near or perhaps far—and it was simply sticking the chair there as a means of introduction. *Hello there, here's a chair!*

It seemed ridiculous but what theory didn't?

Goggins floated as if in slow motion, reaching the chair fifty or sixty yards from Crantor 4, then casually circling, looking at it from all sides before eventually grabbing hold of the wooden back. To Lavender, it seemed as though Goggins was inspecting it very closely, like he was alarmed or confused by something. But then he hit the retraction button and the tether began pulling him back home.

Lavender sat in one of the several cushioned chairs, pulling out her holo-phone and scrolling through the latest Mars news feed. She'd been sitting there less than five minutes when Steely came over the intercom.

"Miss Lavender, may I ask if that is your original name? Your given name, that is."

"What?" Lavender said, looking up at the speaker in the ceiling. "Why?"

"Please confirm, Miss Lavender," Steely said.

"I was renamed at the lunar orphanage when I was three," Lavender said, annoyed, "because they thought it would make me more adoptable for the locals if my name matched my hair and lips. Why, Steely?"

There was a pause. Then: "Is your original name Loraine?"

"What the f—" Lavender started. "How did you—"

That name, so far as Lavender knew, had not existed for the last ninety-two years of her life. Steely may have access to old birth and adoption records in his expansive database, but what would be the point of bringing her name up at this moment?

"Miss Lavender, Captain Hamilton and Mister Latz are requesting your presence in the airlock bay."

Ennis couldn't take his eyes off the damn thing now that it was inside.

Sure enough it looked like the typical chair from a schoolhouse a few centuries back. It was even small as if meant for a child between, say, five and twelve. The size of it, in fact, reinforced the idea that the chair absolutely *should not exist here*. Very few children had ever traveled past Mars. Indeed, most adults weren't typically allowed to engage in space travel until they reached twenty-five, when their brains were fully developed and they could become candidates for the anti-aging serum.

But the size of the chair and its mere existence were no longer the oddest part. It was the fact that everyone's name was written on it, as if penned or carved by children. There were markings of blue, red, and black ink, including an unfinished game of tic-tac-toe and a crudely drawn stick figure with his tongue sticking out. And there were areas of wood gouged out as if by a pocketknife. There was even what appeared to be three spots of hardened chewing gum on the underside of the chair.

But the names ...

Seven names.

There was "Gerald" as in Gerald Hamilton, "Haruto" as in Haruto Latz, "Boris" as in Boris Galloway, "Loraine" as in Loraine 'Lavender' Fender, "Dylan" as in Dylan Goggins, and "Mitch" as in Mitch Ennis. And there was one more name, if it could be called that: AI90875349-ROBO14-SM. It was Steely's product model number, written down the metal leg of the chair in black marker.

"What the fuck is this?" Ennis whispered, not loud enough for anyone to hear. Not that it needed to be asked—everyone was thinking the exact same question.

"It's almost like it's a trick or something," Captain Hamilton said. "But it can't be."

"It has to be what I said," Lavender said. "Alien contact. What other possibility is there?"

"Infinite possibilities," said Latz. "Recursion anomaly, maybe. Human thought loops back on itself until the object manifests. Could be some sort of message or warning from the universe. Could be it followed us through the Kuiper for God knows why."

"Maybe it's not even real," Galloway said. "A projection of some kind. A transmission."

"Maybe," Latz said with a shrug. "Infinite possibilities."

"Why the fuck does it have our names, though?" Lavender said. "Our original, given fucking names, even Steely. Like it knows everything about us. From the beginning."

"What do we do with it?" Ennis said, looking around the room. "We got it here. Now what? It's not like we have the equipment here to do thorough testing. This isn't an archaeology vessel. We're transmitting supposed words of wisdom to the cosmos."

"I can do a basic analysis of the materials in the lab," Steely said.

Everyone stood around it for a moment without talking, lost in their own thoughts of the mystery.

"Steely," Captain Hamilton said finally, "have any of the other broadcasting vessels come across something strange? Maybe not like a chair but—*something*? An odd occurrence of any kind?"

"Not of this sort, I'm afraid. At least, nothing that has been reported across the fleet. The Pascal 2 disappeared, of course. But it's widely suspected they were hit by an asteroid. The Marx 5 succumbed to infighting over rank and power. Three crewmen were killed and the rest were detained by the onboard AI. That's the extent of any strangeness that I'm aware of, Captain."

It was Galloway who finally decided to do something besides blurt out thoughts and theories.

"You know what I usually do when I'm having trouble deciding how to move forward with a project?" he said, moving toward the chair. "I sit down and think about it."

No one tried to stop him. No one reached out or verbalized an objection of any kind. Not Goggins, the risk assessment officer, and not Steely, who was programmed to take into account every possible scenario in a given situation. Whether it was the collective confusion of the situation or a genuine curiosity that stayed everyone's response, Ennis wasn't sure. He only knew that he was watching with interest as Galloway sat upon the wooden seat.

"It's kinda cold," Galloway said with a chuckle as he crossed his right foot over his left knee while interlocking his hands behind his head.

Then, within three seconds, his face changed from thoughtful, almost whimsical, to fearful. Something was wrong. Ennis was sure of it—he could see the concern on Galloway's face. His right foot went back to the floor and his hands came apart, going to his knees. He was on the verge of standing when...he *screamed*, his face turning red with anguish, his jugular veins bulging from his neck.

Everyone took a startled step backward, even Steely, with a collective gasp rising between them.

"What's wrong?!" Lavender screamed at Galloway.

If Galloway heard her, he couldn't answer. His screams were his only response. And he was, Ennis realized, shrinking somehow. Galloway, coveralls and all, was collapsing inward on the chair, like a sheet of paper laid flat on a person's hand that then turned into a fist, crumpling the paper into a ball, smaller and smaller.

Blood exploded around Galloway and from the rear of the chair as he imploded, slivers of meat and fabric littering the floor around him. His screams became so intense that veins in his eyes and cheeks burst. His back and bottom and the backs of his legs were disappearing into the chair, being absorbed by it as he collapsed inward. His arms reached out at the heavens, rigid as steel pipes.

Goggins finally broke ranks and stepped forward, taking hold of Galloway's forearms and pulling back on the man.

"Help me!" Goggins shouted, and Ennis and Captain Hamilton stepped up, each grabbing an arm.

The others fell into place, pulling with all their strength. But the chair was like a powerful, slow-moving machine, sucking Galloway into it with the same ease no matter how much pressure came from the other end.

His waist was gone within the chair now, leaving his top and bottom half to appear as though they were separate pieces entirely, both continuing to implode, with blood and viscera spraying across the floor and all over the fighting crew. When half his abdomen was gone, Galloway stopped screaming and his arms and legs went limp.

The crew of Crantor 4 continued to pull on Galloway's body until it was just his head and arms jutting from the wooden back of the chair and his calves and feet from the seat. But it all sank away no matter their efforts. And as they slinked away, defeated and exhausted, they watched the last of Galloway slip into the chair's surface like he was dipping below the surface of a lake. A bloody smattering was all that remained when his fingers disappeared into the chair's back, and then that too disappeared.

Ennis stepped back, nearly slipping in the giant puddle of gore around the chair. "What the bloody hell?" he said.

"We need to get rid of this fucking thing," Goggins said. "Right fucking now."

"Crantor 4 to Nightingale 3, over," Captain Hamilton said into the mic for the fifteenth time, at least. He waited, and nothing. "Crantor 4 to any available Nightingale, over."

"I'm not sure medics are what we need, Cap," Latz said, coming up behind him on the bridge.

"Likely not," Hamilton said, putting the mic down. "But I've tried contacting all the defense vessels in this zone and they're not answering either. Not even the other broadcasting vessels are talking back."

"There's a reason for that," Latz said, and Hamilton turned to look at the mission leader, noting the sound of defeat in his voice. "Ennis said all of our transmissions systems have been rendered inoperable. We're no longer broadcasting to the cosmos, and none of your calls are leaving the confines of this ship."

"What? How is that possible?" Hamilton looked at the mic, then at the monitors around him. He saw the locations of several vessels noted on the galactic map monitors, all millions of miles away but still signaling. He held his hand out to the monitors. "If we can pick up their signals, we should—"

"I know," Latz said. "But nothing is getting out. Ennis and Steely both have run the tests multiple times. And neither of them have found anything mechanically wrong. But we're flying dark, Cap. Nobody can see or hear us."

"The chair? Could it ..."

"It seems the only explanation."

"Is everyone still in the monitor room?"

"Goggins wants everyone in there until we have a solid plan for chunking that chair back into space."

Captain Hamilton nodded, and together he and Latz boarded and descended the lift to the monitor room.

"Has it done anything?" Hamilton asked as he walked in, seeing three of the room's monitors showed the chair from different angles in the airlock bay, sitting at the center of Galloway's puddle of blood.

"Nope," Goggins said, his arms crossed as he stared at the screens. "It's waiting for us."

Hamilton looked from Goggins to the monitors then to Goggins again. He was seeing a fight on his hands, Hamilton figured, and for good reason.

"It's alien life then?" Latz said, directing his question at Lavender. "You were right. It's mimicking a familiar object in order to—what?—feed?"

"That seems a pretty accurate assessment," Lavender said.

"It's the most logical explanation now," Steely agreed.

"And what's to keep it from turning into something else?" Ennis said. "A bottle of water or a spacesuit or the pillow on my goddamn bed? If it can be a chair, can't it be anything?"

"There's no way of knowing," Lavender said.

"But we got eyes on it," Captain Hamilton said. "And speakers. Steely, we can still access the intercom in the airlock bay, right?"

"Yes, Captain, all internal coms are in good working order."

"Are you thinking about talking to the chair, or whatever it is?" Latz said.

"Actually, mission leader, I was hoping you would do the talking."

He took a deep breath, leaning over the keyboard and looking up at the monitor. His heart was thumping abnormally fast and sweat dotted his forehead and dampened the pits of his coveralls. He waited a moment, searching for the right words, then pressed the intercom button on the keyboard.

"This is Doctor Haruto Latz speaking, philosophical archivist and mission leader of the Crantor 4, a broadcasting vessel of the Echo Initiative. We mean you no harm. And we want no further harm to come to our crew. Please, if you understand and are able to communicate, tell us what it is you want and what we can do to prevent further bloodshed."

He paused for a moment, everyone staring at one of the three monitors showing the chair. But no movement or form of communication came.

"What is your name?" Latz said. "And what is your mission here?"

Silence. Just the quiet whir of monitors and cooling fans. Just the chair and the gore.

"Is there anything we can do to help you?"

A pause and silence.

"Why did you take the form of a chair? Why did you kill Galloway? Do you live in space? Do you have a home planet? Did you interrupt our external transmissions?"

All the questions were asked one at a time, then given a pause long enough for a response. But no response came—at least, Latz thought, no response they were capable of hearing or deciphering. When dealing with an alien entity, communication could happen a thousand different ways. Wasn't the writing of their names on the chair's surface communication?

"Maybe we should try writing to it," Latz said, looking at the others, "showing it messages from the bay window or something." He pressed the intercom button again. "Would you be able to communicate through writing?"

Suddenly, the monitors shut off—not just the ones showing the airlock bay, but those showing the rest of the ship's interior and exterior—and a brief zap under Latz's finger indicated the power to the intercom had been cut as well.

Everyone stood silently for a moment around Latz, and he was certain they could hear his heart thumping against his chest.

"Is that a yes?" Captain Hamilton said.

"Or is it a fuck you?" Lavender said, and all eyes turned to her with the same uncertainty.

Who are you?

It was the fifth message Lavender had scrawled on her digital writing pad, showing it through the square-shaped window on the door separating the supply hall from the airlock bay and the airlock beyond. All the crew crowded around the door looking for a response of any kind from the chair. But nothing happened.

Lavender erased the screen and wrote again with her finger.

Why are you here?

Nothing. But what were they expecting? Maybe Goggins was right—maybe it was waiting. Waiting for some other unfortunate soul to take a seat and get sucked into wherever—into oblivion, into another dimension, into God only knew where. Maybe it was feeding, as Latz suggested. It just wasn't hungry just now, because Galloway was a satiating meal. But the time would come when the chair would get hungry and demand another meal.

"We're not getting anything with this," she said, turning away from the door to face the others.

"We can't really see the surface from here," said Latz. "Maybe it's leaving messages on itself. Like on the surface of the chair."

"You going in to check?" Ennis said.

"No one is touching it," Captain Hamilton said. "That would be a terrible idea."

"Nothing happened when Goggins touched it in the spacesuit," Ennis said. "Maybe it depends on the material you're wearing on what it can do. Or maybe you have to sit on it for it to kill you."

"Or maybe it just wanted on the ship first," Lavender said. "It didn't kill Goggins because he was bringing it on the ship."

"Okay," Goggins said, stepping forward and peering close through the window, "that's enough trying to communicate with the fucking thing. It's killed one crewman. It's turned off our digital coms, both external and internal. As the risk assessment officer, I say it's time to send the fucking thing back out into space before anything else happens."

"What do you suggest?" Captain Hamilton said. "If we go in there and try and toss it out the airlock, there's no telling what will happen."

"That's right," Goggins said, turning around and crossing his arms, "which is why Steely is going."

Lavender turned and looked at the stainless-colored AI bot standing at the rear of the rest of the crew.

He blinked and looked at Lavender with a kind smile, then looked at Goggins.

"You are, of course, correct, Mister Goggins," Steely said. "It is already clear the entity can harm human beings. I, however, am not made of flesh. I am far more durable. Not to mention, I do not need to don a suit."

"What if it can turn off your core processor the way it turned off the monitors and coms units?" Lavender argued.

"Possible," Steely said, "but not likely."

"Steely runs off a supercharged plutonium battery with a billion-year life and no off switch," Ennis said. "He can't be switched off as easy as the coms systems."

"Steely is crucial to the mission though," Lavender said. "He's the only one capable of doing all our jobs."

"The mission now, Lavender," Captain Hamilton said, "is to get that thing off the ship. Goggins is right about that."

"Agreed," said Latz, though Lavender thought she saw doubt in his eyes.

Moments later, the crew was backing away from the door and Steely was moving toward it, grasping the handle. The plan was for the bot to open the airlock, grab the chair, move into the airlock, close the airlock, open the space-passage doorway, and toss the chair out. No fuss with tethers, no pause to inspect the chair for new scrawls on its surface, no wasting of any time. Get rid of the thing—that was the only goal.

Steely slid the airlock bay door open, stepped through, and closed it behind him.

The crew moved up to watch, Lavender claiming the spot at the center of the window.

Steely walked across the room with his typical rigid motion, straight as a post, his arms swinging slightly as he moved past the chair without incident to the airlock door. He punched in the code and the airlock double doors slid open, revealing the small chamber beyond that would open into space when ready.

Then Steely returned to the chair, stepping through Galloway's blood and glancing only briefly at the window, at Lavender, before he turned to face the object. As agreed upon, the bot did not pause to inspect the chair. He simply bent at the waist and grabbed hold of the wooden back of the chair with both hands.

Steely froze suddenly, and the lights of the airlock bay and the supply hall flickered briefly. Then the AI bot was being sucked into the wooden surface of the chair by his arms. He made no sound or movement and his stainless-colored flesh flickered with jagged veins of electricity. As with Galloway, he was being pulled in slowly but deliberately, and flecks and shavings of metal and rubber spewed out around the chair, as if it were a greedy eater, too hungry to not be sloppy as it consumed.

"Jesus Christ, it's taking Steely," Lavender shouted, feeling everyone else crowd around her to see.

"Can't be," said Captain Hamilton as Steely's triceps disappeared into the wood.

"Impossible," Latz said.

"We're so fucked," said Ennis, and Lavender felt those words to her core.

They watched as Steely—his face never changing, never looking to the window at his fellow crew—gradually disappeared inside the chair among a shower of shiny shredded compounds. When he was completely gone, the floor around the chair, previously red with blood and viscera, shimmered like silver glitter, the remains of what was once Steely.

Lavender stood so long against the window that her breath fogged the surface before her eyes. When she at last turned about, she saw Latz, Goggins, Ennis, and Captain Hamilton all leaning in various places in the supply hall, deep in thought.

"What do we do now?" she said, not really expecting an answer.

"We kill it," Goggins said.

"With what?" Captain Hamilton said with a laugh. "It's not like this vessel has any firearms."

"Ennis," Goggins said, looking toward the engineer, "don't we have a plasma cutter down here somewhere?"

"Goggins," Captain Hamilton said, placing a hand on his shoulder, "don't get carried away and point that thing toward the airlock seal unless you feel like dancing around in space without a suit."

Goggins chuckled. "As long as the chair goes with me, that wouldn't be such a bad thing."

The plasma cutter was new and unused, intended for potential hull repair or clearing of debris in odd situations no one on Crantor 4 ever expected to encounter. The power supply fit on Goggins's back like a backpack, with a hose leading to the torch, which he could hold in one hand, his finger on the trigger. It wasn't like the plasma cutters of old, which could take a full minute to cut through several inches of thick steel, but more akin to the mythical weapons once referred to as lightsabers. When the power was tuned to the maximum, as Goggins's plasma cutter was now, it spit out a blue rod of flame nearly six feet in length, capable of slicing through any metal or mixture of metals with relative ease.

In theory, with a few swipes of the plasma cutter, the chair would be in pieces. With a few dozen swipes, Goggins hoped he could reduce the damn thing to shards, sweep it into a dustpan, and expel it into space like a flushed turd.

Goggins nodded he was ready, and Hamilton slid the airlock bay door open just wide enough for Goggins to squeeze through and quickly shut it behind him.

With sweat dripping down his temples, he thought of the Moon Wars all those years ago, of marching into battle with laser packs and sonic grenades, not expecting to ever come out of it alive. He'd been anxious then, scared even, but had he ever felt the way he did now? His heart thumped in his ears and his testicles were sucked up into his belly. Goggins had faced many foes without fear, but now...he simply didn't know *what* he was facing and what it was capable of.

He took one step into the room and pulled the trigger on the plasma cutter, causing the flame to shoot out to its full length. Then he locked the trigger in place and took another couple of steps toward the chair. He eyed it for just a moment from a distance of about five paces, considering where he wanted to slice it first. Down the center, cutting it in half and causing it to fall both left and right, presumably? Or across the seat, cutting off the back of the chair? Or maybe down low, taking its legs off? Not having any idea what the chair actually was, he didn't have the foggiest idea if it mattered where he cut the damn thing.

In the end, Goggins decided to charge the chair like a knight with a sword and take the back off its supports. Then he would turn around and slice it to pieces.

But Goggins did not get that far.

He ran one step, then two, then three, raring back with the plasma cutter, readying himself to slice level with the chair's seat as he ran past, then took the fourth step and ...

He felt a sudden gurgling from his insides, right at the center of himself, not in a particular area of his body but at his core somehow and radiating out to the rest of him, a gurgling all the way to his fingertips. And that was all he knew.

What the others saw from the window was as Goggins took his fifth stride, coming almost alongside the chair, he simply exploded into a billion pieces, blood and guts and bone flying everywhere in all directions, turning a mostly white room into an abstract painting.

The plasma cutter fell to the floor undamaged right in front of the chair, the blue flame jutting out uselessly, burning the floor's surface.

To the horror of the remaining crew, much of the gore that had been Goggins floated through the air to the chair and disappeared upon its surface. Not near all of it, though. The room had once been dominated by white walls. Now they were red.

"What the Christ do we do now, Cap?" Ennis said, backing down the supply hall away from the airlock bay door. "We're so fucked, aren't we? I mean, what can we possibly do?"

"He's right," Lavender said, turning to Hamilton and grabbing him by the coveralls collar. "What the hell can we do? Just avoid the airlock or what?"

"Yeah," continued Ennis, "fucking go to the mess hall and finish dinner and continue on like normal, except just stay off this deck?"

"Continue as normal how, Ennis?" Latz said. "We have no coms. Or did you forget? There is no continue on. This chair—this goddamn thing—is our problem. It's our mission now, like we said before."

"Fuck you, Latz! With no coms, you're not the mission leader. Your whole reason for existence on this mission is to communicate with the universe. Well that ain't fuckin' happening! Hamilton is in charge."

"What do we do, Cap?" Lavender said, tugging on him again, pleading with him.

He thought for a moment, then turned to Ennis.

"If we do a system override—the Crantor 4 has to allow an override with Steely out of commission—then would you be able to open the airlock from the bridge? The vacuum of space should suck the chair out. Theoretically, of course. Nothing is certain with that damn thing."

Ennis scrunched his brow.

"Maybe," he said. "It would take some doing. But maybe. And I would need the monitors on the bridge to be working, or the holo-projectors. I gotta see what I'm doing to accomplish anything."

"Great," Hamilton said, looking back at the airlock bay door as Lavender released his collar, seeing splotches of blood on the window. "Then let's get our asses up to the bridge. I wish Steely hadn't mentioned that chair until we were a million miles from here."

"You and me both, Captain," Lavender said.

As they both turned back from the door to face the other two, something rushed past Hamilton and Lavender. A blur of red clumps zoomed through the air, brushing Hamilton's coveralls and even his hair, splatting against the airlock bay door. They looked.

Raw lumps of meat and blood covered the door, moving across its surface as if looking for passage to the other side. The flesh slowly moved toward the door jamb, the blood and some of the smaller bits of flesh squeezing through. Hamilton didn't have to peer through the window to know where the flesh was going. He turned and looked at the other end of the hallway.

A skeleton, red and slick from the body that had encased it for years, lay several yards away. Beyond it was Latz, backing farther down the hallway, his eyes wide and white. The skeleton was Ennis and so was the flesh across the door.

"Jesus Christ," Hamilton said, then heard a clatter on the floor followed by a heavy splat.

Once more turning back, he witnessed new flesh covering the door and another skeleton right beside him. Lavender, stripped of her meat and sent to the chair. Her blood and guts squeezed through the seals of the door. Hamilton thought perhaps he could hear her screaming. But likely that was just his imagination. For what did he have left but imagination? All hope, after all, was gone.

Then he felt it in himself, a churning, bubbling sensation, followed by intense pain that didn't give him time enough to scream.

Haruto Latz sat at the end of the supply hall for a long while, waiting.

The lights flickered once.

Three skeletons littered the hallway before him.

And what flesh couldn't squeeze through to the other side lay in a sick display at the base of the door.

He waited, but his flesh was not taken. And after a time Latz could not ascertain, the door to the airlock bay slid open on its own. He looked up when this happened, expecting his death, but no. Unmoving, he continued waiting. When the chair was ready for him, whatever it was, it would take him.

Only, it didn't.

He waited so long that the urge to urinate presented itself, and Latz relieved himself in the restroom connected to the hallway. Having given up, he waited longer, not bothering to leave this part of Crantor 4. Soon his mouth was like cotton and his stomach twisted with want for food. But Latz waited longer, until exhaustion was threatening to take him over. And only then, with the courage of defeat and fatigue combined, did Latz venture into the airlock bay.

He stepped in gingerly, cognizant of the blood all over the floor, though most of it had coagulated. Standing just inside the door, Latz looked at the chair, seven or eight paces away. It looked like a chair, nothing more, as it had from the beginning.

Had it forgotten about him? He thought maybe it had. But here he was standing before it to remind it of his presence. He showed no fear or protest if it wanted to suck him from his bones into the abyss. Or *with* his bones, for that matter.

But nothing happened. The chair sat where the chair was left, in the exact spot where Goggins had originally placed it. Was it waiting?

Latz moved forward, one step and then another and another. Another step and a long jump and he could land atop the chair if he wanted. But he did not do this. He took another step, then two more. He was within two paces now. If he strained, he could likely reach out and touch it. The plasma cutter lay on the floor between him and the chair, and Latz kicked it out of the way, the blue flame flickering a protest.

There was his name, Haruto, scrawled on the seat of the chair in blue ink, scrawled with the penmanship of someone no older than nine. If Latz had to guess, he'd written it himself at that age. Only, he never sat in such a chair.

"What are you?" Latz said, and he took one more step forward. "Why are you here?"

Slowly, Latz lowered himself to the floor in a cross-legged position so he could be eye level with the chair's back. He could feel blood soaking into the bottoms of his coveralls. He stared at it for a time. He looked at the names of the other crewmen and that of Steely, written down the front right steel leg of the thing.

"What are you?" Latz said again. "An intrusion of the deadly mundane into the sublime void? A passive throne, a demand for stillness?" Latz raised his voice. "Is that it? Are you telling us to be still and listen? Are you telling us to shut the fuck up and listen?" He breathed heavily, rubbing sweat from his eyes. "No. Punishment for hubris, perhaps. How dare we presume we can find meaning in anything—in Philosopher Rock, in life, in a goddamn chair." He paused, considering something he couldn't quite grasp. "It was just a chair—until we tried to understand it." His eyes rose to the chair, to the wooden face of the back. "Are you...are you the universe? Are you...God?"

Slowly, Latz leaned forward, reaching out with his right hand and placing it upon the seat. It was cold at first. Then he shuddered.

Olaf's Ossuary

Micah Castle

Mr. Bauld

I LEAVE THE MONARCH Theatre through the back exit, and the starless night sky hangs over the city like a thick black tapestry. There's not a star in sight, the moon hiding behind the tall buildings, but there's enough pale light to see by. As I enter the alley, I'm smacked with frigid wind howling through it. My jacket barely does anything to prevent the cold.

Why the hell didn't I wear something heavier? It was a date, that's why. A date. First one in years since the wife left me, so I wanted to look presentable. Good, even. Little did it or paying for her expensive fucking meal help, out here alone in the dark winter freezing my ass off. She's probably someplace warm. Probably with *someone* warm.

Fuck 'em. I'm better off anyway.

Grime stains the red-brick walls the farther I go. Filth pukes from upturned trash cans. A family of rats enjoys their buffet. I smell piss and tobacco smoke, but not a soul's out here but me. Could be me, for all I care.

I turn into another alley, then another, and another. All mimic the first, like the architects of this city said fuck it, let's do them all the same.

The cold becomes more unforgiving. I've lived in Cherry Brooke since the day I was born, and I can't believe I'm lost. I walked these alleys hundreds of times when I was a kid. Tommy, Frank, me, and some other one drinking stolen beer, playing cards, smoking whatever we could get our grubby hands on. The good ol' days.

Nostalgia does nothing for this cold.

Suddenly I pause and see a shop on the corner. If I was fifty pounds lighter, I'd run toward it; instead, I walk a little faster. Closer, I see an old-fashioned oil lamp hanging over a creaking wooden sign and a round, weathered door. It takes a minute to read the sign with the light flickering in the wind: Olaf's Ossuary. Never heard of it, and what the hell's an ossuary, anyway? Something to do with oysters? Whatever, it doesn't matter. I'll give the owner a couple bucks to use his establishment for the night, then I'll leave in the morning.

What a night.

The stench of dust slaps me in the face. I cough into my arm while I carefully move around all the shit shoved onto shelves flanking the entrance. It's so dim in here I only catch glimpses of the thick books sticking out like broken teeth and piled on the hardwood. The last thing I need is to ruin some expensive text and have to pay out the ass for something I probably can't even read. As if I want to.

Entering the store proper, I let my vision adjust to the light coming from candles—really, candles, in this day and age?—in a black chandelier hanging overhead. A large, round table is in the middle of the room with more dusty books, trinkets, kitchenware, and so many other knickknacks heaped atop. Any second, it'll spill, but I ain't cleaning the mess. Inlaid shelves run along the walls, and I think my great-grandfather had the same chipped bowl with the light-blue wavy pattern, and my grandmother definitely had something like that dented kettle. Insane what people will spend their money on. Why buy this when you can buy new for less?

I pick up a diamond ring. There are black dots in the center of each diamond. Kinda reminds me of eyeballs—

"Greetings," a thin man says beside me, and I nearly jump.

"Where the *fuck* did you come from?" I almost drop the ring, putting it back. My heart's thumping like a racehorse in my chest.

"My apologies, sir, I thought you saw me standing over there." He points to a hanging black sheet that must lead to the backroom. I don't remember seeing him, but who knows. "My name's Olaf." He takes a step back. "How may I assist you?"

His bald head has a filmy look to it, like gasoline on water without the colors, and his deep-seated, beady eyes above his beak nose, I swear, twinkle for a second. At least he knows how to dress. His black suit looks new, perfectly fitted too. If it's tailored then this guy has money, so I probably can't lowball him to stay the night. Damn. He has some bony fingers, though, interlaced in front of him.

"I got lost in the alleys somehow." I chuckle. "Just needed somewhere warm to stay the night."

"Ah, yes, the cold—supposed to be the worst winter Cherry Brooke has ever seen."

"Yeah ..." I inhale, and silence fills the room. Somewhere behind the black curtain, something's *ticking*, like a huge clock. "So...how much for the night?"

"Free, as long as you entertain me through conversation."

"Just talk to you, that's it?"

"That's it, sir."

"Well, hell, alright." I smirk. "I can talk."

He grins. "Wonderful, so, Mr. ...?"

"Bauld." The fake name blurts out. Why does he need the real one?

"Mr. Bauld, have you seen anything you like?"

"Ah, no, not really. Sorry, I'm not a big collector."

"How come?"

"Not someone who likes clutter, that's all. My place looks like I just moved in, but I've been there for years now."

"A minimal gentleman. I've met a few of those in my time." He moves around the table and stops, placing his hands flat on top where I swear space wasn't there before. He taps on it with his fingers that seem longer than a moment ago. Either my vision's going to shit or I wasn't paying much attention. I rub my eyes, but nothing changes, so must be column C. "You know, some people are collectors who haven't yet found the right items to collect."

"Maybe." I glance at a disgusting-looking dog collar. Pink, little bulbs are attached to it with what might be cat paws. Cat paws? Christ. "Maybe."

"If you're interested, Mr. Bauld," a breeze wafts through the room, and I look up and he's by the curtain to the back, "I have some special antiques in the backroom you may like."

"Like rare?"

He smiles, revealing too many narrow, yellowed teeth. "Yes, yes, quite rare."

If listening to this weirdo gets me off the hook from paying, then I'll listen to whatever. Anything to keep me out that damn cold. I should've brought a heavier jacket and all this could've been avoided. Well, no, if I didn't get lost, this wouldn't have happened; or maybe if what's-her-name would've been more appreciative of me, I would be at her place with her right now. I shrug. "Sure, why not?"

"Please, follow me." He pulls aside the curtain, ushering me in.

Through a tight hallway with deep-red walls and a strange, dark pattern, we come into a showroom bigger than the one we left. Wide enough to fit probably ten or so cars, it seems to go on forever. Was the building this big? I can't remember; I was too focused on not getting frostbite. A variety of pedestals and stands are placed everywhere, stretching back into infinity, most topped with glass cases protecting a bunch of different things.

Tick.

More old-fashioned lamps hang from red-brick columns, interrupted by shelving built into the walls matching the color of the hall we just left. At least the light's brighter than the candles, making the dark wood floor shine. Must've had someone polish the place recently. This big, now I'm sure he's got money.

The shit back here's more taken care of, though it's about the same trash he's selling upfront. Books bound in a bunch of different materials. Antiques like silverware, dishes, vases. Jewelry like necklaces, rings, a fucking crown. Fancy pens and paper. Some of it looks so old it might've been around when Jesus was crucified. And that clock's still there, louder back here, coming from somewhere. I don't see it. Weird.

Olaf hasn't said a peep, standing there waiting for me to get a good look at the place. "Impressed?"

"Sure."

He puts out his long arm, directing me to a nearby stand, some type of cracked, dark stone rising from the floor. Although it seems like it would be flaky, there's no dust around it. It's almost like it's connected to the foundation, because I can't find where it ends and the floor begins. I gotta find out who did these floors, because they're a master.

I realize I was wrong. It's smooth, not flaky, and the stand isn't cracked. The wavy lines are a design carved into the rock, twisting every which way to where the glass case is. It's almost like it has give if I were to grab it, a softness like a woman's ass in a pencil skirt. My heart races and my skin tingles. Why am I getting a hard-on from this thing? Christ. But I can't stop wanting it, can't fucking stop from reaching for—

"Mr. Bauld?"

Tick.

I look up at him. Reality snaps back into focus. His eyes point to the gnarled thing inside. I shove my hand back into my pocket. How could such an ugly black knot of—muscle, maybe?—sit atop something so beautiful? Wisps of brown and red hair poke out from coarse divots, and little raised orbs or something dot it up its gnarled side. "What is it?"

Olaf lifts the case and pulls it out. "It's not important *what* it is, only how it came to be. Like everything here, it arrives with an origin." His curved thumb rubs it. A lipless smile stretches ear to ear, the skin around it bunching up. What's so important about this damn thing? "There are so many items, but this particular one remains one of my favorites."

Tick.

It's gotten louder, a dull poke in my temples. I take a quick glance around and still can't find a clock. "Really?" I say, entertaining him like I would a drunk at the bar. "How'd you get that thing, then?"

"Yes, really, and if you care to learn, I would be happy to tell you."

Goosebumps rise on the back of my neck. The way he speaks is like a woman's, kinda makes me want to lie down and sleep. He has my full attention, as if I *want* to be here by choice and not obligation. "Sure."

Olaf

I was organizing items out front, bundled in several layers of clothes. It was colder than it is now, the snow unforgiving. I hoped it would let up, but it didn't care about my hopes. Unfortunately the heating wasn't working for one reason or another, and the cast-iron stove I had set up in the front barely scratched the chill.

While I fed more wood into the stove, I heard the door creak open. Wind howled into the store, all the entry books clapping, then it slammed shut and silence fell.

"Hello?" someone called. "Is anyone here?"

I turn to the short man bundled in a dark-blue overcoat and scarf, a knitted cap sparkling in snow pulled down to his auburn eyebrows. In his gloved hand was a handle attached to a box covered in a black blanket.

"Greetings, sir. My name's Olaf. How may I assist you?" I didn't extend my hand to shake, refusing to remove it from my partially warm pocket.

"I heard you buy odd stuff?" His blue eyes took in the shop uncaringly. The snow had already begun melting from his clothes.

"Odd is subjective, but yes, that's correct. But only rare items, ones with value." I indicated with a shrug. "As you can see, I already own many, many items."

The man glanced over his shoulder as though someone may be following him, then set the box on the floor. It rattled like an animal cage, and when he raised the blanket in the front for me to take a peek, it *was* an animal cage. Inside was what I hold now, though it was very much alive. "Do you have anything like this?"

I only caught a glimpse due to the darkness, but it had four short limbs on its underside, more patches of fur, and the eyes—yes, those are what those are—were open, all sharing the same color: teal. It hid in the far corner, whimpering in a gibbering tone like a dozen gasping old men whispering at once.

Then he covered it again, and I straightened. My curiosity was piqued, to say the least. "No, nothing like that. How'd you come about owning it?"

"I found it," he said.

"Found it? Where?"

"At my mom's house." He looked at his slick boots. "She passed away about a year ago—cancer—and I was cleaning out the place to sell...." The man groaned and shook his head. "It doesn't matter. I just want it gone."

"You could've gotten rid of it anywhere. Why my shop? The Refleski is always hungry for more of the unwanted."

"I don't want to kill it. At first, I really wanted to, but I just.... I can't keep it anymore, can't keep *looking* at it. I have to get it out of my life."

"Again, why my shop?"

"You've seen it," he spat. "No one's going to want it, and the last thing I fucking need is for someone to go looking into my life because of it. My mom's gone, her house is for sale, and this is the last thing that reminds me of her, of her lies. So just take it, *please*."

Desperate sellers always make for an easier, cheaper purchase. Money never seems to be their goal, only a convenient part of discarding their burdens. But before I could take it, I had to know its origin. History is important. Without it, I couldn't know what to expect from it, especially when dealing with something *alive*. "Tell me how you obtained it, then I'll consider it."

He sighed, scratching his head underneath the cap. "There's no other way?"

"None."

"Do you at least have somewhere I can sit?"

I procured two fifteenth century chairs that were far too valuable for a simple transaction, but like I said before, I was curious, and we settled before the crackling stove.

"After my mom died, I had to clear out her house before a realtor could sell it. Becca, my sister, couldn't come help because of work, plus she lives in North Carolina. Not to mention, Becca also hated her, but that's a whole other story. For the first couple days it was fine, tiring and frustrating to have to go there, then my apartment, then to work, then back again, but it's whatever.

"Almost everything in the house was tossed. Most was junk, but I admit it hurt a little doing it. Lots of memories of growing up there, the ones that're good, anyway." He snickered. "Probably why it took me so damn long to get to the bedrooms, like if I put it off enough I wouldn't have to do it, but who else was going to? Becca's room was across from mine in the back of the house, and I did hers first. After she moved out, after graduation, my mom turned her room into a second closet. For whatever reason, she loved buying clothes even though she didn't wear even a third of them. Never hung them up, either."

"I'm certain it made it easier to take them out, though."

"Yeah, guess you're right. I shoved them all in trash bags and put them out by my car to be donated. I left the bed frame and mattress for the realtor to deal with, because I wasn't carrying it or tying it to the top of my car. Screw that.

"By the time I was going to start on my room it was already evening. I didn't have the money to pay the electric, so it was hard to see, and I had to hurry up before night. At least I didn't leave much behind, so I hoped to get it all done before dark."

He took off his cap and ran his fingers through his hair. He inhaled then continued. "As soon as that door was open, this thing," he nudged the cage with his foot, "bolted. It was so fast I didn't even get the chance to see what exactly it was. I only knew where it went because it left behind this trail of grayish goo on the carpet. I thought maybe it was blind since it knocked over the stacks of magazines and books running into the dining room. I was wrong, because it found the open window and jumped out. Outside, there was a path of trampled grass going to the steel fence, gunk streaking up it. My mom's is next to this patch of woods, and I assumed it went there. Even if I wanted to find it, I wouldn't out there.

"At the time, I thought it was just a big, wet rat. I heard it happens a lot with places not taken care of, so I didn't really care about it escaping. Also, clearly it wanted out of the house, so everyone wins. But it was night by then, so I had to push off doing my room until the next day. I left the place trashed as it was and went home. A bit later on, I called Becca and asked her if she knew about any pets mom might've had. She said why would she know? She hadn't talked to mom since dad died five years ago."

I apologized for his loss.

He waved me off. "It's whatever. Anyway, Becca didn't know anything, so we hung up and I went to bed." The man adjusted his position in the seat, leaning forward with his elbows on his knees. "Funny thing was that I couldn't stop thinking about it, like it was important but I didn't know why. I actually cared that it might get lost or hurt in the woods, that I might not see it again. It was *really* weird, and no matter how much I tried, I didn't sleep much that night. I called off work in the morning, grabbed some coffee, and went back to my mom's.

"My bedroom was nothing like it was when I moved out. I didn't know what it was, still don't exactly. An animal den or something. Papers and magazines and God knows what else coated in slime covered everything, hung from the ceiling and curtains; a cocoon of the stuff took up the corner where my bed used to be.

"A hole the size of my fist was at the top, ends of blankets poking out. Even in the sunlight I barely could see anything, but there were crumbs of some type of food going from it and the door, and near the cocoon was a dog dish with gross water. And the smell, Christ, like someone locked up a pet store and let the animals die and rot.

"I didn't know what to do or not to do, couldn't imagine this sort of thing existing, let alone in my mom's house. It had to have been there for a while. I tried to remember the last time I saw my room but couldn't. How the hell does something like that happen without me knowing? I didn't visit often, at least every couple months.... The thing about it, I wasn't scared. I should've been really scared, but there was nothing. It felt like looking into Becca's room. It was just *there*; what was inside didn't matter. So I left it the way it was.

"I went straight to my mom's room. I planned on getting to it last because it would take the least effort. She didn't keep much there after dad died. He liked collecting things like rocks, mugs, pencils and pens, notepads, random stuff he liked having around even though he didn't use any of it. Becca thinks he was a hoarder, but it never got that bad. My mom *hated* it being all over the house, so he kept everything in their room. Probably drove her crazy there too." He scratched his chin. "Funny that after he died the house became such a mess, like he was in a strange way keeping *her* from collecting by him doing it...."

"People are enigmas."

"True. Anyway, sorry. I tore her room apart looking for anything about whatever-the-hell was in my bedroom and what apparently lived in it." He pulled a small notebook from his pocket, raising it. It was wrinkled, missing many of its pages. For a moment, I believed he was throwing it in the fire.

"First, I found this." He flipped to the last page. "Only this one is important—the others are just her complaining about us or Dad. 'Ungrateful. Spoiled. They don't appreciate anything that I do. I wish John could give me another. There has to be a way to do it without him. I'd never cheat, but something else.' Then on the back, 'Trish down at bingo knows someone who knows someone who can help. Don't need John at all, only the kids. This one will be the one. They'll know how good of a mother I am, they'll appreciate me—they'll be the one I was supposed to have from the start.'"

"I'm assuming she meant another child?"

He tossed the journal into the flames and pulled out an envelope. "That wasn't a surprise to me. She made it known how bad of kids Becca and I were, and how if she could have another, they'd be the good one," he said, ignoring my question. "We weren't bad, funny enough. We got into normal kid stuff, like coming home late, fighting at school, normal kid's stuff. Nothing too crazy."

He unfolded the envelope and withdrew photographs. "But this surprised the hell out of me. Photos, photos of her and that thing. They're all blurry and it's never fully shown, so I couldn't really see what the thing looked like." He went through them. "Just gray smudges. Cuddling with my mom in her bed." He tossed it into the fire. "Out on the recliner in the living room watching TV." Another. His hands shook. "Dressing it up in mine and Becca's baby clothes." That one too. His knuckles became white. "Spoon feeding it baby food at the kitchen table, its gunk and the mushy food covering the table." He flung the remainder into the stove and shoved his face into his palms. "Fuck, I'm sorry, it's just …"

I wanted to console the man, but I didn't want to overstep my boundaries. I was only a merchant trying to purchase his wares, nothing more. I sat and waited until he spoke again.

"It clicked after going through those photos a dozen times." He sniffled, wiping his eyes on his sleeve. "Becca and I were still *living* there when they were taken. She made that thing and raised it while her own two kids were still there! Not once we ever said she was a bad mother, not once did we ever disrespect her or anything like that. We got in trouble, yeah, but how were we supposed to know her delusions would drive her to do something like this? We were just kids! Like, how fucked up in the head was she?"

"What did you do next, with that information?"

"At first, I thought about burning the house down, but I needed the money, and I wanted at least something good to come out of this insane situation. But it was still out there in the woods, and at the time, I couldn't let it go, that my *replacement* was alive. Mainly, I was so pissed and hurt about what she did I wanted to destroy what she wanted more than her own two kids."

He rubbed his hands together. "I wasn't going to go look for it, but I assumed it'd return to its den at some point, right? Like an animal. So, I went out and bought a rabbit trap, a hammer, and a flashlight and set it up in my room. It was too big to fit into the cocoon, but I put it in front of it and covered it with the gross paper I pulled down from the walls. I washed my hands like seven times afterwards. Then, I left all the windows open and hid out in Becca's room overnight.

"I sat at the cracked door watching the whole night. I probably should've brought more coffee beforehand. I didn't even know if it was going to come or not. For all I knew, the thing might've been run over by a car and I was wasting my time...."

He grinned. "But when it was around 5 a.m. there was scratching on the house outside, and something fell with a thunk in the dining room. My heart was beating so fast. I was worried I'd scare it and have to stay another night.

"It went past Becca's, but it was still too dark to see besides that it was small and had four arms or legs. It went in my room. I held my breath. My blood pounded in my ears. I remember needing to pee so bad, but I'd be stupid to move. Then the trap snapped shut, and a low gurgling, like it was whispering nonsense, came from my room. I ran in there, hammer raised, flashlight on, and pushed all the shit off the cage and looked at it for the first time and wanted to puke.

"It was...mangled, like it'd been hit by a semi but was still alive. Slick with dark goo and all muscle, knotted and twisted. It had tufts of hair coming out one side, and the other there was a row of eyes. So many. I don't know how it was making noise, because from what I can tell, there wasn't a mouth, but there had to be some sort of one if it ate food."

He gazed into the stove. "Some of its eyes were mine, some were Becca's. I know it sounds crazy even though this whole story is already insane, but it does. Blue and hazel. I know they weren't really mine, but it was like I was staring at my sister or my reflection. Then I realized its hair was the same color as ours too. Brown and auburn.

"It started whimpering, mewing, like a dog after being beaten. I couldn't bring myself to kill it. I don't want it to even die. Those fucking eyes ... I hated it, but that strange affection made me drop the hammer. I cried and screamed, broke the flashlight on the wall, kicked the cage. It was everything my mother ever wanted, so what did that make us? Trash? Unwanted? It's one thing to think your mom doesn't like you, but it's another to find out your mom actually hates *you*, hates you so much she replaces you with something not even human."

There was silence. He bobbed his knee and bit his fingernails. I expected him to explode and storm off into the cold, but after a while, he went on.

"I left it in the cage for a couple days. I didn't go to the house, either. I was a mess; I couldn't think straight. It wasn't so much the creature, but my mother and how she felt, what she did. The thing's basically innocent in all this. It couldn't know what it was being born into. I don't think it even has the ability to think like we do. I remembered what the note said, about how Trish from bingo knew someone. That someone was the one who helped her make it.

"So, through some phone calls, I found the guy—Chris something, an old man living out in the fucking boonies. He tried lying to me about it, saying he didn't know my mom or what I was talking about. I was still so angry about everything, I laid into him pretty bad—I was more ready to kill him than this thing here. Finally he says wait and grabs a book from a shelf. He opens it and gives it to me, saying it was how my mom did it. And right there on the page were the ingredients to create it, how if someone used parts of real people and some other weird stuff, a new life can be made. Then I remembered all the haircuts we had at home to save money, or the old clothes we were too big to fit in, or all those teeth that went to the tooth fairy. She had everything she needed. It didn't explain the eyes, but it didn't matter. I had my answer, little good it did. It was my sibling, Becca's too. Its blood is ours."

"Does your sister know about it?"

"No. She doesn't know anything, and I want it to stay that way."

"You're willing to sell your own kin to me?" I said. "After all the turmoil you went through to capture it and discover its history?"

"Yeah." He nodded. "It still reminds me of her, of all those years full of lies, of that damn house. I don't want, it but like I said, I don't want it to die, either. It's innocent. Now please, take it."

Mr. Bauld

I swallow the lump in my throat and wipe my forehead with the back of my hand. This guy has to be lying. No way what he has there is some Frankenstein. We're in America, for Christ's sakes; shit like that only happens in Germany, Russia, wherever. But he still holds it like it's gold instead of the coal it looks like.

"Would you care to hold it, Mr. Bauld? It's completely harmless now."

"No thanks," I say, putting my hands in my pockets. "So, what, did you take care of it after the kid dropped it off?"

He gently places it back within the glass and lowers it back down. "Yes. Its name was Amatus, and it was my companion for many years. It used to run around this room, hiding behind the same stands you see here today." Olaf smiles. "Amatus brought a lot of joy to my life, to this shop, but like all things made by man, sooner than I hoped, it passed away, becoming what you see now."

I don't have a clue what to say, so I blurt, "How much did you have to pay?"

He sighs. "Not much. If I would have known then how much I would love it later on, I might've paid more. There's no price I won't pay for a reprieve from the doldrums of time."

"Ah, well, I'm sorry for your loss, really. I had a pup once when I was a kid that had to be put down, had some sort of sickness. I cried for days."

"You understand then, the loss?"

I nod. "Sure."

Olaf runs his palm over his scalp, the skin folding over his hand and pulling back his face, then breathes in deeply. His chest looks like it may pop out of his shirt, like his body's able to suck in more air than any man should. Maybe he's a swimmer. I hear they can hold their breath for a long time. He lets his head go, and the skin snaps back into place. Is he wearing one of those like-real-life masks? Why would he be doing that? Why does he collect all this weird shit? Why does anyone do anything?

"It's still the witching hour, Mr. Bauld. We still have time for at least one more story, if you're still interested."

Tick.

Has that still been going this whole time? I must've been too wrapped up in his story to tell. It's definitely gotten louder, or closer, but that doesn't make any sense since we haven't moved from this spot. "You hear that?" I point at my ear. "That clock?"

"I don't hear anything but you and I. Not many noises can reach back here; even the heaviest of storms are a mere whisper."

Alright, I must be going nuts then.

"Now, on to the next tale. Follow me, if you will."

We pass by a rusted chain with a worse-off padlock keeping a small purple box with gold accents secured; a white flower with yellow in the middle, only the head, no stem; a bundle of gray, curled roots inside an ugly triangle with chicken scratch surrounding it. I'm extra careful not to knock anything over, because even though it's junk, I'm sure it's worth more than what I make in a year. Don't know if I should be upset with my boss or people blowing their money on shit like this. Probably both.

Tick.

Fucking clock! I run my hand over my sweaty face. Did it get hotter in here or is that the gnocchi I ate at the theater? I'm probably green at the gills. But leaving this schmuck and going back outside wouldn't be any better. I'd have somewhere to puke or shit my brains out, sure, but that's about it. I didn't eat much, so it should pass.

"Are you okay, Mr. Bauld?" He stops, turns to me, and puts his too-long hand on my shoulder. I swear his fingers reach to the other side of my back. Those beady fucking eyes are deeper somehow, wavy crow's feet spreading to his forehead and cheeks. "You don't seem quite well."

"I'm great," I say, the lines on his face gone, "just peachy."

"Would you prefer to stop?"

"Stop? There's a choice?"

"Certainly, Mr. Bauld. Everyone has a choice of whether they want to do something or not. It's only the outcome they fear."

"What would we do if I wanted to? Stop, that is."

"I would return to my work, and you would return to the outside."

I chuckle. "You'd seriously toss me out for not listening to a story after I've listened to one already?"

His skin ripples, like something in a flash passing just beneath it. "Unfortunately I would, Mr. Bauld. I uphold all my bargains even when the other party may not."

"It's just a story, though. You could go do whatever you were doing, and I can sit on the floor and be totally out of your way."

"That wasn't the agreement, and I don't believe in retroactivity."

I breathe in as much stale air my lungs will hold and sigh. "Alright," I wave my hand at him, "then let's get a move on."

Tick.

"Wonderful." He continues onward.

My legs are weaker, and rubbing my eyes doesn't take away the sting. Why am I suddenly exhausted? What time is it? I would've been better off sleeping at the theater than being in this place. If only she would've been grateful....

We pass a fancy black wood pedestal holding a thick open book with a picture of an eyeless woman kneeling over a weird symbol, an ugly, big piece of purple crystal sitting on a white cushion inside glass, wide silver cords burrowing through it like worms, an old, ordinary violin set in a dark stand, its stick tucked under the strings. What the hell is that doing here?

"At last we arrive," Olaf says, standing behind a small, glossy ball in a three-tiny-claw holder twirling up from the ground like some sort of wizard's staff. "Open your hand, Mr. Bauld." Olaf plucks it up like an egg and sets it in my palm. "Whatever you may believe this is, it is not."

Slippery and has some weight to it, it's like an oiled-up golf ball. Twirly indented lines cover it, forming a round symbol on the bottom. I rub it with my thumb, and it's oddly cool. "I better not be holding some type of weird testicle."

"No, no, nothing man-made."

Tick.

"I give up. What is it?"

"On second thought ..." He puts his finger to his chin. It curls backward up his head, blending into the lines around his eye, or I think that happens. The lights are darker here, or have they always been like this? Is my vision going to shit from not sleeping? And that damn clock's not fucking helping!

"It'd be better for me to tell its story, if that's alright with you, sir?"

"Like I have a choice."

Olaf

This was before the man with Amatus, many, many years in fact, although I can't quite recall what year it might've been. Existing for so long, time becomes frivolous. Still endless, unfortunately, in some cases. I do remember it was a cool autumn, far from summer and closing in on winter. I had the door propped open to allow the breeze and soft evening light in.

I was doing something—again, memory lost to time—and a man entered. He wore a lab coat stained red and yellow, its tail shredded and an ugly tear by his chest. Underneath were loosely hanging scrubs torn at the end, his pants ripped at the knees. The strangest thing of all was that he wore no shoes.

"Are you Olaf?"

"I am."

He adjusted his crooked glasses, panes spiderwebbed, while looking up at me with his left eye. Half his head was wound in frayed bandages covering the other eye. "I've heard of you through the grapevine of collectors. Do you still purchase oddities?"

"For as long as the Ossuary exists, yes."

"Is there criteria, or do you take anything off the street?"

"Many great items have come from the foulest parts of the city, but they must have intrinsic value for my interest to pique enough to make a purchase."

"And that's all? Intrinsic doesn't always equate to worthiness."

"I assure you, sir, that's all."

He opened his hand before me. "Does *this* pique your interest, Olaf?" The fingernail from his thumb was missing, and his calloused palm had many nicks.

My attention finally turned to the object he held, the very one you hold Mr. Bauld. I hadn't an inkling of what it was. The pattern was familiar—I had come across numberless labyrinthine patterns on more items than I could possibly name, but the sphere wasn't. It could've been anything or nothing, but nonetheless, my curiosity had awakened. I raised my hand to touch it, but he snatched it back. "What is it?"

"I don't want to reveal that until you've agreed to buy it," he said.

"If you know of my work, sir, then you must know I'm no fool."

"It's possible you won't buy it if you know what it is."

"And what leads you to that conclusion, Mr. ...?"

"*Doctor.* Dr. Trushel."

"How about this, Doctor. If you tell me how you procured it, but not what it is, I will purchase it without question." For playing games, I had every intention to pay as low as possible. I had dealt with unpleasant customers longer than he had been alive, but to demand that I purchase it on his terms in *my* shop? The audacity.

"Really?" He grinned.

"Certainly. So, if you would be so kind, tell me how you came to obtain it."

The doctor shifted from one foot to the other.

I eyed a thirteenth century broadsword leaning against the shelf near the front door. I wondered if it was still honed.

Then, finally, he started his tale.

"Like I told you before, I'm a doctor, and one morning, a new patient came in complaining about his eye. He wore an eye patch because he claimed when any sort of light touched it, it felt like 'a fire raging inside his head.' In the office, with the lights off and the window curtained, I had him remove the patch. His eyelid and the skin around it was swollen and pink, obviously very inflamed. Some blood vessels were popped in both too.

"I had him open his eye. His sclera was beet red, and the iris also had a tinge of red, mixing with his natural brown. His pupil had the beginnings of cataracts. Soon his whole eye would have it. I asked him what happened, and he said he was a construction worker, and a steel rod had slipped out from the wrapped bundle being lifted by a crane and hit him directly in the eye. If it hadn't been for his coworker pulling him out of the way in time, the rod would've went clear through his body."

The doctor spun his hand in circles in the air. "I ran him through vision exams and found his sight in that eye was gone, more than likely permanently. The hit must've severely damaged his optic nerve. It was the only thing that could cause the pain in his head, so I determined if the eye was removed or replaced with a false one, he'd no longer have any pain.

"I gave him another option of the wait and see approach and prescribed him painkillers. It's possible it might've healed over time and the pain would go away, but I doubted his eye would ever be normal again. He elected for surgery. He said he didn't have the time to wait. If he couldn't work, he'd lose his house; he needed the money. So, I scheduled him for the surgery a week from that day. He thanked me and left. About an hour later, I locked up, said good night to the secretary, and went home."

He looked around the empty showroom as though someone had materialized from the shadows. "No one knows this—colleagues, friends, family, any women I've been with—but in my library, there's a false shelf that opens like a door to a room. In there, I do the work I actually enjoy. Shelves against the walls holding odd trinkets, strange books, etcetera. The worktable in the middle had tinctures, jars of deformities in formaldehyde, and pages long forgotten by historians atop." The doctor smiled. "It was such a beautiful space. Took me so long to collect everything...."

"Anyway, under the table was an old wooden chest housing all the odds and ends I couldn't find a purpose for. I hoped eventually I would, and finally I did with the construction worker. I dug through the chest's contents until I found what I needed: the Sphaera Visus—the item I showed before—tucked in the bottom corner. Coincidentally, I got it through a trade from a patient years prior for removing his teeth. At the time, I didn't know what the Sphaera was, but it looked like it could potentially have value."

He shrugged. "Using the instructions in *The Elongation of Sight and Other Transmogrifications of Vision* by E. Alley, I used a blowtorch to heat the Sphaera until it was white hot, then using a baster half full with a green concoction I prepared, I squeezed single drops onto it until there was no more. The carved lines glowed as the substance filled the indentations until the symbol on its underside was entirely colored. With prongs, I quickly picked it up and plunged it into a bucket of cool water by my feet. Iridescent steam billowed, and it sizzled as it sunk to the bottom. I tightened a lid over the pail, covered it in a thick, black blanket, and pushed it against the wall underneath the table. I turned off the lights on my way out, sealed the room, and didn't return for five days. When I removed it from the water, it was ice cold. The lines had dimmed, but were still noticeably green. I placed it into a small box and two days later brought it into the office for the patient's procedure.

"I didn't divulge to him his eye would be replaced with the Sphaera, only that his vision may be greatly improved after the operation. He consented to a false eye, yet ... Don't look at me that way, Olaf. A half-blind construction worker would be replaced quickly by another with full sight. He would've lost his job. Then what?"

I didn't look at him in any way besides my usual stare. Perhaps he saw himself in me, the excuse to justify involuntary implantation, to alter another's physical form based on his own selfish beliefs.

The doctor scratched his greasy head. "I was doing him a favor," he repeated, "and the surgery went well and easier than I expected. The Sphaera connected seamlessly to his optic nerves. And besides the bandaging around his head, he appeared fine after it was over. When the anesthesia wore off and he woke up, I explained how the operation went, what he could expect, and not to touch or remove the bandaging for at least ten days. At that time, he'd need to come into the office to see me again. He thanked me, and I left him with a nurse.

"Ten days later, I was excited as I undid his bandages. I had to force my hands to stop trembling. It felt like when I undressed a woman for the first time, that...*rush*. Once it was removed, his face was bruised blue-black, and the closed eye leaked a lime-green pus I wiped away. It took him four tries to open his eye.

"He said it still hurt like he was being stabbed in the eye, but it wasn't as bad as it had been. I did some basic vision assessments, and the Sphaera moved like a normal eye should. Its etchings weren't green anymore, but a bright yellow.

"He said everything looked weird, like all the edges were now smoothed down and color bled into the outline of things. I assured him that was normal and it would become clearer overtime. I told him to contact the office if he experienced any problems, and he should return in about a month for a check-up, or earlier if he believes he needs to."

The doctor rubbed his closed eye with his palms. It was only then I noticed the bag beneath it, how haggard he was, but I didn't ask from what.

After stretching his back, he went on. "It was three weeks since I saw him in my office, so I assumed his recovery was doing well. But one night, I came home to find it in shambles.

"Initially, I thought maybe my crazy ex-wife broke in and ransacked the place, but she moved away with the kids years ago, so I doubted it was her. Cautiously, I went through the foyer towards the kitchen. I had only one home defense, which was a loaded pistol stored underneath my bed upstairs.

"In the silence, there was a rummaging noise coming from the stair-well only a couple feet away. Whoever it was was still in my home, upstairs. I gave up going for my gun and turned back to leave and call the police, but immediately I was smashed in the head. I spun, trying to grab something to stop my fall but found nothing, and smacked the floor and blacked out.

"When I came to it was still night, and a weight pressed my head into the ground. I smelled stool and rotten meat, tasted the foul scent along with my own stomach bile. I managed to move my head enough to see above. It was the construction worker, bathed in pale light. His unwashed hair hung over half his black-smeared face. A patchy beard ran up his cheeks like overgrown ivy, and cut out from the mess of facial hair was salivating, yellow teeth. His eyes were wide: the normal one wild, the Sphaera spinning like a sphere on a gyroscope, endlessly rolling and rotating in place.

"He shoved his face against mine and screamed, 'Get it out!' Spit went all over me. 'Get it out, get it out, get it out!' His voice became shriller and shriller. 'No colors,' he continued. 'No shapes, no forms, no counterssss.' He ground his teeth, raked at his cheeks with chipped fingernails.

"'It can see, *It* can see beyond and through and gaze upon me, you, us.' He groped his face like it wasn't his own. 'This place, this world to burden. I don't want It, I don't want to watch and know and see, and take it out, take it out, take it out!'

"'Lines without purposes, colors without colors—limbs, so many growing and withering and growing and withering and dying and re-birthing, searching, searching for something to hold, to grasp, something to burden It, someplace to give passage into and out and through, to purge and empty and fill and *grow and grow*—take it out, take it out!'

"I shouted I would, but we'd have to go back to the office to do so. I didn't have the necessary tools to extract it. Then, suddenly, he looked at the ceiling, mouth agape, tears trickling through his beard. He hollered gibberish until seemingly his throat became raw and his voice became a whisper.

"'Too long, too long,' he croaked, raising his hands towards the sky. 'If not now, too long; can't, can't, It can't and I can't and must be gone, must be gone.' His fingers bent into claws, and I closed my eyes before he dug them into his eye.

"He mumbled something as I listened to him dig around the eye. I heard skin tear, and I felt his blood hit the side of my face, then another tear before he smashed me in the head again. I blacked out, and when I came to this time, I was ... I was ..." The doctor quieted and rubbed his left wrist where gray fragments held to the sleeve.

The faint rain pitter-pattered on the door, and thunder grumbled in the far distance. I frowned. Autumn was my favorite season here, and to miss a day of perfect weather was a travesty. Alas, such was life.

"What followed, sir?"

"I was strapped to a kitchen chair with duct tape by my wrist and ankles, around my forehead to the backrest, my eyelids and my mouth. The construction worker stood over me, blood and pus draining from his empty orbital socket onto me. His hair framed his face and touched mine. I tried ... I tried to move, but nothing would budge.

"'No one deserves to see like this,' he said in a trance. 'Nobody deserves an eye like this.'

"I shouted apologies, although they were muffled by the tape. He didn't care. He raised his hands," the doctor looked up, "and in one was the Sphaera and the other was a scalpel he must've stolen from my emergency bag I left in the house. I couldn't move. I couldn't look away. I couldn't ..." Tears welled in his eye. "It was excruciating, like my entire body was full of magma, every nerve, every fiber ablaze and raw and rubbed with salt and boiling oil. Impossible agony. Unmeasurable. So much blood. It clogged my nose and my throat and I was drowning. Drowning on my own blood. And I watched from two different points as he severed the nerves; then I could only see from one. He tossed my eye on the floor carelessly, forced the Sphaera in, then sealed my eyelid with more tape."

"What did you see?" I said.

"It was everything and nothing, a transparent colorful but black mist overlapping and devouring and rebirthing and far away, so far, things grew outwards and forwards and back and crumbled and were replaced by more and more, and from somewhere inside me, a discordant symphony unlike anything I've ever heard played on instruments with no name."

He cleared his eye and sniffled. "It was horrifying and beautiful, and I was only able to stop watching It consume when my neighbor undid the tape. She saw the door open and the mess inside and came in to find me like I was. I collapsed to the floor and told her I was fine, that she didn't need to call the police. She kept asking about my eye, why I wouldn't open it, and the blood on the floor and ... I screamed to leave. When she finally did, I avoided my eye on the floor, grabbed the scalpel he abandoned, and went to the mirror in the bathroom."

He glanced at his hand holding the sphere. Taking a deep breath, he went on. "Once it was out, I dressed it and went to the office. It was destroyed, and blood spattered the walls. I didn't even know the secretary was there until I went past the desk to find her unconscious. The side of her head was swollen, her face bruised, and hair stuck to her skin with congealed blood, but she was still breathing. In the exam room, I tended to my wound, gathered what necessary things I needed, then left."

"What happened to your practice, your home?"

He shrugged. "They didn't matter. Once I saw what I saw, it changed me fundamentally. I couldn't care about anything—life lost meaning from just a glimpse. I tried to care, but it was impossible. When that man tore out my eye, my past didn't matter. But I'm sure the office is closed and my belongings stolen or sold, except for what I have with me."

"If this item is all you possess, sir, then why sell it? It seems as though it's the most important part of your present existence. As you said, once you had peered behind the curtain, nothing else mattered."

"I still see," he said, almost a whisper. "Even in my hand, I still see." The doctor coughed, then said, "I want to want my old life back, and getting rid of it may do that. I know I could toss it in the river or throw it away, but I want something in return, something to help me back on my feet, and the only person who would possibly do that for me is you."

"What about the other collectors? Certainly they'd pay more than I would."

"I don't want them to see me like this, knowing that they probably know what happened. Also, if my things were stolen, I'm positive they would be the ones who'd do it."

"One last question," I said, drawing it out for curiosity's sake. "What will you do if I take the item from you and you still see It?"

His bloodshot eye fixated on me. "Then the Sphaera is parasitic and infected my brain, and the problem doesn't lie with It but with me."

"If that's true—"

"Enough of the games. Are you buying it or not?"

Mr. Bauld

"I paid him a modest amount for it, less than what it was truly worth. His imprudence with the poor worker soured my empathy for the man." Olaf takes the ball from me and places it back into the display case. "He left the shop soon thereafter, and I haven't heard from him since."

Tick.

I rub my temples. My stomach gnaws at me. The ground's shaking, or I'm so fucking tired I'm imaging it. It has to be close to morning. I think I can deal with the cold more than with the damn clock and his damn stories. "What time is it? I think I should be hitting the road."

From a pocket inside his overcoat, he slips out a golden watch, pops it open, glances at it, then shoves it back home. "There's yet still time for one more, Mr. Bauld."

Tick.

"But I don't ..." Words feel like motor oil coming out. My head is filled with fluff, pouring out my ears, my nose.

"Mr. Bauld?" Olaf stands a couple feet away. "Are you coming?"

Tick.

"No more. I'm done with your shit." I swivel toward where we entered from, but there's only dark fog there—no more cases or stands or the wall or door. Where the fuck did everything go? Where did *we* go? I lick my dry lips and focus—fucking focus—on walking to where the door must be. "You can take your crazy stories and shove 'em."

"What about our deal?" Olaf calls. "It's yet not dawn."

I throw my hand over my shoulder. "Deal schmeal."

Inside the fog there's only fucking more. Everything's eaten by it. It reeks of exhaust and smoke and duck shit. Something's crying from somewhere, high-pitched, like an animal, maybe a kitten or baby squirrel? I don't know. Drawn out whining overlapping rustled trees. Soft distorted laughter behind both of them, barely there. Maybe it's not trees but that? On and on they go and—everything quiets like they weren't ever there.

I gotta leave.

Tick.

My legs are so heavy like I drank the whole bar. Everything's going downhill. Tonight's been one long joke. The theater. The broad. This place. Why'd I think it would be any better than before? I should've stood her up and played cards at Jimmy's game, or picked up Bobby and drove out to the boonies to shoot shit, or...

How *stupid* do I have to be to believe that things can change for the better? That those fucking banshees won't drag me to the pits of Hell where they gargle come like it's mouthwash. I can't win. Treat them like royalty and they just shit on you.

They had it coming. Some more than others, but at the end of the day, they deserved what they got.

Tick.

Finally the fog thins. Shapes come into view. I move my fat ass faster, and out of the haze, I arrive where I started. Olaf's waiting there, thin as a toothpick, and so...tall. His back bows like my great-grandmother's, and his head hangs from a long neck, arms bent wrong at the elbows, hands spilling over the floor. I don't know why I expect him to be any different.

"Will you follow me, Mr. Bauld?" His voice is the air, in my ears. "I'm certain you'd enjoy this one the most."

"What—" I spin around, and there's a brick wall an inch from my face. I jump back and almost fall. Nothing else. No door. No lights. Nada. I touch it like it's a...what's the word? Mirage. Yeah, mirage. Gritty and hard, no give. I put my ear to it, and machinery clicks and clinks and clacks and pops and whispers and

TICK.

"—the fuck's going on?"

Cold hands wrap around my shoulders, spread like wiry roots down to my belt, and Olaf's face appears beside mine. His smile reaches the top of his head, sinking into the churning of his mask. I blink away sweat. It's a sauna inside my clothes. "Mr. Bauld, once man has made a pact, it must reach its terminus."

"I don't want to," I think I say. "I didn't mean to. Really. Just let me go, okay? I got a dog to feed, kids to let out, a wife—a wife to walk ..."

TICK.

"So many lies," he hisses. "However, I place no blame unto you, Mr. Bauld. It's of your kind to mislead for one's own benefit, woven into the fabric of the vacuous primordial pool in which you blindly crawled out of." His fingers wrap around my waist and turn me, and I almost stumble forward when the floor tilts even though nothing else budges. "It's obvious you're so very tired, so let me be the courteous host and move things along."

TICK.

A blur of ugly misshapen things fly past, stands and pedestals and lights poof into smoke and spin and rotate, and I don't feel but hear the ground grind against rock and drag across my shoes and another wall is in front of us. This...this is *massive*, higher than any mountain I've seen. Above sits impenetrable black fog. Does it have a top? An end? Does tonight? This can't be happening. It can't. This is America for Christ's sakes; this doesn't happen here.

Did he drug me?

TICK.

Hypnotize me?

TICK.

Is this a dream? A nightmare? Am I really in that girl's bed, knocked out? Maybe she was appreciative. Maybe she was grateful. Maybe she saw the error of her ways before I went down the alley and we caught a cab and did the you-know and now I'm out like a light while she does whatever girls do after getting the ol' wham-bam. Must be. Has to be. God, I hope so.

TICK.

Oh God, oh Christ—where, what? My body's gone, empty. I'm a puppet, and Olaf's the strings and, "Poleaste." Words, how do they work? If I could lift my hands, would there be a face to feel? Am I even seeing with my own two eyes? "Oleafse."

TICK.

Olaf walks around me, his normal tall, two-legged self, while I'm trapped in place by his grip. There are no bent arms or wild smiles or bowing back. Weird looking but regular. He stops before the wall and faces me, eyes no more beads but charcoal. Embers. Smoldering like coals. His skin moves like the jelly atop of milk gone bad.

TICK.

"Behind this wall lies the final item, Mr. Bauld, the item that gave everything fruition—the Ossuary, my ancestors, some believe this very city and the alleys—like roots deep in the foundation of man. Always flourishing and subsuming, creating a perpetual labyrinth in its own image, change begetting change until all's ash and rust, and even then it will continue on under the desolate black skies and through barren deserts while gods are audience from the echelons of propagation."

TICK.

"Denizens don't discover the Ossuary because they found it themselves. They only discover it because it allows itself to be seen. It knows what it wants and knows what I want. The items you've seen, touched, could you possibly fathom what would transpire if any imbecile could enter these walls and view them? Purchase them? Gods—"

It—Olaf's no man, no human, he's an *it*—shakes its many heads. Slivers open like big blinking eyelids across its chest, and smoky, delicious-looking water rolls inside it. "There's not a word strong enough to describe the madness that would ensue."

TICK.

It sighs a cloud of purple-black. "I've grown weary of this place, Mr. Bauld." A never-ending blooming bouquet of hands lowers from above. One bends back, and it rests its head against it. "It too wants change: scenery, time, species. Man has worn out its welcome, the entertainment they once held now lackluster."

TICK.

"The Ossuary revealed itself to you tonight." It turns to the wall, raises its arms, and its dozens of fingers reach toward it. "Deep down, you must have had a reason to find it, had a purpose it sought after, like the boy, the doctor, the thousands of others who've crossed its threshold. Yours may not be here for the items it contains, but perhaps it was to simply serve as audience to the severance of the Ossuary's tether to the city, to be a watcher, a reader, a listener." It breathes in deeply, and its back swells and gorgeous slits run down it. Black water gurgles as a million fingers rise from the goop and clench onto Olaf's back. "It makes sense, however nothing truly matters on the precipice of an Origin."

TICK.

Olaf's fingers stretch longer—more than I've ever seen anything do. The tips split down the middle like pulling apart an orange, and wiry veins squirm all over the brickwork and burrow into the shaking mortar. Dust rains down, and bricks clatter like shivering teeth, and rock grinds against more rock behind the wall, but Christ almighty, *finally* the ticking stops. It's gone. I think I sigh, but I'm sure there's relief; the calmness in my chest, the aching in my joints and the pounding in my head—gone like that.

The worms scurry back into Olaf's fingertips, and he steps back as a crack bolts down the middle of the wall, breaking like a bajillion knees being smashed.

I wince when a warm, white light blares from the widening opening.

The back of Olaf's head sinks into its skull then snaps back in place, and its eye sockets are full of wiry, dark things tangled together, swimming out into the air.

Olaf's other hands let me go, and my useless legs collapse under me. I look up at the monster Olaf has become, a shadow against the light behind it. I want to move, but—who am I kidding? I *don't* want to. What little I'm leaving behind isn't worth the trouble trying to get out of this hellhole again. I'm cooked. Caput.

And not to mention, the light's so beautiful. I don't know how I didn't see it before. For Christ's sake, I'm crying from how smitten I am with it. It tastes like a fine red wine, smells like cigars, feels like a naked woman who has more than a handful; it makes everything better. My date, the guys, all of them ain't nothing compared to this, and really, I don't want them to be. They're not important any more, fuck 'em. I put in too many damn years dealing with their bullshit, and finally—finally life's giving what I rightfully deserve.

Something coils around my gut, the wonderful light eats everything, and, willingly, I'm pulled in.

Feeding the Beast

Robert Essig

Now

WADE SALMONSON FEEDS THE beast.

It has only been a matter of months, and still he doesn't understand why the beast manifests in his attic like some creepy conjuring in a cheesy horror film. These things don't seem quite so impossible when they're happening, when the texture of the thing is flesh and not latex. The impossible becomes quite easy to accept when you're the one feeding the damned thing. And it's a whole lot scarier in the flesh than latex and foam on the TV screen.

Wade stares as it eats. He's captivated and repulsed in equal measures. The captivation comes from the sheer absurdity of the thing in his attic. The repulsion has a lot to do with the measures to which he has devolved to feed the thing and keep it from devouring his son.

Standing far enough away from the thing as not to be in danger, Wade grips the jawbone tight like it's a talisman. He can feel the enamel teeth digging into his palm. He always clenches the jawbone in his hand as the beast eats, as if by doing so he's reminding himself that this is reality, because the thing in his attic has to be something that escaped from his worst nightmares, the ones so dark and deep he has no recollection of dreaming them even on his worst nights of sleep.

The crunching of bones coming from the beast causes Wade to shudder. He stares on as if he has to see what he has wrought, as if this is a part of some evil punishment for a circumstance in his life that he didn't apply for and yet hasn't properly petitioned.

The eyes that stare at him from the beast have a touch of pity to them at the start of every feeding that quickly turns to ecstasy once flesh is ripped and bones are crushed enough for it to swallow the bloody mess without much chewing.

Wade squeezes the jawbone.

How many more times can he feed the beast before he just gives himself over to the thing? Would it even accept his flesh as a sacrifice? He wonders that, especially during a feeding or right after. He can't follow through with such an act of selfish sacrifice, not with his son still in the picture. What would become of Trevor? Would *he* be in charge of feeding the beast, or would the beast eat him too?

Trevor has enough problems to deal with being twelve and openly transgender in a world that's still grappling with the idea that people sometimes don't feel comfortable in their own bodies. Add to that his mother and sister going missing and a father who's preoccupied with some freakish manifestation in the attic and the poor boy doesn't have a chance. Wade can't leave him to the fate of this thing that haunts him. He has to find a way to hand his burden off to someone else.

"Dad?" Trevor's voice drifts up the stairwell to the door Wade has left open just a crack, just enough that he can hear approaching footsteps or his son calling for him.

Wade stares at the monster as it finishes its meal. He takes tentative steps backward, toward the attic door. He doesn't like letting the beast out of his sight. It isn't that the thing has ever been aggressive toward him; it's more that he feels threatened by it and fears turning his back on it.

At the door, Wade hollers down the attic stairs. "Give me a few minutes. I'll be right there."

It's almost time for baseball practice. Trevor is a stickler about punctuality, something most young boys are oblivious of. But he knows not to come up to the attic. He knows it's forbidden. Most of the time the attic is a perfectly safe place to be, no more dangerous than any other room of the house.

After the beast is sated.

But when the beast becomes hungry, Wade cannot only sense it but also hear the thing in his mind, calling to him. He's tried ignoring the calls, but that was when the first tragedy happened. That was when Wade realized the beast calls to him and him alone, as a sort of warning that if he provides food, it will retreat into the ethers until again it requires nourishment. It will call to Wade, and Wade alone can feed it.

Or else it will call to whoever is close by and feed on them.

"Daaaad?"

Trevor's voice drifts from below again. It's faint enough that Wade figures he's on the first floor. The attic is at the top of a small staircase from the second floor, hidden by a door that looks as if it leads to a coat or linen closet. The door is always locked. The attic is Daddy's workshop. At least that's what Wade has convinced Trevor into believing.

As the last of the shredded flesh and broken bones are consumed, slithering down the strange gullet of the beast, it begins to fade as if it hasn't been there, as if it doesn't have tethers to Wade's mind. As if it doesn't torment him with its pleas, its hungry calls.

Its threats.

Wade places the jawbone on a table that has been stored in the attic since his wife redecorated the living room five years ago. The patina on the bone is the color of French vanilla ice cream with the grime of who knows how many hands that have been unfortunate enough to hold the strange artifact and beckon to the call of the thing gazing upon Wade with human eyes in a face that looks as if it has been half-blown away from a shotgun blast. The tongue hangs grotesquely from where its jaw is missing, tendrils of flesh and snippets of muscle dangling like the roots of a tree fallen from over saturated ground.

As the thing fades, it stares at Wade with sad eyes as if it too bears the other end of some awful curse that forces it to feed in such a grisly manner just to remain on this Earth, and for what?

Then

The second time Wade fed the beast, it felt as if he had given the thing a part of his soul. He was sick about what happened, and as much as he tried to push the event out of his mind, it was there, taunting him at all times.

He was raising his son and baby girl solo since Brittani's disappearance. His mind had been all over the place. After all the detective interviews, police tape, and investigation, he was mad with guilt and yet there wasn't a thing to tie him to her disappearance. Life moved on.

Wade told Trevor that his mother had probably been abducted by someone and that they would do everything they could to find her. The problem was there was no evidence to support that assumption. Even the police were stumped. With such a jarring lack of evidence, it was as if she had merely vanished one day.

Trevor's baseball season was in full force, and that was a great way for him to deal with the pain of losing his mother.

It burdened Wade that his baby girl, Donya, wouldn't know her mother. She wouldn't remember anything about her, the way she smelled, her smile of reassurance. Donya wouldn't have fond memories and cherish the comfort and love. For her, Mother would be a photograph and nothing more, just a picture of someone she would have been told all her life was a great woman.

That broke Wade's heart.

In the weeks after Brittani's disappearance, Wade found himself slipping further into a void of denial. He would drop Donya off at the babysitter's house—there was no way he was having someone watch her at his house, not with the possibility of the thing in the attic showing up and sending ethereal messages—then he would take Trevor to practice, where Wade was assistant coach.

He hardly fit in as it was considering baseball wasn't exactly his favorite pastime like so many other men who volunteered for such responsibilities. His decision to vie for the assistant coach position was primarily fueled by the treatment some of the kids on the team gave Trevor when they found out he had been born a girl. Wade and Brittani had gone to great lengths to have the league allow Trevor to play, and he feared backlash. With Wade present at practice and games, the other kids were less likely to tease and taunt Trevor.

Wade was distracted by current events in his life but also the voice that called out in his mind—a hungry voice that spoke no discernible language and yet very clearly wanted to eat.

Wade put the lock on the attic door to keep the thing out of the rest of his house as much as it was to keep Trevor out of the attic. Wade had no idea whether the beast could get out of that unfinished room on the third floor of the house, and he didn't want to find out.

He stayed away from his house as much as possible, attending vigils for his wife and doing TV interviews when they came up. It had been several weeks since her disappearance, and she was becoming forgotten about. She was just another missing person in a world where people went missing every day.

He had always worked from home, and that was becoming a problem. During the day, while Donya was at the babysitter's and Trevor was at school, Wade would sit in his office delving into his work just to blot out what a nightmare his life was rapidly becoming. The problem was, day by day, the voice in his head swelled. At first it was a mere whisper that invaded his thoughts, a touch of madness so slight it was acceptable, palpable even.

But the whisper grew and grew into a pained moan of hunger like a beacon. And then it became angry. Demanding.

Many times, Wade found himself at the top of the stairs, staring at the attic door. The beast would speak to him in its unique tongue. Words that made no sense instilled in him an urgency, a need that only he could suffice. It was an unspoken chant to bring human flesh.

The longer Wade denied the beast what it wanted, the angrier it got and the more Wade felt like he was losing his mind. He had read Lovecraft in college, and he felt as if he was in one of those stories. Only he couldn't just lose his mind after scribbling a rambling manifesto and be done with it like one of Lovecraft's unfortunate protagonists. He had children to care after, to protect.

It was a Wednesday when the babysitter called early in the morning to let Wade know she had come down with a cold and wouldn't be able to watch Donya. Wade told her that was okay, he would take care of his little girl until the sickness passed, but he didn't believe her. She was putting it on a bit thick with the strain in her voice, like she was on her deathbed. The cynical side of Wade figured she had the brown-bottle flu, but he was kind and told her to take all the time she needed, figuring she would have a miraculous recovery the following day. At least he hoped so.

The beast was making him nervous. The voice in his head was more than a mere taunting. It was a thrum, a force that was not only distracting but also maddening to the point that he feared he would do something stupid.

He made calls to get a babysitter on the quick only to find the incessant howling of the beast too much to handle. Wade could hardly speak on the phone without sounding like a man insane, or at least a man deep in the throes of meth addiction or on a tranq bender. It was as if he had to talk above the demanding voice that dominated the echo chamber of his mind, screaming about finding a babysitter but unable to hear or comprehend the people he was calling.

The next step was to leave the house all day, but what good would that do? Wade would have to return or move himself and his kids out entirely, and he knew the thing would follow. Somehow. So long as he had that damned jawbone it would follow, and he had tried getting rid of the damn thing. Like a boomerang, it always came back to him and with it, the beast of limitless hunger.

The way Wade remembered it, he had packed a diaper bag and was headed for the garage door to get in the car and leave. He knew that would only earn him enough time to figure out a method in which to feed the beast that didn't require sacrificing one of his loved ones, but the beast had something different in mind. It wasn't the garage door Wade found himself at. It was the attic door. And it was unlocked.

His memories of what happened were filed like an old film missing frames. It was as if the beast had caused him to lose control of his mind, moving him around the house like a chess piece.

The attic door was open. Wade was in the attic. The beast stood in the corner like something birthed of a thousand nightmares. It was taller than a man and larger in girth, but it bore a striking resemblance. Wade had never seen it like that before. It was never appealing to the eye but certainly was more so when it was sated. The thing stood on spindly legs of raw muscle, wet, glistening, and streaked with throbbing, purple veins. Its gut was open and its rib cage split down the center, meaty ribs splayed out like spider legs. Dripping intestines and thin tendrils of its nervous system reached out from the gaping cavity like eager tentacles, whipping around like cats' tails. Wade had never felt so terrified in his life as he approached the monstrosity with his baby girl thrust before him like an offering. It was if he could sense his movements but was powerless to flee. It was almost like watching himself make the worst decision of his life through the lens of a movie camera just waiting for the director to yell *cut*, only no one did anything as he got closer to the beast.

Closer still, he could feel the sticky tethers of its nervous system as it grabbed for Donya. And Wade did nothing to protect her. He handed his daughter to the beast, watching as she screamed and cried while the veins and arteries and ligaments wrapped around her body. Mummifying her in its fetid clutches, her little body was pulled away from Wade and squeezed until her little screaming voice was stifled and her flesh oozed a consistency the thing could manage with its lopsided head that was missing its jaw. As pieces of Donya were sucked into the throat, the beast's body began to coalesce and take shape, repairing itself before it faded away as if it had never been there in the first place.

Wade could have easily thought it was all a figment of his imagination or that he was going insane—well, he was pretty sure of the latter, regardless. But Donya was gone without a trace and only he knew why. At some point there would be an investigation, and it would look awfully suspicious that both his wife *and* daughter went missing within a period of several weeks.

It was clear the jawbone was to blame. Wade couldn't understand why, but that was the only explanation. It was to blame, and he had to do whatever he could to be rid of it.

Only it didn't want to be rid of him.

The words of his friend, Singer, echoed in his mind.

Singer, you bastard.

But what bothered Wade more was a deeper regret that was probably to blame for all of this.

Had he brought this beast upon himself? Upon his family?

Now

Trevor has always been into baseball, going back to before he announced to his parents that he felt more like a Trevor than a Lindsey. Brittani and Wade accepted their daughter's admissions with caution, assuming it was a phase she would grow out of. Once Trevor was old enough to play softball, they signed him up under his birth name for a league. When he found out softball was a different version of baseball with a larger ball and all-girl teams, he was devastated.

It was then that Brittani and Wade truly accepted that their little girl was indeed more comfortable as a little boy. Trevor even explained to them that he didn't find joy in the things little girls were interested in. He didn't like playing with dolls or wearing dresses and cute clothes. He wanted to get dirty and play baseball. He wanted to go fishing and climb trees.

At first, Brittani was sad, feeling almost as if she had lost her daughter, whom she had envisioned getting married in a gorgeous dress and shopping for clothes and doing all those girly things that she enjoyed. Depression hit her hard, but Wade was there to talk with her and let her know the only thing that mattered was Trevor's happiness. What would his life be if he was trapped in a body he didn't feel comfortable with?

"I miss Mom," Trevor says from the passenger seat on the way to baseball practice.

Wade glances over at his son. "I do too."

He wants to tell Trevor the truth but knows he can't. He can't tell anyone the truth. It's a burden for only him to bear, one he isn't sure he can live with.

"The police are doing everything they can," Wade reassures.

Trevor's getting tired of hearing that over and over again. To him, it feels like nothing's being done. Life moves on. Another baseball practice awaits. Meanwhile, both his mother *and* sister are gone, vanished as if they disappeared into thin air.

"You're getting pretty good on the field," Wade says, changing the subject.

"Coach Henrickson puts me in left field all the time. No one hits balls out to left field. It gets so boring."

Wade nods and takes a deep breath. "I know. I'll talk to him. I really wish he'd let the kids switch positions a bit so they can all experience and try out new things."

"The other kids get to change positions. I'm always stuck out in left field. No one wants to be in left field."

The truth is Tyler has a hell of an arm. He's pitcher material, but Coach Henrickson only allows his son, Aaron, to pitch, and sometimes Aaron's friends. Wade doesn't like that, and he's spoken up about it, but Henrickson just laughs in his face. Wade knows the type. He had likely been a bully in school and carried that torch into adulthood, passing it on to his offspring to perpetuate a vicious cycle of hate and intimidation. Wade isn't proud that he, as an adult man, can be intimidated by the likes of Henrickson, but Trevor's well-being matters most, and Wade doesn't want to be kicked off the team for not getting along with the coach. He has to be there.

What are you going to do when you can't be there for Trevor? Wade thinks. *What if that damn thing in the attic doesn't allow you to be there?*

Wade's mind often returns to the creature in his attic, the things he's done to keep the damn thing away, the sacrifices that have been made. How long can he live with that thing taunting him? With every feeding, it goes away, and just when things begin to get normal again—well, as normal as can be in a tumultuous life where his wife and daughter have gone missing and only he knows where they've gone—it calls to him again and again and again, always hungry for more.

"Dad?"

I will never leave you. A mere whisper cuts through Wade's mind like a razor.

"Dad?"

I need to get rid of it, Wade thought. *I need to get rid of that fucking jawbone. Damn you, Singer!*

"DAD!"

Trevor's voice brings Wade out of his thoughts just in time to slam on the brakes to avoid a collision with a Dodge Ram at a stop sign.

Wade looks at his son with haunted eyes. "I guess we both have a lot on our minds."

Then

Before it took Donya, Wade had been trying to feed the beast other things: rats, cats, dogs, even a snake he wrangled from the backyard. Nothing sated the beast like human flesh. It would dissipate sometimes after being fed a pet, for instance, but snakes and mice and organic matter did nothing to satisfy its insatiable appetite.

Singer's words echoed in Wade's mind. *It wants what hurts you, what you love.*

Wade hardly remembered the man saying those things to him. It was on the night he was given the damn jawbone, what he thought was some strange offering, a mere joke between a couple of buddies out having a drink. At the time, he didn't think Singer knew about Wade and Singer's wife, Marta. He didn't think anyone knew about them aside from he,

Marta, and the motel room they met at a few times.

At the time, before his little girl had been consumed by that damned thing in the attic, Wade was only just recovering from the police interviews and media storm that followed his wife's disappearance when he saw online that Newton Singer had killed himself.

Wade grabbed the bone, idly passing it between his hands. He was intimately familiar with the smoothness of it and the shape of the remaining teeth. On first glance, one would think it an animal jawbone, but closer inspection revealed it was more alien in nature. Not alien like little green people from outer space, alien as in not from this world, wholly unique in structure of the bone and the teeth it held in a mammalian fashion.

Singer gave him the jawbone at the bar that odd night they met for drinks, something they used to do regularly before their individual married lives became too hectic for things like meeting up with friends and having a few beers over the game, a few laughs and time to let off steam. Wade especially didn't have that kind of time because when he did go out to blow off steam, he was seeing Marta.

She had stopped talking to Wade weeks before he met with Singer, and though he was fairly certain Singer was setting him up to call him out, he agreed to meet in a very public place for drinks. Singer didn't say anything about Marta and Wade didn't ask, but he could tell. There was an underlying current between them that screamed of something unspoken, which caused Wade to drink more than he intended.

Enough to accept the offering of a jawbone of all things, to which Wade laughed about even when the exchange was finished and Singer sighed in apparent relief, a response which, at the time, Wade hadn't understood.

Wade even laughed off the warnings that got lost somewhere in his alcohol-saturated brain that night.

Now

Wade loves seeing Trevor so excited about baseball and playing the game. He knows deep down it must be hard for Trevor, considering what he had to overcome to play with the other boys in the first place. Wade knows many of the boys on the team don't see Trevor as one of them. And the ones who accept Trevor for who he really is aren't vocal about their support, especially since the hot shot of the team, Aaron, is the manager's son. Getting on Aaron's bad side means being stuck in outfield or deep in the batting rotation, both of which Trevor often complains about.

Despite being positioned in left field, a no man's land that sees little action during games, he never throws his glove up in the air or spins in circles like so many young outfielders do when the boredom of baseball sets in. Trevor is always locked into the game, ready for anything.

After a ball comes his way and he catches it with no problem, which would have been an out during game play, he throws it to second. It's a good, straight throw, but Aaron, from the pitcher's mound, says, "You throw like a girl."

A few of the other players laugh.

Wade looked at Henrickson, who snickers.

"Aaron," Wade says—he can feel Henrickson's eyes eating into him, "that was a good throw and you know it. You're a team—better start acting like it. I don't want to hear that kind of talk on the field anymore, got it?"

Aaron gives him a shitty smirk he learned from his meathead father, who is also giving Wade the same goon expression. Like father like son, perpetuating a cycle of imbeciles.

Wade doesn't often speak up like this knowing Henrickson doesn't like it, but he's tired of those little jabs and knows they wear on Trevor, who is doing his best to fit in and giving more effort than half the team even though he's given half the chances.

"Boys'll be boys," Henrickson says under his breath. "She wants to play on a boys' team, she's gonna have to get used to it." He smirks again—a look Wade detests. "Needs to grow a pair."

Anger fills Wade, and he puffs out his chest. There have been several times he was close to punching Henrickson square in the jaw, and this time it takes all his resolve to keep his emotions in check. He doesn't want to make a bad example for the kids, especially because they aren't privy to what Henrickson is saying. If he would be more vocal about his prejudices, Wade would clock him in the nose just to make his point very clear that asshole bigots won't be tolerated.

At the end of practice, Henrickson says, "Wade, don't forget the trophies. Last game is next weekend, and we'll have the pool party at my house."

Wade nods. The trophies are on order already and Henrickson knows it. He's throwing around his authority like a mall cop.

"And Wade, let's give out a big one this year for MVP, one that really stands out, you know?"

Wade nods, knowing what's coming next.

Henrickson grins big and bright, which makes his puffy red face look like a target. "I think we know who the MVP is, right?"

Trevor? Who has more heart and desire for the game than half these kids? Who gives 110 percent despite knowing the team looks down upon him? Who would be a great asset if he was allowed to play shortstop like he wants to?

Wade just stares at Henrickson, who doesn't understand what that condescending stare means.

"Aaron's MVP." Henrickson garbles out a gravelly laugh and slaps

Wade on the shoulder like they're in on some great secret. "We both know it. He's our starting pitcher, so it only makes sense. Let's get him a nice big trophy, 'kay?"

Wade nods and turns away to finish collecting gear and get the hell out of there.

Then

Wade tried to break the jawbone.

After the beast ate Brittani.

Even before that he tried to get rid of it. Once he saw the thing forming in the attic, speaking to him ethereally, louder and louder every day, he began to understand what Singer had told him, the warnings, the method in which to get rid of the jawbone that Wade had laughed about.

The method was not to throw it in the garbage. Wade tried that anyway, but the jawbone made its way back into the house. He chucked it out the window one morning while driving to get a coffee. It was waiting for him at home on his desk by the time he got back. He tried burning it outside in the firepit, but it showed up the following morning, free of soot. He smashed it with a hammer, watched the bone splinter and teeth shoot out like popcorn kernels, only to find it in his underwear drawer the next day.

Brittani thought he was placing the damned thing around the house as a joke. It creeped her out, but she would laugh about it. He couldn't tell her where he got it. He couldn't tell her about the beast in the attic, the beast that spoke to him and him alone, that slurred out words without a jaw, slavering onto the attic floor as it demanded nourishment that Wade wasn't willing to offer.

Eventually, the damned thing took what it wanted.

Wade didn't know exactly how it happened. He had been keeping the thing in the attic a secret from his family, hoping he could rid himself of the curse by destroying the jawbone, but nothing was working. He installed a lock on the door but didn't say anything about it. That would have caused too much suspicion. It was such a rarity anyone went up there that he figured he had enough time to get rid of the damned thing. Somehow.

Until he came home one day to find Baby Donya crying from her crib, which told Wade something was wrong. Trevor was still at school. He hollered for Brittani, but there was no answer. That was when he saw that the attic door was open. That was when the incessant voice in his head ceased for the first time since the damn beast entered his life.

Wade rushed up stairs, Donya's cries echoing through the house. What he stepped into was a horror scene. It was a bloodbath of epic proportions that became etched into his mind like something engraved in granite. The beast held Brittani's body with two gangly hands, thick ropes of its intestine around her waist. Her head was gone, having already been consumed. Blood saturated the hardwood floor so thick it was pooled. The thing used the teeth in its humanoid head to shred her flesh before sucking the fatty tissue down its throat, bones and all. Unable to chew, considering it lacked the hinged jaw that Wade held in his hand—he had no recollection of grabbing the damned bone when he got home—it slurped the shredded meat, working its way down after finishing her chest cavity. Its intestines snaked away from the body and recoiled within the beast's gut. Veins and arteries from its legs seeped out of the flesh like rapidly growing sprouts and tethered to Brittani's legs while the thing continued gnashing its teeth into her torso and sucking the slick, red pieces of her body into its cavernous mouth.

Wade wanted to do something, but what could be done? Brittani was dead—beyond dead. She was mutilated. Yet Wade couldn't turn away. He watched as the thing ate his wife right down to her toes. The blood that saturated the floor absorbed into the monstrous thing, leaving no trace as its body slowly faded into nothingness.

Wade broke down and cried while his baby girl did the same from her crib.

He threw the jawbone through the attic window with a scream. He went downstairs to comfort his daughter only to find her cooing in her crib, fascinated with the jawbone clutched in her delicate little hands.

Now

Wade loathes the idea of getting a bigger trophy for Aaron. The little shit doesn't deserve anything but a good whooping to set his ass straight, and even then he has no chance with an asshole father who's more than eager to instill his prejudices on his offspring.

Trevor has been quiet since practice. He doesn't like when Wade stands up for him like he did. Trevor is stubborn and wants to integrate himself into life as a boy without his father there to cover for him. He told Wade that makes him feel uncomfortable.

Wade just wants the best for his son. That's why he and Brittani fought so hard for Trevor to be accepted into a little league that had no precedent for trans players participating. After threats of a lawsuit, the league agreed on it so long as there was no mention that Trevor is a girl on his birth certificate. It was kind of a "don't ask, don't tell" sort of thing, which Wade and Brittani accepted just to avoid what would likely become a litigation nightmare.

The jawbone manages to find itself into Wade's hand like a sneaky cat eager for back rubs. He strokes it and fondles the teeth on a subconscious level. The thing calls to him constantly. Wade is growing used to the calls and how they escalate through the days until tragedy strikes. The voice is getting louder as if attempting to blot out his thoughts, but he learns to compartmentalize and reorganize his mental facilities as to push the beast into the background. But it's constant and hungry, and when it eats, a part of Wade dies. He's trying to get over the tragedies of losing his wife and daughter, to move on and provide for Trevor as much as possible. He tries and yet he feels hollow inside.

The gnashing of the beast's hungry pleas causes Wade to drift off. He comes back to reality by pushing his thumb into the jagged edge of the teeth in the jawbone. He knows there isn't much time. He knows what will happen.

Wade dials the number to the trophy store.

"Hi, I need to make an expedited order."

Then

Wade lost touch with Singer months before their fateful meeting at the bar. The call to hang out over a few drinks came out of nowhere. Wade was sure he knew why. Though he had lost touch with Singer, he had run into Marta at the little league field after a game one day and they started talking. She was eager to share with him her displeasure at home, and Wade couldn't help but pick up on her advances. Wade was happily married, but his sex life had suffered after two children. Brittani always seemed to be too tired or just not in the mood, and he was frustrated. There was no good excuse for adultery, but Wade convinced himself that his intentions were justified even though he felt like a complete asshole after each meeting with Marta. They met three times for sex, and that was three times too many.

The bar was called Dirk's. Wade figured it was a public place and safe enough that Singer wouldn't kill him on the spot. If a fight broke out between them, someone would stop it before it got out of hand. He was nervous but had to face Singer rather than avoid what could turn into quite an ordeal.

They had a few beers, catching up and talking about old times. Singer was acting weird. Wade knew he was going to drop the bomb soon enough, which caused him to act a bit odd as well.

"Have another drink," Singer urged. Wade obliged. Finally, after too many drinks, Wade's vision blurring and speech slurring, Singer said, "I have something for you, but you have to *accept* this gift, Wade. Do you understand?"

Gift? Like a slug from a .45?

Wade almost made an inappropriate comment about Singer blowing him away, but his reserve held him in check, even with the beer loosening him up.

The jawbone came out of a hidden pocket in Singer's coat, almost like magic. Wade's eyes went wide. It was a ghastly looking thing, a bit larger than a human jawbone and lined with teeth that looked more animal in nature. Something about the thing repulsed Wade.

"Do you accept it?" Singer asked.

Wade stared at it with question marks for eyes.

"Well," Singer urged, "do you?"

"I ..."

Wade wondered if this had something to do with the affair but couldn't figure an angle in which a jawbone would fit into the equation. Why was Singer offering him the vile thing to begin with? Wade didn't want to accept it if for no other reason than he was inherently repulsed by it. On the other hand, he wanted to be done with this night. The constant fear that Singer was going to confront him was too much to handle, and the beer hardly washed away the feeling of impending doom that clouded over him.

"Sure," Wade said, reaching his hand out and grabbing the jawbone. The feeling of it beneath his fingers caused a shiver to cascade up his spine and down his arms. He sighed heavily. "I'll take it." He offered a goofy smile as if he should be excited to be given such a thing.

Singer let go of the jawbone and seemed to deflate as if the burden of all the world had been on his shoulders and had suddenly relinquished.

After a moment of silence and a few sips of warm beer from the bottom of their glasses, Singer said, "I'm sorry."

Wade's droopy eyes darted to Singer. "Sorry? For what?"

"Give it to somebody, but remember that they have to accept it. You can't just...mail it to someone or something." Singer chuckled nervously. "It'll just keep coming back to *you*. They have to accept it in person, like you did tonight."

Wade's brow wrinkled and he tilted his head. He tried to blink away the foggy blur he was left with by being over-served. He lifted the jawbone, cringing at the feel of the thing in his hand. "What are you talking about?" Wade asked.

"I could tell you, but you wouldn't believe me anyway." Singer swallowed hard then went to take a drink of beer, but it was all foam at the bottom of the glass. "I'm not even sure I *can* tell you. That's why I'm being so cryptic."

Singer stood on wobbly legs. He looked at Wade with almost sorrowful eyes, and then a sick smile dipped his wet lips. "By the way, I know about you and Marta."

Now

It's Sunday, the day after the final game. The team had a mixed year and knew a win wouldn't clinch their spot in the finals. They played for fun more than to win and ended up with a blowout. Trevor, stuck in left field against a team with no leftie batters, saw very little action but was more attentive than any of the other outfielders. During cheers and high fives after the game, he's noticeably pushed to the side and ignored by his peers.

The pizza party at Henrickson's house is in an hour. Trevor doesn't look forward to it. He knows how the boys will be in a social situation. They'll glom onto Aaron, especially because the party is at his house, and treat Trevor like dirt.

They were awful to him at the mid-season party they had after a Saturday game when everyone met at Fuddrucker's for cheeseburgers. It was as if Trevor didn't exist despite how much he tried to be a part of the conversation and fun. It had left him feeling detached and lonely, but he came to practice a few days later as if nothing had happened, always trying his best to fit in and be a part of the team.

On the dinner table, a box of trophies sits, waiting to be carted to the truck. Beside the box of small participation trophies is one huge trophy. Trevor peers at the inscription on the large trophy and sees it has Aaron's name on it. He assumed it wouldn't be for him, but at the same time, he feels a pit in his stomach grow larger just knowing that prick would be getting the MVP trophy. It seems like the bullies always get the rewards, especially when their fathers are in positions of power. So why hasn't Trevor's father done more to make his season better? Besides, if anyone deserves the MVP trophy, it would be Grayson Harris. He has the best batting record and made two of the best game plays of the entire season.

Wade rounds the corner, buttoning his shirt. "Hey, buddy," he says with a smile. "Ready for the party?"

Trevor looks up from his gaze upon the trophies. His face is expressionless. Wade remembers that look going back to when he and Brittani were still calling Trevor by his birth name. They had recognized something in their young girl that wasn't right. She was depressed when she should have been having fun being a child. They had taken her to the doctor and even to a therapist before she confessed she didn't feel comfortable in her skin. Even then, it took time for Wade and Brittani to understand the ramifications of her personal strife and her desire to make a change. Though both Wade and Brittani were vehemently opposed to any kind of surgical procedure, they were open to their daughter adopting a male name and changing her appearance to match how she felt inside. The results were astonishing. It seemed that overnight Lindsey became a happy little boy named Trevor, ready to take on whatever the world had to throw his way.

The look on Trevor's face, staring at the huge trophy on the table, reminds Wade of the months leading up to Lindsey confessing she was Trevor. Wade would do anything in his power to wash that look from his son's face.

"I'm not feeling so good," Trevor said. "I don't think I want to go to the pizza party, anyway."

"Oh, come on, Trevor," Wade pleads, but his son turns his back on him and walks out the door.

There's no time to chase after him. Wade has to get the trophies to the pizza party.

I'm hungry. Bring me someone. Anyone. I'm hungry, damn it. Hungry, damn it. HUNGRY, DAMN IT! HungryHungryHungry!HUNGRY!

He has to get the big trophy to Aaron, and Aaron has to accept the gift, along with the jawbone that's encased in resin inside the trophy's cup.

Trevor hangs out in the overgrowth where he can see when his father's car leaves the house to go to that stupid pizza party. There's a pool at the Henrickson's house, and the team has been told to bring their swim trunks. Trevor knows they don't accept him as one of them no matter how hard he tries. He can't think of anything good that will come out of a pool party. He had accepted the fact he would have to sit in a chair while the other boys frolicked in the pool, but seeing that giant trophy and knowing it's going to that asshole Aaron is too much for Trevor to handle. It isn't that Trevor thinks *he* deserves the trophy. It's that he knows Aaron *doesn't* deserve it, and he's getting frustrated with little things like nepotism and playing favorites.

Look in the attic, boy. See what your daddy doesn't want you to see.

A chill scales up Trevor's back, rippling down his arms in a tingle of gooseflesh. The voice speaks to him almost as if someone snuck up and whispered in his ear, yet he knows confidently that the voice came from within. It wasn't that of his inner dialogue but originated within his thoughts, nonetheless.

The attic has been locked since his mother left. He has no idea what his father does up there. He never really sees Dad go up into the attic, but Trevor certainly has been given instruction *not* to go up there. All after his mother went missing. Such strange behavior for his father to be so adamant about not going into the attic after his mother left.

Or was he told she had left?

Trevor looks up at the dormer with the little window at the top of the house as if he would see his mother standing there like a ghost in an old horror movie.

Come see what's in the attic. Your mother came up to see. So did your baby sister.

The urge to investigate the attic is so strong that Trevor finds himself at the attic door as if he has been swallowed by a fold in time and transported from the bushes outside to that door in the house.

Wade explains that Trevor doesn't feel well, but no one really seems to care that his son isn't there. The lack of compassion puts a knot in his stomach and makes him wish he could give each and every one of them their own cursed jawbone attic demon. Fuck 'em all! If Trevor wants to play ball next season, Wade will do everything in his power to manage the team, and he'll do things right.

He's nervous as the trophy ceremony begins. Each kid is given the small participation trophy after a congratulatory run down of what they accomplished throughout the season. There's talk of cannon arms and deep mitts that can catch anything, jokes about being caught spinning in circles in right field and trying to steal too many bases. It's one trophy after another, and all Wade is concerned with is Aaron accepting that damn MVP monstrosity. And why wouldn't he? Of course he'll accept it.

Right?

Trevor finds the attic door is locked.

He can hear something inside. He places his ear to the door and tries to hear what's making such noises within. The sounds from the attic feel as if they're inside his head. Whispering sounds rustling within. Urging him to open the door. To come in. To see what happened to his mother and sister.

The deadbolt his father put on the attic door retracts with a click so loud it almost hurts his ears. The house is quiet except for the voice in his head, urging him to investigate the attic, to see what it is his father is hiding from him.

Trevor grabs the handle and turns it, pushing the attic door open to reveal wood stairs leading up. The sounds from within are louder; clearly, something is up there.

Or someone.

Mom?

Wade wears a fake smile as he holds up the MVP trophy. The look on all the boys' faces indicates hope that any one of them thinks they could be the recipient. How sad that they haven't figured out how it all works yet. They still have hope. Wade knows which players deserve it. They know they deserve it too, and they'll be crushed when they get their first taste of how unfair the world can be. It will make the blow of losing a promotion to an ass-kisser a little bit easier to manage when they're in the workforce later in life.

Aaron's smile is bigger and more confident than all the others, for he knows he's the one being awarded the biggest trophy of all. Maybe Henrickson already told him. Maybe he's making assumptions. But he knows.

What if he doesn't accept the gift? What then?

And why has the thing in my attic stopped...stopped speaking at me?

"And that's why the MVP trophy," Henrickson says after a longwinded speech, "goes to—"

What happened to the voice? To the hungry urges? What's going on?

"—Aaron Henrickson!"

Everyone cheers even though several of the boys wear scowls, clearly feeling slighted for not being rewarded for their efforts on the field.

Aaron, all smiles, approaches Wade, who holds out the huge cupped trophy. Beads of sweat form on Wade's forehead.

Trevor approaches the beast, terrified and somehow enchanted, as if unable to turn away. Something about the creature beckons to him, drawing him forward just like his mother before him. Just like his father had been drawn into the uncanny temptation of the thing in the first place.

Come closer, the thing chides.

It doesn't speak with its mouth for it has no jaw. It's hideous in its vile rendering, and yet Trevor can't turn away. It towers there in the attic, crouched with the crook of its neck wedged into the corner of the wall and ceiling. Its rib cage opens like the legs of an arachnid. Slimy lengths of intestine slither out like strings at the hands of an invisible puppeteer.

Come closer, it urges.

Trevor takes a few steps toward the thing. His heart races, yet he can't deny the pull. It's like nothing he's ever felt before.

Come see where your mother went, boy.

Arteries and capillaries snake out of the thing's skin like tree roots, whipping around and curling. They're a spectacle all their own in some psychedelic manner that has an almost hypnotizing effect on Trevor as he takes even more steps toward the beast.

"Do you accept this MVP trophy, Aaron?" Wade asks. "This...gift?"

Aaron scrunches his brow, either perturbed at the strange offering of a gift or maybe the jawbone buried beneath the resin causing an unsettling feeling that Wade is very familiar with. A hush falls over the boys, all staring at Assistant Coach Wade and Aaron and one giant trophy the likes none of them have ever seen before. It's more like a trophy champions would get.

One big enough to hide secrets in.

Then Aaron smiles and yanks the trophy out of Wade's hands. "Of course I do!"

Have a Heart

Jay Bower

One

MARK GRIPPED THE STEERING wheel of his jet-black Challenger with a white-knuckled death grip. The speedometer bounced between 120 and 140 miles per hour. It was the middle of the night, and the few cars out on the interstate seemed to be moving in slow motion as he passed them.

Only an hour ago, he was sitting at home reading a book, trying to ignore the powerful voice inside of him, but now he was trying to outrun the evil spirit he had invited in. He knew when he took off from home that it was an impossible task, but he did it anyway. He couldn't sit still with the demon in his head.

The regret that he experienced for the past few months after calling on the demon had manifested itself into daily drinking. He considered something harder but chickened out. His fiancé would have kicked his ass.

Metallica's album *Ride the Lightning* blared through his Bose speakers on repeat. Mark wanted nothing more than to drown out the wicked voice within, the evil spirit that wouldn't leave him alone. That was what he was running from, and he was doing a terrible job of it. He never should have invited it into his life.

The highway curved sharply to the right. He struggled to hold his car in the lane, drifting to his left. With his window partially open, sweat streamed down his face despite the chilly March night.

Mark fought with the steering wheel as he navigated around a semi. When he passed it on the left, he hit a giant pothole and lost control. The Challenger slammed into the concrete median and flipped. Everything spun in a wild, chaotic mess. When he landed on the concrete in a loud, terrifying crash, the last thing he heard before his life slipped away was the opening riff to "Fade to Black", and he smiled.

Two

When I ended the call, I placed a hand on my chest, feeling the rhythmic beat of my decaying heart. My wife, who was seated across from me, leaned forward on the couch with her hands clasped in her lap and an excited, hopeful look on her face. I couldn't speak the words. Was it finally ready to happen? All of my hopes and prayers felt answered in that one short call from the transplant coordinator.

"Are you going to make me wait?" Debbie asked.

A single tear rolled down my cheek, and I nodded.

"We have a match. I'm getting a new heart!"

Debbie bolted from her seat and lunged at me, wrapping her arms around my neck. She smelled of tropical lilacs.

"Is this really happening?" she said through her tears.

"I...I think so. The coordinator said we need to get to the hospital immediately."

"Oh god, Bryan, I can't believe it. A new heart!"

My tears flowed faster, the emotions within me stirring at the thought of my life suddenly changing for the better. We had been waiting for this moment for months, and if I was being honest, I was also starting to lose hope that it was going to happen. But the good Lord works in mysterious ways, and one thing I had learned in this process was to be patient.

"I'll get the bags." Debbie bounded from the living room, and I sat there saying a quick prayer for my good fortune.

Of course, that also meant someone had to lose their life for me to gain the heart, so I prayed for them and their family, thanking them for the gift and hoping that the family could find strength at such a terrible time.

Within fifteen minutes, Debbie and I were on the road to Mercy General Hospital, a quick two-hour drive from where we were staying. Home was much farther, but we had to remain within four hours of the hospital for when the time came for the surgery. I didn't know how much longer our finances were going to hold out paying for two places to live, but in my euphoria at having a chance with a new heart, those worries slipped away.

It was a quick drive to the hospital filled with talk about our future, because we now had a future to look forward to. All thanks to a generous donor and the goodness of God.

Three

I awoke from the surgery with my mind swirling. I had been dreaming the entire time I was under, and it wasn't pleasant. I was in another dimension, almost as though I was no longer on this planet. Or maybe under the planet.

I was surrounded by walls of flames and hideous, grotesque creatures that evoked thoughts of Hell and damnation. I saw winged creatures with blood-red skin and black wings that flew overhead. Smaller, ground-dwelling creatures with gnarled, black talons scuttled all around me like vicious dogs.

Then I saw one creature larger than all the rest. He had legs like a goat and was bare chested. His body gleamed like it was oiled, but I soon realized he was covered in blood. Thick, twisted horns sprouted from his bald head, one on each side. His eyes were yellow with black slits, like cats'. Long fangs protruded from his mouth, and when he opened it, he had two sets of jagged teeth.

The creature, what I suspected was a demon or even the Prince of Hell himself, tilted his head back and laughed. It was a loud, booming sound that rattled my bones. It sent a bloodcurdling fear throughout my body. I heard an unfamiliar word echo around me: *Asmodeus.*

The horrific nightmare was chased away by the warm light of the recovery room and the sweet timbre of Debbie's angelic voice.

"Bryan? Can you hear me?"

I blinked my eyes, allowing them to adjust to the room. I was relieved to be free of my hellish dream and thankful for Debbie's comforting presence.

I nodded slightly, as everything hurt. I felt a pressure on my chest from the surgery, grateful to have made it back out from whatever I had been dreaming about.

"Dr. Williams said everything was a success. Oh, Bryan, I'm so happy!" Debbie leaned close and gave me a kiss on the cheek.

Rehab would take several months, but this was the first step toward recovery. As long as my body didn't reject the heart, things would get better. Maybe one day our children might have kids of their own. Becoming a grandpa was something I was ready for. With my new heart, that was a real possibility.

But the powerful vision I had while under anesthesia wouldn't leave me. It was so vivid and detailed that I almost thought it was real, but that was impossible. I tried to forget it and dismiss the vision as my overworked and anxiety-fueled mind playing tricks on me. I'm a God-fearing man and didn't ever expect to visit Hell. My eternity lay in Heaven.

Four

A week after surgery, I was at home with Debbie, sipping water on our back deck and watching our dog chase after a ball. I had thrown it for him a couple of times, but I got winded quickly, and Debbie, ever my caregiver, scolded me and took over ball-throwing duties.

It was a pretty day outside. The leaves were just beginning to come out of hibernation, and the world was morphing from death to life. Sort of like me.

I patted my chest slightly, thankful for every moment. Without the donor heart, who knew if I would still be alive? I asked about the donor, but the hospital claimed it was a matter of confidentiality. At first, I wasn't sure if I now possessed the heart of another man or a woman, though I guess it didn't really matter in the grand scheme of things.

However, for some reason, this bothered me a lot when I was in recovery, and one of the nurses, Nurse Tabitha, told me it was from a man, though she swore me to secrecy and if I ever told, she would revoke my sponge bath privileges. I love my wife Debbie quite a bit and have never been unfaithful to her, but Nurse Tabitha was an attractive woman about ten years younger than me and always smelling of sweet perfume. Her sponge baths were...special. I wouldn't dare jeopardize those, so I kept it to myself.

"Hun, are you ready to go inside?" Debbie's voice cut short my daydream, the vision of Nurse Tabitha chased away by guilt. It was unusual for me to fantasize about other women like that. Debbie was more than enough of a woman for me.

"Huh? Oh, yeah. Sure."

"Are you feeling ok? I was talking to you, and you just zoned out. It was like you were gone."

"Sorry. Just trying to figure out this new heart," I said, patting my chest. "Don't wanna do anything that'll nullify the extended warranty."

Debbie shook her head and smiled. I was in the clear. I also needed to be careful. I shouldn't have been thinking about other women like that.

Five

Just two days after my vivid Nurse Tabitha experience, I was overcome by a powerful urge to drink. I was directed by my doctor to avoid all alcohol as it might interfere with my medicines, among other complications. But the desire to drink an Old-Fashioned hit me like a freight train.

I was never much of a drinker. Occasionally I would get pretty drunk, but those days were few and far between, especially after the birth of our twins, Jared and Julie. I determined early on that I wanted to be a father that was there for his kids, and being drunk wasn't part of that playbook. For eleven years, I followed that commitment.

But for some reason, all I could think about was how wonderful the bourbon burn would be on my tongue, of how wonderful it would taste sliding down my throat.

Debbie and I had taken our kids to a birthday party at a friend's house. We were close with the Robinsons, and their little girl was turning ten. Our daughter Julie got along with her, but Jared could care less. Still, it was good to socialize and be around others.

It was there, at the party, that the urge to drink kicked in.

My mouth watered. I could almost taste the smooth alcohol, touched by sweetness. I looked down at the red plastic cup in my hand and scowled at the water.

"Hun, is everything ok?" Debbie asked.

"Huh? Oh, yeah. Yes. Sorry, my scattered thoughts since the surgery seem to overcome me at times."

"Do we need to see Dr. Williams? Is this normal?"

I waved a hand, dismissing her concern. "We don't need to bother him. It'll pass, I'm sure of it."

I didn't want to alarm her with my sudden powerful need to drink. She would tear into me up one way and down the other. I guess I couldn't blame her, but I was in no hurry to let her.

"Dad, can we go now?" Jared asked. His sullen face and shrunken shoulders told me all I needed to know about how little fun he was having at a girl's birthday party. He was the only boy there and had remained on his own for most of the time.

"Go play with your sister," Debbie said before I could speak. Jared looked to me, to Debbie, and back to me before he hung his head and slowly walked away.

"Poor kid, he's not enjoying himself at all," Debbie said. She took a sip of her water. "It'll be good for him to get out of his comfort zone. He's too tied to those stupid video games."

I nodded, barely engaged in the conversation. My thoughts remained on the alcohol that I was missing at the moment. The yearning was strong.

Then, the urge disappeared. It was like a magician's trick or an illusion bursting. It was just...gone. The thought of having a drink repulsed me. In my current health condition, it felt like the worst decision I could have made.

What was I thinking? How could I have been so stupid?

For the rest of the party, the urge never returned.

Six

Debbie and I had a strong relationship. Neither one of us had been extremely adventurous in the bedroom, and that was fine with me. I had never wanted to branch out into some of the weirder and darker forms of sexual pleasure. Not that I cared if others did; it just didn't appeal to me. I had always been more focused on the intimate bond Debbie and I shared when we were making love.

That was why when I daydreamed about having anal sex with Debbie and watching as she went down on another man it was so startling.

We were at home watching an old episode of *Matlock* (not the newer one!) when my thoughts drifted into something bizarre. Instead of watching Andy Griffith save an innocent man from wrongful conviction, I pictured Debbie in our bed.

She was bent over, begging me to enter her. She even pulled open her cheeks to give me a better view. I was shocked. Horrified. And aroused.

I couldn't focus on *Matlock* anymore as my erection started growing. I shifted myself a little to better accommodate the growth in my pants. My heart beat faster, and that scared me too. Was my new heart ready for such activity? It had only been a few weeks since the transplant. Though things had been going well, I wasn't sure if I should push it.

Then the vision shifted, like a blurred movie scene. Debbie was sitting on top of me, her legs spread open to reveal her vagina, though I wasn't penetrating her there. I watched as she adjusted herself on my erect penis and it disappeared within her behind.

I had never once in my life imagined us doing something like that. It was scandalous and yet...intoxicating.

My heart beat faster at the vision.

"Do you think that's the killer?" Debbie asked, breaking my lurid vision. I glanced at her with large eyes, wondering what triggered my thoughts and if any of that was grounded in a reality I had been denying.

"Hun, are you ok?" It was the question Debbie seemed to ask every moment since my surgery.

"Why do you ask?" I tried to calm myself and will away the erection that had formed in my pants.

"Your face is flushed. Is something wrong?"

I swallowed hard and took a deep breath to calm down. "I'm perfectly fine. Just thinking about you and how lucky I am to have you by my side." A half-truth to smooth over what was really happening in my head.

She smiled—her eyes were so bright. "Aww, thank you." She got up from her seat across the room, planted a kiss on my forehead, then went into the kitchen to get a glass of water.

I watched her leave, and my eyes instinctively dropped to her behind. The lust-filled thoughts returned with a vengeance. It was then that my daydream turned even more graphic.

I had visions of her naked and on her knees in front of a man I had never seen before. He grabbed her head and pushed her all the way down on him as she performed oral sex. He leaned back and groaned while bobbing her head up and down.

I couldn't recall the last time we had done that. Debbie was never a fan of it, and though I enjoyed it, I wasn't the type of person to make her do something she wasn't comfortable with. That was what made my vision all the more perplexing. Debbie seemed to want to do that to the man, even pulling off of him and using her tongue to lick all up and down him.

It startled me yet also excited me to no end.

Just as the man was about to ejaculate in her mouth, the real Debbie returned from the kitchen and handed me a glass of water.

"Here," she said, placing it on the table next to me. "I thought you might need this."

The moment she set the water down, the image fled from my mind and the erotic excitement I felt dissipated. It was like a balloon had slowly deflated.

What was happening to me? Why was I having these pornographic thoughts about my dear wife? We weren't those kind of people. Our sex life was nothing like what I just imagined. Nor had I ever imagined it to be that way. Not until now.

I had no idea what it meant. I only hoped it didn't mean I was going crazy. There were no transplants for that.

Seven

The images that infiltrated my mind that day stuck with me for several days after, though I was careful not to let them overwhelm me. I still wasn't sure what my heart could handle, and I didn't want to end up in the hospital because I got worked up about a vision. I never told Debbie about them. I didn't want her to think I was some deviant.

A week after my latest episode, I was scheduled to meet Dr. Williams for a checkup. A new heart needed a lot of care and attention.

Debbie drove us, and as we waited in the waiting room, she reached over and grabbed my hand. It was such a sweet gesture and reminded me of when we were young. It brought a sense of warmth and kindness that I appreciated. It was one of the things I adored about her.

Debbie had always been a good church-going girl and was instrumental in getting me to go. I didn't grow up in church, but it appealed to me, and Debbie's experience was kind of attractive. I started attending with her and had been going ever since.

Her touch in the waiting room rekindled those innocent, virtuous feelings, and I was grateful for it. The thoughts that had intruded on me lately were nothing like that.

"Bryan Weaver," a nurse with a clipboard called out.

"That's us," Debbie said quietly to me. We got up and followed the nurse through the door to our room.

After taking my vitals and asking me the standard round of questions, the nurse left with assurances that the doctor would be in soon.

Surprisingly, he was.

Dr. Williams breezed into the room, looking down at his clipboard. "Good morning, Bryan. How are you today?"

He glanced up and smiled. He was older, maybe close to sixty, with a crown of peppered hair and thick glasses. "Have you had any problems? Any concerns?"

I shook my head no. "Honestly doc, I've felt...wonderful. Rejuvenated even. It's amazing what a new heart will do for a person."

Dr. Williams chuckled. "Yeah, they give new life, don't they?"

"And how are you?" he asked Debbie.

She smiled at his concern. "I'm doing well, thank you."

"Is the patient taking it easy like instructed?" He gave me the side eye but with a smirk on his face.

"Well, he has been playing fetch with the dog. But honestly, he seems to be listening to instructions."

Dr. Williams raised an eyebrow. "Is that so? Remind me later, and I'll share with you my secret to keep that going. Maybe it'll help around the house." He winked at Debbie, and she giggled.

"Deal."

"So, let's check you out." The doctor ran through his battery of questions and poked and prodded until he seemed satisfied with the results. He typed into a computer on the desk and then turned to us.

"Bryan, I have to admit, this is stunning. Everything seems to be far and above where we'd expect your recovery to be at this point. You're progressing at an excellent rate. Keep this up and you won't have to see me so often."

"Really?" I was quite surprised by his words.

"It seems we matched you with the perfect heart."

I gave Debbie a quick look and then quietly asked, "How soon until, you know, we can ..."

Dr. Williams leaned back and smiled. "Until you and Debbie can make love again? Honestly, I'd say you're good to go as long as you don't do anything wild."

Debbie gave my leg a playful smack. "Bryan!"

"Debbie," Dr. Williams said, "it's quite alright, and we get these questions all the time. It's an important thing to know and quite natural."

Debbie's face had turned bright red. I hated making her uncomfortable, but the visions that had assaulted me lingered, and a desire to have sex with my wife burned within me.

We finished the visit and left. As we reached the doors to the waiting room, I patted my front pockets.

"Oh damn. I left my phone in the room. Go ahead and schedule the next visit if you want. I'll go get it."

Debbie went ahead, and I went back to the room. Not because I left my phone, which was in my pocket, but because I needed to ask Dr. Williams something without Debbie around.

I found him as he was about to go into a room with another patient.

"Dr. Williams? Can I have a minute?"

He approached me with his bright smile plastered on his face. "Bryan, what can I do for you?"

I coaxed him into an empty room and closed the door. "Sorry, I needed to talk to you in private. I have been experiencing...I've been having...I see odd visions. And...and I have unusual urges. I've never experienced these before. Could it be something with the medicines or the surgery?"

Dr. Williams clasped my shoulder with his hand and his smile lit up even further. "Sometimes when we expect death and find out we're still alive the brain has a funny way of reacting. I suspect you're experiencing an awakening due to how close you were to death. As long as these episodes don't interfere with your daily life or cause you to do something illegal, I encourage you to embrace your awakening. You never know what you'll find." He squeezed my shoulder then let go.

"If you have any pain or adverse reactions to the medicines, get in touch with me immediately." He opened the door and left.

Maybe he was right. Maybe my body was telling me that with another lease on life, it was time to enjoy it.

Eight

I tried to take what Dr. Williams told me as truth, but my experiences were telling me otherwise.

Every day, I struggled to keep my thoughts pure. Of course I loved my wife and thought she was an attractive woman, but the powerfully lurid daydreams I experienced were something else. Even when I was a blossoming teenage boy with hormones running rampant through me, I had never experienced a sexual awakening like I was now. It got so bad that I had to masturbate several times a day just to keep it in check. Even then it still bubbled under the surface like a serpent ready to strike.

And then there was the urge to consume alcohol.

I woke up in the morning and instead of wanting coffee, which had been changed to decaf since my operation, I craved hard liquor. Especially whiskey. My mouth watered at the need, and it became a need, no longer a want.

We didn't keep anything stronger than wine in the house, but that didn't appeal to me.

The deep, constant cravings were only cut short by the even more powerful sexual urges I was experiencing.

On top of that, I felt stronger.

I couldn't explain why, since I hadn't worked out in months and had become mostly sedentary because of my transplant. My muscles started to show as though I spent hours in the gym and ate nothing but chicken breast and broccoli.

As confused as I was about my mental and physical changes, I welcomed my changing body. I remember looking in the mirror and thinking I could pick up any woman I wanted and then immediately feeling the guilt and shame of such a thought. What would Debbie think?

Nine

"My god, what have you been doing?" Debbie asked.

I embraced my new look and ordered fitted shirts online. I decided to stop hiding my body and enjoy the gift I had somehow been given.

It was late May, and we were getting the kids together to go to a local beach on the lake. I was ready to get out and show off my bod.

"What do you mean?" I replied.

Both our kids stared at me.

"Dad, you're ripped!" Jared said. "I wanna look like that!"

"Since when have you been working out? Should you have been doing that considering your health?" Debbie asked.

For the first month and a half, Debbie had taken personal time from her job as a financial manager to care for me. Once we realized I would be ok, she went back to the office, but that was only three weeks ago.

"I...Dr. Williams said as long as I don't overdo it, I'd be fine."

"You look done to me!" Julie said, echoing her twin brother's astonishment. I guess I didn't realize how careful I was about hiding my appearance from my family. Baggy sweatshirts did wonders.

"I'm stunned," Debbie said. "And I've seen you naked!"

"Gross," Julie said.

"Yeah, Mom, that's not cool," Jared added.

She shrugged and narrowed her eyes. "You aren't on any drugs, are you? I swear, if you do anything to hurt that new heart—"

I held up a hand to stop the inquiry. "I promise you that I am not doing anything unnatural to myself. I want to protect this heart and the new life it has given me."

"Huh," Debbie said. "Well, come on kids. If we wait too long, we won't get a good spot." Debbie gave me a judgmental look, as though suspicious of me. I had seen it many times before: eyes narrowed, lips tight. If I hadn't known better, I might have thought she was accusing me of something.

I couldn't explain my change. All I knew was that it happened and it made me feel more alive than at any time in my life.

Ten

I couldn't help myself. My urges grew uncontrollable. If I didn't give in, there was no telling what I might have done.

Debbie was off to work, and the kids were at the Robinson's for a playdate. I was home alone, and my thoughts would not stop focusing on sexual gratification. Masturbation had lost its effect. I needed more. And badly. What was I becoming? How had I ended up as this addicted, broken man?

I couldn't stay home. The walls were suffocating.

I grabbed my keys, hopped into my Camry, and took off.

I didn't know where I was going or why, just as long as I wasn't at home where I had nothing but time to let the obscene thoughts fester in my mind.

Before long, I noticed a strip club down the road. I gripped my steering wheel tightly. I had never been to one in my life, but seeing the video screen with a scantily clad, young, blonde woman smiling at me was more than I could handle. I headed for the Pink Pony and parked in the nearly empty parking lot. There probably wasn't much business at ten thirty in the morning.

What are you doing here? I scolded myself when I turned off the ignition. I almost changed my mind but knowing that just beyond the walls of the building were half-naked women ready to dance for my pleasure was more than enough to squash the thought.

Please forgive me, I thought as I entered the dark doorway.

There were only two other patrons in the club: an old man with a cane and a fistful of dollar bills and another man close to my age dressed in a navy-blue business suit.

One dancer was on the stage, and my initial desire was shattered. She was sickly skinny with hardly any curves at all, and I swear when she smiled she had to have been missing several teeth. She was topless, but that didn't help as she had small breasts that clung to exposed ribs. She needed something to eat badly.

The place smelled like cheap perfume and stale beer with a hint of cigarettes.

This was a bad idea. I should never have gone in there.

I turned to go and felt something move within my chest, like a gas bubble shifted. It was the oddest sensation I had ever experienced, and for a second, I worried that maybe my new heart was turning on me. What would Debbie think if she found me dead in a strip club?

I placed a hand on my chest as though it would stop it, and then a deep, terrible voice spoke.

Don't you dare leave this place. It has been ages since I've tasted another. You will not deny me.

I spun around looking for the source of the voice, but no one was near. The old man was busy stuffing money in the skinny woman's G-string, and the businessman had a hand under the table moving in a slow, rhythmic motion. The bartender was cleaning the end of the bar with a cigarette hanging out of her mouth.

Where did the voice come from? Maybe it was another hallucination, like all the others. Maybe Dr. Williams was wrong and this was something more than just my body reacting to the new heart.

I must be losing my mind, I thought.

You take one step out of this place, and I will kill you.

My heart raced. Who was speaking to me? The bubble sensation in my chest changed, and then it felt like someone was grabbing my heart...and squeezing. I clutched at my chest with both hands as though I could remove it.

"Hey, new guy, what's wrong with you?" the bartender asked. "You ain't gonna do something stupid, are you?" She reached under the counter and placed a shotgun on the bar. "I suggest you think twice if you are."

I nodded. "No," I said between trying to catch my breath. "No, I'm ok. I'm not going to do anything."

The song ended, and the dancer left the stage, upsetting the old man, who let out a string of cuss words.

Now that I have your attention, you will listen to me. Proposition the dancer and get us into a back room. I must have her.

"Who are you?"

The bartender narrowed her eyes and glared at me. Her hand ran along the shotgun's wooden stock.

My name...is Asmodeus.

Eleven

I didn't know who was speaking to me and how I was able to hear it, but the experience with the invisible hand gripping my heart shook me to my core.

A memory flashed in my mind, and I gasped. Asmodeus. That was the word I heard in my awful dream when I was in surgery. The hellish visions that assaulted me and the large demonic figure that glared at me. The word spoken was Asmodeus. Was it not a word, but a name?

I found the dancer near the side of the stage. She was smoking something in a small glass pipe. I didn't dare ask what it was.

Go to her now.

"Umm. Hi," I stammered. I still wasn't sure what I was doing or why.

She glanced at me with bloodshot eyes. "What do you want? Cash only."

I nodded. What did I want? Asmodeus wasn't explicit in his request, if he was even a real entity.

Tell her you want to have sex with her and you're willing to pay double what she's asking.

I swallowed hard. I had exactly four dollars in cash in my wallet. How was I going to pay anything? How was I going to do that to Debbie? I knew I went to that place to release some pent-up sexual tension, but I wasn't really going to have sex with anyone. Asmodeus must have heard my thoughts, because he squeezed my heart again.

Now!

I wanted to believe this wasn't real, but I was starting to have my doubts. And it frightened me. I obeyed his command.

"I...I was hoping we could have sex."

She giggled, but it turned into a cough. "What do you think I am? I dance; I ain't no prostitute."

"I'll pay you double what you want."

Her eyes opened wide. "Double?"

That's it. Agree!

I nodded. "Yes."

"Honey, I got five minutes until I take the stage again. Come back with me."

I heard a deep, evil cackle in my head. Asmodeus was pleased. I was terrified.

I followed her down a dark hallway lit only by red lights. At the end, she opened a door into a small dressing room with one well-worn and used couch. Rips crossed through the cushions, and some of the filling had spilled out.

She closed the door behind me.

"Let's make this fast. You want oral, regular, or anal? I'm game for anything, darlin'."

My mouth went dry, and words refused to come out.

Asmodeus jumped with glee at each option. Finally he said to me, *Anal.*

It was like my daydreams with Debbie were coming true, though with a woman I didn't know.

"Anal," I squeaked out.

The woman grinned, showing off the gaps in her teeth.

She wasted no time ripping down her G-string and grabbing a bottle of lube from a small table next to the couch. She applied a liberal amount between her cheeks and handed me the bottle. "The last thing I need is my ass bleeding when I'm up there dancing. It won't take much lube—I take it in the ass often."

I had grown an erection despite how unappealing the woman was. I also started to feel a powerful lust building up within me, sort of like how I felt when my daydreams took hold. I wanted to be repulsed by her, but something inside was different. I had to have her.

I pulled my pants down and applied the slick substance all over my erection.

The woman bent over and pulled her ass cheeks apart, exposing what I could only describe as a well-used hole.

Asmodeus roared inside me, and I felt my heart tighten, but not like he was gripping it to get my attention but as though in anticipation of what was to come.

I grabbed her waist and plunged inside of her.

It had been so long since Debbie and I made love, and the intimate sensation of being inside of a woman felt amazing and shameful all at once. Especially since we were doing something Debbie and I had never done.

It felt glorious, and I closed my eyes, imagining Debbie instead of a woman whose name I didn't know. It made my thrusts harder and faster. She moaned and reached between her legs, playing with herself and occasionally stroking my balls.

Asmodeus panted in my head. He groaned as though he could feel every thrust. *That's it*, he said. *More! More!*

The woman may have been used to anal sex, but she kept a tight grip around me, even with copious amounts of lubrication.

Every thrust brought me closer and closer to climax. The woman moaned louder, so loud that I thought someone might hear us.

Asmodeus moaned as well, his deep voice reverberating in my head.

She gripped me tighter, and my heart raced faster. I worried I might be overtaxing my new heart. I had another fleeting moment of me thinking about what Debbie would do if she found me dead in a strip club. But that thought was wiped away as a building orgasm took over.

My balls tingled, and I added my groans to the chorus already verbalized. A moment later, I knew I couldn't stop myself.

"I'm gonna come!"

The woman tightened around my erection. "Fill me up!"

I had no choice and exploded inside of her. She moaned louder, rubbing her hands all over her tiny breasts and between her legs.

When the orgasm finally faded and I had expelled all of my built-up tension, Asmodeus spoke, and it chilled me to the bone.

Kill her.

Twelve

"What?" I said out loud.

I need her blood. You will need it to live.

"I can't do that!" My erection had instantly gone away, and it slipped out of the woman's ass. She expelled my semen in a great show as though I cared at that point.

"Not bad," she said. "That'll be $200." She went to grab a towel that was crumpled on the floor when Asmodeus spoke again.

I said to kill her. To emphasize his command, he squeezed my heart again, making me lose my breath. *I am inside of you now, and you must obey or you will die. And if you die, your soul will be tortured forever. If you'd like to avoid that, you must serve me.*

"But...why? How did you get inside of me?"

"Darlin', it was you inside of me," the woman said. "Now pay up!"

Kill her or suffer. Kill her or your wife and kids will have a worse fate than you.

I didn't know what to do. How could I possibly kill another human being? I had already gone down the path of sin by having sex with the woman.

Yet Asmodeus had done so much for me already.

My body was in excellent shape despite not having worked out. I had more muscles than ever before. My desires were being fulfilled. What I just finished doing with the dancer was something I dreamed of doing with Debbie, and it was all made possible by Asmodeus.

Still, murder was something entirely different than having sex with a stranger. I wasn't sure I had it in me.

A tight grip on my heart snapped my attention back to the command.

Kill her.

I glanced around the room. I needed a weapon or something to use for what Asmodeus wanted. I spotted a toppled beer bottle next to the table. I grabbed it, smashing the bottom on the table and leaving behind a jagged half in my hand.

The woman saw the weapon, and her eyes widened. "Fuck," she murmured.

Do it now!

I followed his command.

I didn't think when I attacked her. I didn't see her as a person with hopes and dreams. I saw her as an object that needed to die at the request of the voice in my head, a voice connected to something powerful, if it was indeed from that monstrous creature I had seen in my nightmare. It was easier to do what I had to do when I didn't think of her as a person.

She was no match for me. With my physically gifted body and her much weaker one, I overpowered her easily, and with the jagged glass, I cut into her flesh with little resistance.

Soon she was covered in deep cuts. Crimson crossed her pale body everywhere. It splashed on my arms, my face, my chest. I tasted her warm, salty blood on my lips, and it both repulsed and excited me.

A red filter covered my vision and bathed the entire room in a crimson cast. It wasn't her blood but like someone dropped a veil over my eyes. I attacked more ferociously, hoping to snuff out her life quickly to avoid thinking too much about what I was doing.

All I knew was that I wanted to save my family from a horrific fate while appeasing the thing inside of me that seemed capable of making it happen. I was in a terrible situation, but it was better to take this woman's life than what the alternative presented.

When I was done and she breathed her last, I dropped the broken bottle to the floor. A deep sorrow filled my soul. I killed someone.

The dancer's body lay on the floor in a pool of blood that was growing quickly. Deep gashes crossed her nude body like angry rivers. I felt a powerful shame at what I had done.

Now drink her blood.

"What?" I had already gone way too far. This was a step I couldn't do. I wouldn't.

I need her blood. It's the only thing that will save you. And your family. To prove his point, Asmodeus flashed images of my family in my head. My twins were tortured by demonic-looking creatures, both of them being torn apart and violated in ways far worse than what I had done with the dancer. My wife appeared and was surrounded by red-skinned monsters that took their turns raping her. It twisted my stomach and made my blood boil. I had to stop them!

Do you understand me now?

Tears rolled down my face. I hated what I had done. I hated that I was in this position. I hated what I was about to do.

I dropped to my knees and lapped at her blood like a dog.

Asmodeus groaned inside of me, sounding like he was close to an orgasm himself.

The taste was awful. I wanted to vomit. My stomach tightened, and I felt sick.

You have done well. My thirst is slaked. For now.

I used the towel the dancer had used to clean herself with and wiped off all the blood from my body. I got dressed and rushed out of the club as fast as possible before someone went looking for the woman.

I was a monster, and it pained every ounce of my soul.

Thirteen

I wanted to say that was the last time I committed such an atrocious act, but I would have been lying. Whenever I felt like I might be free of the curse, Asmodeus made sure to remind me that he was in control. I worried that one day it might go too far, as though murder and drinking the blood of the victims wasn't bad enough.

I also worried I would be caught. How many bodies could I leave strewn about before the authorities came after me? Asmodeus assured me all would be well, but I still wasn't convinced that one day the police wouldn't show up at my door.

Ever since Asmodeus's "appearance," I wondered how our relationship came to be. Where did he come from and why did he choose me? I never dabbled in the occult, and I was as straight an arrow as you could imagine.

One Sunday, while we were in church listening to Reverend Dale exhort us to live our best lives and lift up our fellow man, I rubbed my chest. It was an action I had done a lot since my transplant, running my fingers along the scar. It was a subtle reminder of what I had endured to attain a longer life.

Then I wondered. Could Asmodeus have come to me with the surgery? Had he found a way to enter me through the incision?

I gasped, and Debbie looked at me like I had grown another head.

What if it was the heart?

It had never occurred to me that the original owner of the heart might have been in contact with Asmodeus. With that person's death, maybe the connection was passed to me.

"Are you ok?" Debbie whispered, looking around to see if any of our fellow church members had heard us.

I nodded, though everything was surely *not* right with me. I was a murderer. I was a fornicator, having sex with more women—and men—than I had ever hoped to. I drank the blood of my victims to serve a voice in my head, a voice connected to a demon that threatened not only me but my innocent family.

For all of my efforts, Asmodeus gave me a chiseled body that I didn't have to work for. He gave me pleasure beyond my wildest dreams. Yet it all came with a steep, steep price. How much longer could I pay it?

I looked up at the reverend and the cross on the wall behind him and wept inside.

I determined then that I would find out more about my donor, the man whose heart beat within me, so that I might find a way to expel the demon and save my family. Fleeting mortal gifts were nothing when eternal damnation was on the line.

Asmodeus was quiet for the next few days, and I was grateful for the break.

I went back to the hospital to see if I could find the nurse that confessed to me that my heart came from a man. She was my only hope of finding out more information.

I roamed the halls for hours as sickness and pain closed in around me. I felt so bad for all of the patients and said quick prayers for their healing.

When I wanted to give up, Nurse Tabitha turned the corner in the hall and headed toward a far room.

Hope blossomed in my chest. I raced toward her.

"Tabitha? Tabitha!"

She turned at her name and smiled when she recognized me.

"Hi! How's the heart? Is everything working out? Oh, sponge baths are only for patients, so if that's what you're looking for, you're out of luck." She giggled, but I didn't smile.

"What can I help you with?"

"I need to know where my heart came from. I need to know about the donor. It's crucial to find out."

"I'm sorry Mr. ..." She tried to think of my name. I was sure she saw a ton of patients every day.

"It's Bryan."

"Well, Bryan, as I recall telling you before, that information is confidential."

"You don't understand. Something is...happening."

"Are you having problems? If you think your body is rejecting the heart, you need to speak with the doctor. He'll—"

I held up my hand and shook my head. "No, everything is fine with that."

"Then the problem is ..."

I rubbed a hand on my face. How much could I tell her?

"I hear a voice. I think...I think it's a demon."

A smile crossed her face. "A demon? That's a new one for me. Honestly, it's probably a side effect of the medicine. It's not unheard of."

"No! It's not that. It's real. I swear it."

She cocked her head and thought for a moment. "Maybe you need a psych consult. There's no shame in that at all. We could all use some help at times."

"Please, just tell me whose heart I have." I poked my chest to emphasize the point. "Please. That's all I'm wanting to know."

Where do you think the truth will lead you? Do you really think that will end our bargain?

Asmodeus's voice startled me. My eyes went wide, and I looked around to see if anyone else had heard it. Nurse Tabitha didn't act any differently. He must have spoken only to me, as he had all along.

"Come with me," Nurse Tabitha said. She huffed and grabbed my arm, pulling me into a small room, closing the door behind me.

"This is highly unethical, and I'm sure I can get in a lot of trouble, but your heart came from a man in a car accident."

I hope you're happy about this.

I shook my head, trying to clear Asmodeus's interruption.

"Do you have a name? Any details about him?"

Nurse Tabitha's face blanched, and I could tell by how she shifted on her feet that she was still reluctant to tell me.

"Please."

She lowered her head. "Let me look."

She approached the computer terminal on the desk and brought the screen to life. "I really hope I don't get into trouble," she muttered. Several keystrokes later and she seemed to have found what she was looking for.

"Mark Whitten. Thirty-five. White male."

My excitement jumped within me, though I got a sense from Asmodeus of calmness. The competing sensations were difficult to understand.

"Mark Whitten," I repeated. "Do you have an address?"

She shook her head then closed the program. "I've already said way more than I should."

"Ok, I understand. Thank you. This means so much."

She brushed past me and opened the door, holding it open. "No more questions. I gave you what you wanted."

I nodded and left the room with the name etched in my brain.

Fourteen

Later that evening, I opened my laptop after Debbie had gone to bed and searched for Mark Whitten. It didn't take long for me to find a possible match for my donor. Nurse Tabitha mentioned he was killed in a car accident, and with a news report about a man with that name dying in a car accident, I just knew I had the right person.

Asmodeus confirmed it.

Ah, Mark. He was a good and faithful servant. He tried to outrun me, but you see how that turned out.

I swallowed hard, then answered out loud. "How did you...why him?"

Asmodeus laughed. *He invited me in.*

"Couldn't he have asked you to leave?" I really hoped Debbie didn't hear me talking to myself. She would have me committed immediately.

I leave of my own accord, and I was not ready to go.

The hope that I could rid myself of this curse faded. I was stuck with it until *he* thought it was time to go. How would I know when I had done enough? My stomach twisted, and a sickening feeling came over me. I would keep murdering and drinking blood as long as he wanted me to. My only choice was to follow his commands or do what Mark did. But what about my family? Would the curse fall to one of them?

I glanced down at my heart and shook my head. I would've been better off dying instead of getting my new heart. I had unwittingly allowed a demon inside of me, all because I wanted to live. My selfishness brought this on. I had no one else to blame other than myself.

Tears rolled down my cheeks at the realization of what all of it meant. I was a murderer, and unless I was willing to die, I had to keep doing it until Asmodeus was done.

I told you earlier that you didn't want to know all of this. Rest tonight. Tomorrow, we search for blood.

I knew then that I was too weak to say no. Too weak to resist him. Too weak to take the curse with me to the grave and doom my family.

Fifteen

My weaknesses were soon too much to bear. Going to church was painful. Asmodeus filled my head with terrible, lustful images, and I couldn't concentrate on the sermon. I even lusted after the thirteen-year-old daughter of my deacon! Asmodeus wanted more than I could handle.

When we got home from church the Sunday he had me lusting after two boys seated in front of us, I had had enough. New body or not, it was time. I knew then that Asmodeus wouldn't ever leave me. Considering how I got his curse, I didn't think it likely that he could do anything to my family if I died. I prayed to God that I was right.

I created an excuse to get out of the house.

"Debbie, I forgot I was out of decaf coffee. I'm gonna run to the store and be back in a bit."

"Grab some toilet paper while you're there too, please."

"Will do. Debbie," I said, hesitating a moment, going into the bedroom, where she was changing her clothes, "I love you. I love our family. I'm so glad I got this new heart so I could be around a little bit longer."

Debbie smiled. "It's been a blessing."

I gave her a kiss knowing it might be the last time I ever did. Then I left, but not to go to the store. It was time.

When I got in the car, Asmodeus spoke. *You can't outrun me.*

"I know, but I can end this."

It's a mistake if you do. Think about your family. Think about your soul forever tormented.

"It already is. But I trust in God. He can forgive me."

I got onto the highway, and the moment I merged with traffic, I slammed on the accelerator.

You're making a mistake. You're dooming your family. He sounded panicked, almost worried.

"I can't take it anymore!"

I spotted a bridge ahead and aimed for the pillar in the median. It was my only hope. I pushed the accelerator to the floor, maxing out the speedometer of my Camry. I said a quick prayer for forgiveness a second before I smashed through the yellow barriers and into the concrete pillar while Asmodeus screamed in my head.

Sixteen

The paramedics that pulled up to the grisly scene of the car crash knew immediately that their services weren't going to be needed. The mangled car left no doubt about the death of its occupant.

When they approached the officer on scene, he shook his head.

"Sorry, boys, there ain't no saving this one. He was an organ donor, though. Maybe there's still time?"

One of the paramedics took the information and checked on the status of the dead man, Bryan Weaver.

"His heart won't work. He got it from someone else. What a shame to have received such a gift only to die like this," the paramedic said.

The other paramedic, an older man, spoke up. "Let's get him out of here and take him to the morgue. They'll do what they need to there."

Within moments, they pulled the broken and bloodied body of Bryan out of the wreckage and sped to the county morgue. They left him in the hands of the coroner, Earl Connors.

Earl knew the heart wouldn't be useful for normal people, but he had a connection that still needed organs, and Earl needed money. He texted his contact then got to work.

He extracted the heart and placed it in a cooler, working fast, as time was running out. Any harvested organ needed to be used quickly, before it was no good.

Within moments, a man in a black suit entered the morgue. He had a scar on his face and was built to intimidate with his thick muscles and permanent scowl.

"The boss thanks you for your business," he said, dropping off a small bag of cash and taking the harvested heart. "We got a patient that needs this pretty bad. You just saved someone's life. Or not. I don't care as long as we got his money and he gets this heart."

"It was already transplanted once," Earl said. "I let your boss know that."

"Don't matter to me. I ain't getting it."

With that, the man left.

Earl was grateful for the cash. His debt was getting out of control, and with this stroke of luck, he would be able to clear most of it. And who knew, maybe the heart would work out for the next person. At least he did something good for someone else.

The Obscure Lens
Megan Stockton

MARI SIPPED HER GLASS of red wine as she walked through the quiet kitchen, circling the island like a shark. Her cell phone lay there, face dark. Her fiancé was supposed to have been home hours ago for their anniversary dinner, but he kept getting delayed at work. At least that was what he said. Mari didn't believe him; she stopped believing him a long time ago. She hated the way the female employees in his office whispered when she would stop by, like they assumed they were getting away with their scandalous affairs. Mari wasn't stupid, she was just tired of pretending to care.

The deepest knife in the wound was that he had started spending more and more time on "projects" with Mari's friend Kara. At the same time, Kara had become colder and more distant, only further confirming Mari's suspicions. A double betrayal.

The phone lit up, but it was just a text from her *best* friend, Jean, who just went through a nasty breakup with his own douchebag boyfriend. He'd kind of gone radio silent for a week or so, immersing himself in his work, she assumed. He was a photographer, and a damn good one at that. She knew he needed some space and he would reach back out to her when he had gotten through his mourning period. It was time for them to start shit-talking the ex.

She sat the glass of wine down and retrieved the phone, squinting at the message that showed up under Jean's name.

help pelase

"How did autocorrect miss that one?" She laughed, dialing his number. The message didn't immediately concern her—they goofed around with dramatics pretty frequently. It wasn't unusual for one or both of them to send messages that said things like: kill me now, I hate this place, I'm dying, dear God please help me.

The line hardly rang at all: two brief tones followed by the click of the receiver. Jean didn't say anything, but she thought she could hear someone breathing heavily on the other end of the line.

"Jean?"

"Mari," he responded, voice low and harsh.

"Are you okay? You sound...I don't know, out of breath?"

A muffled thud on the other end suggested Jean dropped the phone, and everything went quiet. She looked at her screen to see if the call had disconnected, but it hadn't.

"Jean? You're kind of freaking me out."

Mari was already putting on her sneakers, snatching the car keys from the island. She bolted out the front door, keys rattling in her shaking hand. Her car's headlights came alive as she unlocked the doors with the key fob, phone still to her ear.

"Jean? I swear to God I'm going to kill you. Hello?" She strained against the static, trying to hear something on the other end. Anything. Maybe he dropped the phone down into the couch or behind the bed, but she knew that if that were the case, he would be yelling that he was trying to find it. There was nothing but silence on the other end.

It was pouring the rain, but she hadn't taken the time to grab a coat. Her short red dress was saturated, water pouring down her body as though she didn't have the thin fabric as protection at all. She stuck to the leather seat as she jumped inside, tossing the phone onto the passenger seat and turning it on speaker.

"Jean!"

She yelled his name again, jerking the car into reverse as she backed out of the driveway. The tires skidded on the wet asphalt, and she reminded herself to calm down. Luckily, Jean lived relatively close by, in a neighborhood several streets down. It was a fifteen-minute drive, but she'd made it in twelve before. Tonight, every second felt like it was scraping against the inside of her scalp, anxiety drumming up all kinds of terrible scenarios.

She was going to *have* to get back on her meds.

The windshield wipers slapped back and forth, barely keeping up with the sheets of rain that assaulted her car. She blinked, trying to focus through the blur. Trees and streetlamps pulsed in the darkness like ghosts, appearing and disappearing as she flew past them.

When Mari pulled into the driveway, she noticed the house was dark. Not a single light on inside. She slammed the car into park, sure she stripped some gears because she hadn't even waited for it to come to a complete stop, and jogged to the front door.

She fumbled with the doorknob, trying to force her spare key into the keyhole with shaking hands. A motion light had come on as she had approached, making it so much easier to see what she was trying to do.

"Jean, I'm coming in." She yelled the warning as the door opened and she slipped inside.

The house was quiet. As she shut the door, she felt like she had entered another world: the sounds of the rain disappeared, and she was left with the gentle creaks and pops of a settled house in the storm. Her own house was composed of too many glass panes and windows—rain sounded like the march of a million tiny soldiers. Jean's house played that kind of faint drone that would help you sleep at night.

She didn't like the lack of life she felt, the way Jean hadn't come down the stairs or called to her from the living room.

She entered the kitchen first, noting the half-drank glass of red wine. *Twins!* she would have remarked to him. She walked into the dining area and then the living room, moving as quietly and slowly as she could. She felt a chill of nervousness creep down from her scalp like cold water.

Mari stopped, lifting her foot as it made a tacky, clinging sound like weak Velcro. Was that blood? Blood wasn't sticky, was it? The dark droplets made a distinct trail to the sliding glass door that led to the backyard. She was going to be sick.

She realized she left her phone in the car. She paused, clamping her eyes shut as considered going to get it before pursuing the trail of mystery substance. Excess water dripped out of her loose strands of hair and dripped against her closed lashes.

She released a deep breath and continued out onto the back patio.

Light immediately flooded the area, blinding her as she spun around in surprise. She shielded her eyes from the glare of the motion lights, heart thrumming in the base of her throat. She blew out another nervous breath, turning to survey the backyard.

The pool was illuminated by lights along the walls beneath the surface. She had spent many a summer day in this very pool...but in her fond memories, the water was clear blue.

Tonight it was red, and she saw the fully clothed body of Jean floating along the bottom.

"Mari?"

She blinked when Brent said her name, flinching against the sound as though it was offensive. He was leaning over the counter toward her, elbows resting on the granite surface. He reached over to squeeze her hand gently.

"I've got to go into work. Are you sure you're okay?"

She nodded. "Of course I am. Why wouldn't I be?"

He grimaced, moving around the island to pull her into a hug. It felt stilted, like hugging an inanimate object. He was wearing a black turtleneck that felt itchy. It was all she could do not to pull away. He had been impatient with her since Jean's death. Of course, on the surface he was doting and sympathetic...but she knew him. They had been dating for over five years and had been engaged for nearly two of those. When he asked how she was feeling, he disengaged about thirty seconds into her response. When she slept in a little he would intentionally make noise and apologize before insisting it was really time she got up anyway. *Bed rot isn't good for you. By the way, can you iron my slacks?*

"If you're sure. I'll have to work late tonight, so don't wait up. I've got a lot to catch up on."

"Do you have anyone helping you?"

He paused, putting on an exaggerated thinking face. "Ramirez, Stroud, Patrick ..."

"Kara?"

"Hmmm...I don't know her schedule for the week. If she's there, she'll probably help too."

What *bullshit*.

"Love you, gotta go." He blew her a kiss as he headed out the door abruptly.

She huffed a sigh, and her eyes roamed around the quiet house. A box on the coffee table had been waiting for her: a box full of Jean's things. He hadn't had any family other than his mother. She had gone through and taken things with sentimental value, some photos, things like that. This box contained random stuff that Mari had tossed together in a hurry to look at later.

She collapsed onto the couch with a sigh, opening the top of the box and sifting through the contents. It felt almost wrong, as though she was violating Jean's memory, but at the same time, it was the only way she could hold on to him. His absence was a constant weight that seemed to drag everything in her life down with it. She ran her fingers over the items, picking up a small, cracked photo frame with a picture of the two of them laughing in a bar. She smiled faintly, the memory of that night rushing back. Jean had been so full of life then, his laugh contagious, his eyes alight with mischief. He had joked he was going to print the photo and frame it, and it looked like he had done just that.

A deep ache settled in her chest, and she shoved the frame aside, grabbing the next item: an old ticket stub from a concert they went to in their twenties. It was faded, the edges worn down with time, but the memory it carried was sharp. Jean had insisted they go even though they were both broke, and they ended up laughing their way through the show because neither of them could afford drinks. She found an old mixtape, too, the kind Jean used to make for her when they were younger. The cassette was marked with his messy handwriting. *For Mari—Music for a Rainy Day.*

"Jean," Mari whispered, her voice shaky as she held the tape in her hands, turning it over and over like a relic. She couldn't believe her oldest friend was just...gone. She refused to believe this had truly been suicide as the police insisted it appeared to be. Jean wasn't suicidal, was he? Did you ever really know what a person was going through?

The next object she pulled from the box was a silver Leica camera. It was surprisingly heavy for something so compact, and the leather strap was worn from use. She ran her fingers over the smooth metal, a strange twinge of nostalgia hitting her. Jean had been passionate about photography, always capturing the world through his lens in ways that felt so raw, so alive. He had a way of seeing beauty in the mundane that she could never quite replicate. The weird thing about finding this camera, however, was that Jean preferred film. He said there was just something about film that couldn't be replicated. She had never known him to use digital.

She turned the camera on, flipping the viewer on the back around so she could see the images he had taken. She saw a few photos of random things: plants, buildings, shadows. The last image was blurry, the edges warped in a way that made the photo look...wrong. A self-portrait. Jean, but different somehow. His face was twisted, the features warped, as though something had been distorted in the image. His eyes looked hollow, his mouth contorted in a grimace that sent a cold shiver down her spine.

It felt wrong. Something felt like a physical, sinister presence pressing onto her shoulders.

Her breath caught as she stared at the photo. Jean hadn't been the kind of person who took dark or unsettling photos. But this? This was something else entirely. The warped image seemed to reach out from the frame, pulling her in, and for a moment, she couldn't breathe.

"What the hell is this?" she muttered to herself, her hand trembling as she held the camera closer, trying to make sense of it.

The room felt cold, and she wasn't sure if it was the air conditioning or if it was the weight of the photo, the haunting reminder that something had been off with Jean for longer than she knew. She could hear her heartbeat pounding in her ears, a steady, unrelenting rhythm that felt like a warning.

Her cat jumped onto the couch, startling her so much that she dropped the camera. It made a clattering sound, and she heard the muted sound of the shutter. It sounded more like a gasp than an actual shutter sound, and it caught her off guard. The orange cat hissed and jumped back onto the floor, winding itself between her ankles.

"You scared me, you little shit."

Most days she forgot she had a cat. He always kept to himself.

She bent down to scoop the cat up. Her fingers were trembling, and her pulse hadn't slowed. The cat squirmed in her arms, but she held him close for a moment, trying to anchor herself to the present with the warmth of his fur and the prickle of his nails through her shirt. She set him on the couch beside her and turned back to the camera.

The camera had landed face down on the rug, the lens catching just a shimmer of light on its surface from the lamp like a silver fish in dark water. It looked unscathed, but the fall had somehow definitely triggered the shutter. She picked it up carefully, blowing a bit of lint off the lens, then turned it over and tapped the gallery button again.

The display blinked once, and the new photo popped up.

Her stomach tightened.

It was the cat, but not how it should have been. Caught mid-leap, frozen as it jumped onto the couch, but the photo had glitched somehow. The cat's body was elongated, warped at strange angles, the eyes pitch black and sunken, mouth open and hanging as though the jaw was broken. There was a doubling effect—something behind the cat had tried to take shape but didn't finish forming. The background was smeared, almost as though time itself had bent during the shutter click.

Mari stared at it, breath shallow. She tapped the preview button to zoom in. The distortion only got worse. The pixels at the cat's edges bled into static, digital snow flickering for a second like the image might collapse altogether.

Her cat, now curled up beside her on the couch, was purring softly, oblivious to the super-fucking-creepy photo of himself.

"Jesus," she muttered, voice hoarse. "Well, that's it then. It's just broken, old. Something like that. That's all."

She set the camera down beside her with a trembling hand. Her eyes drifted back to the box, heart still racing. She proceeded to dig through the items again, trying to distract herself from the camera. Something near the bottom of the box caught her attention: a thin, dark object pressed flat against the side. A small, leather-bound journal.

Unlike everything else in the box—pictures, trinkets, old SD cards—it looked to be untouched on the outside. She flipped it open, expecting sketches, notes, something of Jean's usual brilliance. The spine cracked as though it had never been opened.

The first page was blank.

She frowned and turned to the next one.

Then the next.

Still blank—

—until the fourth.

Don't look into the lens.

Mari blinked. The handwriting was Jean's. *Definitely* his. She would recognize that messy, angular scrawl anywhere. But the tone...something about it was wrong. It was slanted. Shaky.

She turned the next page.

Don't look into the lens.

The same words, but this time darker with an obviously heavier pressure: the lines dug into the paper, leaving wide scars around the ink.

Page after page the words repeated—over and over, each time more frantic.

Don't look into the lens.

Don't look into the lens.

Dont look

dont look

Dont

The handwriting became manic. She flipped faster, heart hammering, watching Jean's mental unraveling ink itself onto the pages. Some were scratched so hard the pen tore through. On one page, the ink had bled as if he had been crying or sweating while writing.

The last pages weren't legible, just black scribbles and what looked like bloody fingerprints dried orange onto the paper. But she knew what they said. *Don't look into the lens.*

Mari slammed the book shut. Her mouth was dry.

She stared at the Leica sitting innocently on the coffee table. God, Jean *had* been having a psychotic break. How could she not have known? How could she have missed it? What was it? Some kind of loss of identity? Had he been taking drugs? She buried her face in her hands, breathing in her own hot breath.

Why did she want to touch the camera again? The journal had warned her, but the warning was so *unreal*. She knew this was a psychosis, not actually about the camera...but she couldn't shake it. It was just ink, just words on paper, right?

Her pulse quickened as she grabbed the Leica again, cradling it in her hands. It felt almost alive, heavy, like it was pulsing with energy. She had to blink and take in a deep breath when she felt like a million tiny fingers crawled across her hands. She turned the camera to face the lens toward her, flipping the digital display so that it illuminated her face in the low light.

She stared at herself, feeling the faintest tremor of unease crawl up her spine. Her face looked normal at first—just her reflection on the camera's display—but then the edges of the display began to shimmer. The image wavered. The color in her cheeks drained a little, and the image *shifted*.

Her eyes began to look hollow. Her skin pulled taut, pale and stretched.

Her lips twisted into a grimace even though she hadn't moved.

Her breath caught in her throat. Her own reflection was warping, the way a funhouse mirror distorts a body. It looked like her flesh was melting away from bone, maggots pulsing beneath like an erratic heart.

She tried to pull the camera away from her face, but her hand felt as if it was glued there. The longer she watched, the more the distortion seemed to *grow*. Her face was no longer just a warped image; it was dynamic, moving, shifting unnaturally on the screen. Her mouth stretched wider, her eyes sank deeper into her skull, and it seemed to repeat over and over.

She felt a strange heaviness in her chest, like something cold pressed against her ribs. She tried to look away but she couldn't. Her eyes were locked on the screen, drawn to the grotesque version of herself. The edges of her vision grew fuzzy. She could feel her finger, as if of its own volition, moving toward the shutter button. The compulsion was unbearable.

She had to press it.

It would only be a second, her mind whispered. *Just press the button.*

Her finger hovered over the button, the pressure building, the weight of it unbearable. It felt like something was pulling her toward the lens, toward whatever lay behind it as if the camera was a portal, a doorway she wasn't supposed to open, and yet everything in her body screamed for her to *do it*.

A sudden loud knock on the door caused Mari's heart to leap in her chest. The camera almost slipped from her hands again, but she clutched it in her sweating palms. She quickly turned her head, gasping for breath like she had been underwater. She blinked, trying to clear the fog in her mind, her pulse racing, trying to push the heavy sense of dread down.

The knock came again. Firm. Persistent.

She felt dizzy. Everything in her body screamed at her to ignore it, to just stay still to gather her bearings for a moment.

But her legs moved before her mind caught up. Mari crossed the living room in a daze, her hand reaching for the door without thinking.

As her fingers closed around the handle, a sharp, hot pain flared in her chest—like something was tugging at her insides, forcing her to act.

The camera still dangled in her other hand.

She opened the door.

She wasn't sure who or what she expected to be on the other side. She was spooked, and her imagination was running wild: dark figures, mangled best friends, twisted reflections of herself. But a man stood on the other side, a few inches taller than her, wearing a worn trucker's hat and a thick, flannel shirt that clung to his broad shoulders. He looked weathered but friendly, with gray hair peeking out from under the hat, a thick mustache, and a deep tan from hours spent outdoors. He smiled when he saw her, revealing a row of slightly yellowed teeth.

"Evening, miss," he said, his voice rough but polite. "I'm real sorry to bother you, but I got a flat out there." He gestured vaguely toward the street. "I'm just down the road, and I can't seem to get the tire changed. Can I use your phone to call for a tow?"

She didn't respond immediately. Something about him felt *off*, but that could have been her paranoia. She glanced at the clock and realized she had been sitting there for hours although it had felt like minutes. It was late, but not too late for a random knock at her door. The man didn't seem dangerous, just tired. She could see the weariness in his eyes, the oil stains on his shirt. He looked like a working man, like someone who had been on the road too long.

"I know this has to feel like the start of one of them scary movies, and I know I don't look the freshest." He laughed apologetically.

"You don't have a cell phone?" she asked, trying to keep her voice soft and polite.

"Out of minutes." He sighed.

"Okay," Mari said, shaking her head slowly. "I have to grab my phone. I'll meet you at the road and call a tow for you. You broke down at the right place… There's a shop just a few blocks down."

He smiled, clearly grateful. "That's mighty kind of you. I'll be waiting just past the corner."

The trucker walked back to the road, and Mari nodded and closed the door behind him. She walked quickly to the kitchen, snatching up her phone from the counter. Her fingers trembled slightly as she unlocked it and dialed for a tow truck.

The tow said it would be five minutes. Just five minutes and she could get back inside, lock the door, and maybe take a long bath before turning in for an early night.

She headed outside and walked down the street, letting the camera dangle over her shoulder by the strap. It had such *weight* to it. She reached the corner where the man was standing, his truck sitting on the side of the road, the front tire flat. He was leaning against the door, looking tired but not exactly stressed. His truck was a workhorse: dirty, covered in rust, but obviously well-loved.

"Thanks for coming out," he said, tipping his hat toward her as she approached. "It's a hell of a time for a flat, isn't it?"

She gave him a tight smile. "Yeah, especially this late. Tow's on the way, though. They said five minutes."

They stood there in awkward silence for a moment, watching the headlights of oncoming traffic. The air was thick with the sound of rain in the distance, a storm on the way.

"Where are you from?" she asked. "Your accent reminds me of West Virginia."

"Tennessee," he said, puffing his chest proudly. "You from West Virginia?"

"No, but I have family there. An aunt and uncle, cousins."

"You a photographer?" he asked, his voice warm and curious as he motioned to the camera hanging at her side.

Mari paused. "No," she said, shaking her head. "My friend was. He was the photographer. He was a really amazing photographer. He passed away recently, and I kind of...inherited this camera, I guess. I just can't put it down yet."

The man chuckled. "Ah, well, it's a beautiful camera. Looks expensive."

"I think this brand is, but I don't know much about cameras. Just point and shoot on automatic settings."

He smiled a little wider. "You know, I've never had a real portrait done. Not once in my life. I've had plenty of pictures taken, but never one on purpose, you know? I'm always in the background doing something stupid, or half of my arm is in the corner. Why don't you snap one of me now?"

She shifted on her feet, feeling a twinge of discomfort. "I don't know. I'm not a photographer. I don't have the eye for it."

But the man didn't seem to hear her objection. "Please, just one. I'm not getting any younger. You'd be doing me a favor, miss. Just a quick shot. For the road. For the memory."

His voice was smooth, insistent, but not demanding. She could tell he wasn't used to being told no, and there was something about the way he spoke that made her reluctant to refuse. He was one of those good old boys, those genuine people.

What would it hurt?

She let out a sigh, holding up the camera with a reluctant smile. "Alright, just one."

He stepped into the street, positioning himself casually, but with an exaggerated tilt of his head. The smile he wore was practiced but genuine enough.

She raised the camera to her face, squinting slightly through the viewfinder. As she focused on him, the same sickening distortion crept into her vision. It wasn't on the screen…it was in her eyes. She pulled her face away from the viewfinder, instead turning on the display for a better view. His face began to warp even more intensely. His eyes darkened, his skin pulled tight, the colors of his features faded into grotesque shades of gray. His mouth stretched wider, the image flickering as though his reflection was being swallowed by the screen.

Her finger hovered over the shutter button. *No,* she thought, panic rising in her chest. *It's just a glitch, just a glitch, nothing more.* But the compulsion returned, even stronger than before. Her finger was *already* pressing down, her vision swimming as she captured the photo.

The screen went black for a split second, then it flashed the distorted image back at her—his face, twisted and warped, staring at her with an expression that could only be described as agony. The distortion made him look like he was *reaching* out, pulling toward her as though he was being consumed by the lens itself.

She froze, an awful sensation crawling under her skin. She didn't want to show him the picture. She couldn't. Not after what she had seen. She quickly lowered the camera. "Uh, sorry," she said, trying to recover. "The picture didn't come out right. The lighting's all wrong."

She deleted the photo and turned the camera off.

The man didn't seem to mind. He waved it off with a chuckle. "Ah, no harm done. My wife always says I got a mug that'll break mirrors."

Before she could respond, the tow truck appeared in the distance, its lights flashing. Mari felt a rush of relief wash over her. "There's your rescue! I'll leave you to it, then," she said, offering him a tight smile as she backed away toward her car. "Good luck with everything. Be safe going home. It was so nice to chat with you."

"Thanks for helping an old man out, miss. You take care now."

As Mari walked away, she heard the screeching of tires followed by the sickening sound of metal crunching against metal, a *bang* that sounded far too close. Her head snapped around toward the source of the noise. Smoke rose from the man's truck as she jogged toward it, a feeling of dizziness overtaking her.

A car had swerved off of the road and struck the man's truck and was on fire. The driver, just a kid, stumbled out of the car and vomited into the grass as he complained about neck pain and begged someone to call an ambulance.

But Mari wasn't looking at him.

She was looking at the trucker, who was pinned between the car and his own truck, body consumed by gasoline-fed flames. He screamed, melted flesh peeling off of his hands onto the hood of the car as he tried to push it off of himself. His mustache and hair sizzled like sparklers, smoke pouring from his mouth. Other vehicles stopped to gawk, several people already on their phones.

The trucker looked over at her, wails turning frantic, and he reached toward her and screamed. *"Don't look!"*

Mari stumbled back toward her house, her mind spinning, unable to shake the images of the burning man, his screams reverberating through her head. Her heart raced, but it wasn't just the shock—it was that *compulsion* again, gnawing at the edges of her thoughts, that pull toward the camera. She had to get it out of her hands. She didn't understand what was going on, but she felt insane.

Sirens wailed as the fire department, rescue squad, and EMTs arrived on the scene. The noise was an icepick to her brain.

Don't look. The trucker's last words repeated in her mind.

She stepped inside the front door, her legs feeling heavier with each passing second. The storm was approaching; thick, black clouds hung ominously in the sky.

The camera dangled from her neck like a noose, placing a heavy and constant weight against her hammering heart.

Without thinking, Mari opened the box on the table and threw the camera inside. She shoved the box onto the floor and pulled the phone out of her pocket with shaking hands. She found herself feeling for the camera's weight around her neck as she dialed Brent. She knew she had put it into the box, but the phantom weight remained.

"Hey, babe, what's up?" He sounded annoyed already, sighing in exasperation.

"I need you to come home. Now." Her voice cracked, raw with emotion. "Please. Something happened...I—please, just come home."

His voice softened, but she could hear the low hum of background noise, a murmur of people talking, maybe office chatter but it sounded far too lively. "I'm swamped at work, Mari. You know I can't just—"

"I don't care!" she snapped, the words flying out of her mouth before she could stop them. She clamped her hand over her mouth in surprise. She was shaking, a deep, hollow ache growing in her chest. "Please. Just come home. I need you here."

There was a pause on the other end. She could hear him exhale, the weariness in his voice catching her attention. "Alright, alright. I'll head out. Just...calm down, okay? I'll be there soon."

"Thank you. Thank you." She barely whispered the words, but they felt like they were ripped from her lungs. She hung up, leaving the phone screen glowing in her hand as she stared at it in a daze.

With her heart still pounding, she climbed into the tub and let the water pour over her. She closed her eyes, trying to let the warmth soothe the pounding in her skull.

The gentle sound of the water filled her ears, but no matter how hard she tried, she couldn't escape what she had seen. The image of the trucker, his skin melting, his final scream—a *warning*, she thought. A warning that she hadn't listened to.

She could have stayed in the bath all night, finding the warmth of the water a comfort she hadn't felt in days. She exhaled against the surface, and it rippled around her.

The sound of a car pulling into the driveway caught her attention, and she opened the drain. She was out and half-dried before the tub emptied. She walked into the kitchen with her still-damp skin clinging to an oversized T-shirt, realizing she must have left the door open because Brent was walking through it.

"Hey, you're home," she said, her voice cracking slightly with relief. She tried to smile, but it felt unnatural.

He just stared at her.

"Something's wrong. I don't know what's happening, but I saw something." She stopped, her breath hitching. "There was a man outside, and he just needed a tow truck." She felt the weight of it all, the dread that followed her inside, the sensation that everything was unraveling. "I don't know how to explain it. The camera...I think it's cursed. There's something about it...something *wrong*."

His gaze dropped, avoiding hers for just a second.

"Are you listening to me?" she asked, her voice rising in frustration. "Please! I'm not crazy, I—"

His voice softened from the tone he used on the phone earlier, almost apologetic. "I am so sorry..."

Mari furrowed her brows. "What? What's going on?"

He slowly lifted his hands.

She gasped as she saw the blood on his palms, still wet and streaked with red. "What—what did you do?"

"I was rushing home, Mari," he whispered, his voice low and ragged. "I didn't want to make you wait. I was speeding. And I—I *ran over the cat*."

Her stomach twisted, a wave of nausea crashing over her. The blood on his hands made her dizzy, like she was seeing it everywhere. Her cat.

Her poor, quiet cat that always stayed out of the way, had been a casualty of her desperation.

"You left the front door open," he added, voice accusatory now. "I was fucking scared shitless because of how you sounded on the phone. I wasn't paying attention."

She walked past him into the living room and collapsed onto the couch, the world spinning around her as she broke down. Her chest ached, and the tears wouldn't stop coming. There was still orange fur clinging to the gray of the couch where the cat had sat next to her earlier.

Where the camera had snapped a photo of the cat earlier.

He sat beside her, awkwardly reaching out to touch her shoulder. "We'll get another cat."

"You can't just replace him like that," she snapped.

He sighed. "Hey...I thought maybe we could watch something. You know, a rom-com or something to take your mind off of everything. I'll make some popcorn."

Mari wiped her eyes, trying to steady herself, but the last thing she wanted was to pretend everything was okay. Brent was ready to move on to whatever was easy. How many times had he gaslit her into thinking she had overreacted when he was trying to be supportive? He'd start a movie and excuse himself thirty minutes in.

"Do you want to tell me what happened today?" He reached for her, but she recoiled from his blood-stained hands.

"Christ. Let me take a quick shower."

"What did you do with his body?"

"I laid it in the bushes," he responded, voice even.

"Okay." She sniffled. Could she convince him to bury the cat later? Would photographing his corpse bring him back to life? She shook away that morbid thought. *What the fuck.*

Mari's hair dripped onto her T-shirt, leaving droplets on the fabric.

She squeezed the tips onto the carpet, watching it fall like artificial rain. She needed to wring it out just a little more. She headed into the bathroom, slipping in as Brent showered. She quietly dried her hair with the towel.

Brent's phone buzzed on the counter.

She turned to the shower, where he seemed oblivious to the incoming message. She took a deep breath, biting her lower lip as she leaned over and swiped up, typing in her birthdate for his pin.

The screen flashed brightly with a message that caught her breath.

It was from Kara, his coworker, Mari's only other friend. It read: *You owe me big time. I didn't get all dressed up for a quickie like that.*

She didn't need to read any more. That was all the confirmation she needed.

Mari's fingers trembled as she set the dinner table, her movements stiff and deliberate, as though she was preparing a feast for strangers rather than the two people who should've been her closest (living) companions.

The kitchen was steamy, the oven heating up to an uncomfortable warmth, the stove eyes glowing red, casting long shadows across the countertops. She had insisted on a gas stove when they bought appliances. More even cooking, better temperature control. Mari now wondered if she had somehow known she would need it for other applications.

Brent had already voiced his objections about tonight.

"I don't think this is a good idea, Mari," he had said, his voice strained, trying to appear calm while avoiding her gaze. "I just don't know if—"

But Mari wouldn't let him finish. "No. Both of you." Her voice was a quiet, insistent command. "We're doing this."

There was something strange in the air between them, a tension that made the space feel smaller, the walls pressing in. Brent had been pacing, but now he stood motionless, his face pale. He looked like a man who had no escape, cornered in his own home.

"Please, Mari—" he began, but she interrupted him, her voice cold.

"Don't argue with me. It's too late for that."

She had been able to tell he was terrified. He didn't know what she may have known or what she had planned. But he agreed. "Alright, alright...I'll call Kara."

The front door opened now, and Mari nodded to herself, her eyes already focused on the empty stove eyes in front of her. She cracked open a bottle of red wine, pouring generous amounts into two glasses before setting the bottle on the counter for easy access.

Kara was shaking off her coat at the door, Brent retrieving it as it slid down her arms. He was moving like a robot, just as uncomfortable as Mari but without the resolve. Kara thanked him, touching his wrist with a lingering brush.

Mari didn't miss it, but she didn't care.

"Dinner's almost ready," Mari announced, a thin smile on her face that didn't quite reach her eyes. "Have a seat."

Brent and Kara hesitated but eventually made their way to the table. The tension was thick, heavy, like they were all actors in some dark drama, the lines already written and the ending inevitable.

Mari returned to the stove, her hands shaking just slightly as she retrieved two plates from the neighboring countertop. The smell of roasted chicken and vegetables filled the air, mingling with the scent of the wine and the acrid undercurrent of something else—something neither Brent nor Kara could name.

"This smells divine, Mari…but is everything alright?" Kara asked, trying to sound casual, but the hesitation in her voice was obvious.

Mari's smile remained fixed. "Perfectly fine." She slid into her seat, lifting her glass. "I know you're fucking."

Both Brent and Kara exchanged another quick look, but neither one said a word. The color drained from their faces.

Mari took a long sip of her wine, savoring the taste as she let the moment linger. "Oh, don't look so worried. I don't care. In fact, this is a toast to new beginnings, to leaving the past behind."

She took another long drink, draining her glass.

Brent cleared his throat awkwardly. "Mari, this is…a little strange, don't you think?"

"Is it?" she asked, her voice quiet but piercing. "I don't think it's strange at all. I think it's a fresh start. Don't you?"

The silence in the room grew heavier.

"You look like you're enjoying this," Kara said, her voice laced with an edge of discomfort, as if the air was too thick to breathe.

Mari's eyes narrowed. "I am," she said, and she reached for the camera sitting on the table, the same camera from the day before. Her fingers lingered on it, the cool, metallic surface like an old friend or, perhaps, something more sinister.

"Let me take a picture of you both," she said, her tone almost too sweet. "You both look so…happy."

Kara shifted uncomfortably, but she didn't protest.

Brent, however, hesitated. "What's going on, Mari?" His voice was raw, defensive, like a child caught in a lie. "You're not yourself today."

Mari's smile persisted, and she gestured for them both to scoot closer together. "Come on, let's make it a memory," she said, her voice thick with mock cheerfulness.

Brent and Kara reluctantly complied, their shoulders touching awkwardly as they sat side by side.

Mari raised the camera and clicked the shutter button. The photo flashed back to her, distorting their faces, twisting them into grotesque masks of horror. She studied it for a long moment, a strange satisfaction curling in her chest. The distortion seemed to deepen their expressions, the agony written clearly on their faces even though they hadn't moved an inch.

Kara cleared her throat, shifting in her seat. "Is it any good? Let's see it."

Mari didn't respond immediately. The oven beeped, and she got to her feet, carrying the camera and the wine bottle with her.

"It's *beautiful*. I'll be right back," she said softly, her voice slipping into something colder than it had been before.

Brent glanced back at Kara, but when he turned again to speak to Mari, she was already gone.

Mari stepped into the kitchen, the camera resting heavily in her hand, her mind oddly calm. She felt like she was watching everything from a distance, as if she was no longer part of the scene unfolding in her own home. She hung the camera around her neck and turned the already heated stove eyes on high.

She walked out the front door, the cool evening air crisp and invigorating. She barely noticed the soft crunch of glass underfoot as she passed over the bloodstained pavement, the spot where the trucker died just the night before.

She took a long swig of the wine, the taste sharp and bitter as it slid down her throat.

Behind her, a sudden flash of light followed a deafening explosion as her house erupted into the night air. Mari felt the heat even at a distance, but she didn't flinch. Even as the sound of wood and debris clattered to the pavement, she didn't turn around.

She continued walking, the bottle of wine in her hand and the camera around her neck, while the night swallowed her whole.

Deadphones

D.W. Hitz

One

1990

THE MUSIC WAS HEAVING in Andrew Underwood's ears. It was just what he needed. He put pen to paper as the four-track played back his improvised song and he transcribed the notes. It was a goddamn hit, Zombie Goat's comeback hit if he handled it right.

The band had been stuck in a downward spiral over the last four years, ever since Maggot Kisses hit number sixty-six on 1986's Best Selling Metal Albums chart. They had made two more albums since then, and around fifty songs, but no matter how hard Andy tried, he felt like he was sinking in quicksand and the label assholes were just watching him go down and laughing.

This was going to change things. He knew just by the sound of the notes in his ears. This song was going to be the first in a new breed of hits that would get them back on top. He could already taste the champagne and cocaine at the after parties.

He finished scribbling down the last quarter note, and the four-track went to hiss after his final chord faded. He pulled off his headphones, leaning back against the oversized, burgundy leather couch

He was in a room he had grown to hate in a house he had grown to

"

despise ever since the last time the label had rented it for the band to live in while they recorded. The house had come to feel like a prison of failure, a place where so many songs had been birthed that later turned to shit. The place was the karmic equivalent of a mouth full of ash and dog shit.

But somehow, it felt better at that moment.

He studied the headphones, then the recorder the label had given them to capture their thoughts. The small deck was no different than any other four-track he had used in the past, a small set of reels and a clunky line of buttons that were probably designed back in 1969. The headphones, though—those felt different.

They were large, encapsulating his ears in cushion. They were red with a long curly cable, and they had no corporate branding or words on them, just a graphic on one side that looked kind of like a horned goat. Metal indeed—and it definitely fit the band. By the style of the things, he would have guessed they were as old as the four-track's designers, but there wasn't a scratch or a scuff on them. They looked brand-fuck-ing-new.

He nodded. He was going to tell the label he was keeping them when the record was done.

Andy rewound the tape and played the song again. He spread his arms wide and closed his eyes, letting the sound take control of his thoughts.

The song was killer. It was Zombie Goat's future. He could see crowds from his spot on the edge of the stage, and they were headbanging along. They were moshing and punching. They were as much animals as they were back in the days of Maggot Kisses.

Fuck. He couldn't believe he had come up with this song. It was good—no, better than Maggot Kisses.

A hand touched Andy's leg, a female one from the compact size and gentle touch. He opened his eyes and saw her sitting beside him: big, black, curly hair; plump, luscious lips; sparkling green eyes; and tits that begged to be squeezed.

Her mouth was moving, and then it rested in a somewhat pouting expression.

Andy had seen and done more women than he could count since his first record deal back in '82, but for some reason, the look of this one sent shivers down his spine. He hadn't heard a word she said, but he wanted to. He needed to.

He slipped the headphones off, and she scooted closer. She took the headphones in one hand and tightened her grip on his leg.

After that night, Andy's life was never the same.

Two

2025

Zach Mathers closed his eyes, absorbing the vibe of Jesse's double bass drum stampeding in his headphones. His fingers hovered over his frets, his pick above his strings, his heart racing, pushing him into the groove that only the best thrash metal could.

He hit the chords once, twice, and his pick was off in a fury, a thunderous wave, riding the rhythm of electric crunch at 140 beats per minute. He headbanged, his long hair like a chestnut cloud in the studio's control room.

He saw the music. He felt it in his soul and his muscles and his blood. He let it flow in and out of his body like breath as his fingers slid and pressed and picked and strummed like a precise berserker. He was the rhythm. He was the soul of the song. He was a god making sounds that had never existed and broadcasting his energy through fingers and strings into pickups and pedals onto tape to forever hold his passion—immortal.

He paused as the drums slowed; there was only the occasional bass thump during the lead solo. He kept his fingers at the ready, pinching the strings to their frets and waiting to come back in.

There was a crunching noise that distorted the kick drum in his ears. A loud crackling rose between beats, and each kick forced the crackling sound harder and harder, then as he was about to shred once again, nothing.

Zach's ears rang in the silence coming from his headphones.

"Shit."

He looked around the control room, growled, and rolled his eyes, setting his guitar on the stand beside the mixing console. "Really?" He pulled the malfunctioning headphones from his ears and examined them. The old Sony studio headgear had lasted him so long he didn't remember exactly when he bought them anymore, but as he tugged and manipulated the cord, he heard static cracking from the tiny speakers, and that was it.

They were dead after more than a quarter of a century.

His heart was slowing and his energy fading.

"Finally bit the dust." He shook his head, set the headphones on the side of the console, and hit the stop button on the transport controls for the reel-to-reel.

The red record light blinked at him. Track seventeen was armed and waiting, and he knew without another thought that he was done for the night.

"Shit."

Zach had other headphones; he had a dozen in the cabinet in the control room, dozens more in the studio, myriad types for the pickiest of musicians. He had to accommodate all kinds of personalities—including the prima donnas—if he was going to keep his small studio in business. But none of those other 'phones were his lucky pair. None of them were the pair that got him through engineering school or accompanied him on every live gig he worked or guided him through every recording session, whether his own music or for clients. None of them sounded the same as his now-deceased pair.

It was a stupid sentiment, and Zach knew it. Every pair of MDR-7506s was manufactured with the same feel, the same frequency range, and the same QA testing. There were literally millions of them out in studios, clubs, and arenas around the world, including his cabinet. But dammit, his were special. And the thought that they were dead hit a note of depression that sucked every bit of energy out of his soul. It was as if their loss meant the loss of something bigger that would kill him if he accepted: his musical career.

He, like so many other young engineers, had gotten into the business as a way of earning money with his love of music while keeping the hope alive that one day he would break through the invisible barrier that separated the technicians from the stars. It was a way of holding onto a dream, denying that it was potentially dead, and believing his future success was just on pause while he earned and learned his way onto the other side of the control room glass.

But if those 'phones were dead, so well-used for so long, bought when his career was ahead and bright, what did that mean for him, a graying engineer with so many more failed ideas than successes?

He sighed. It was a question for tomorrow.

He packed up and locked up, headed to his car, and checked the time on his phone. He was hungry, and at almost two in the morning, the only restaurant open in Custer Falls was Lucky Shot Burger's drive-thru. He wasn't in the mood for it, but he wasn't in the mood to go home and cook, either. A half-hour later, he was walking into his apartment with a cheeseburger and fries in a bag and crashing on his couch to soothe his growing depression.

Before long, the food was gone, and Zach found himself in an endless loop of scrolling through streaming apps, watching trailers, and deciding he might like it but it wasn't right for right now. Then, somehow, he found himself staring at a low-budget horror preview about a band whose members were being knocked off one by one, and he remembered his headphone dilemma.

He needed a new set, but what was he going to do? He didn't think another pair of 7506s were going to cut it. They definitely weren't going to rekindle his hope of being more than he was: a middle-aged engineer with possible delusions of grandeur. He loved the things like he loved his music, and he couldn't escape the looming suspicion that they were both dead. But he couldn't think that way. He had a studio to run and friends in his band. He had to keep going. But if he did, he knew he wanted something different this time—or at least, he needed to try something different.

Zach pulled out his laptop and started searching.

The usual sites like B&H and Sweetwater had a thousand options, drowning him in search results. He read some articles on what was new and hot, and he hated everything he read. He liked modern metal okay, but his heart was in the '80s and the sounds of that time. He decided he needed something that sounded like he imagined his music should, warm while loud and thrashing your soul. Maybe it was something vintage he was after?

It was strange. Almost as soon as the thought came to him, he noticed the ad on the side of the webpage. It didn't even give him a chance to type his query into the search bar.

"Vintage Gear to Rock Your Socks Off," he read aloud. There was an image that looked AI-generated of a Les Paul electric guitar, some tube processors, a reel-to-reel, and a chunky old set of headphones. He hated clicking ads; they always felt slimy to him, like he was feeding the machine and encouraging them. But what did he have to lose? Somehow, that AI-generated picture of headphones was calling him.

"Fuck it." He clicked the link.

Three

There was a knock at Zach's apartment door at around ten the next morning. Normally, he would have yelled for whoever it was to piss off, but he knew what was out there.

He opened the door in nothing but his boxers, the gap in the front window nearly letting his manhood slide out, and there it was on his *Go Away* doormat: a brown box.

Zach couldn't believe the site last night had offered next-day (practically same-day) delivery, but that had been on the bottom of the scale of unbelievable attributes listed for what was in that box. Supposedly, the pair of headphones in the package on his doormat had been owned by his all-time-favorite guitar player, Andy Underwood, and they had been used to record the best thrash metal album of all time.

Zach wasn't generally so gullible as to believe any random thing he read on the Internet, but for some reason, there was something on that site that called to him. There had been a feeling as he looked at the pictures of these things—and he did do some homework, searching old images of the band and he saw the proof. Clear as day, in a grainy old shot from *Rolling Stone*, he saw Andy Underwood wearing the things in the middle of the studio with the caption: "Underwood overdubbing a solo of "Mad Hatter"."

"Mad fucking Hatter", possibly the greatest thrash song of all time, and Andy Underwood was wearing what that website claimed to be contained in the box on his doorstep.

He picked up the package, and it was like they were vibrating inside it. The sensation of holding the box as he walked to the table was surreal. He could feel the power through the cardboard and packing material. There was still some doubt deep inside his mind, some worry that he had been tricked and that at any moment he was going to be the target of an asshole on the other side of the Internet laughing at his dumb ass. But more than that, he believed.

Zach set the box on the kitchen counter and grabbed a pair of scissors from his junk drawer. With them wide open, he sliced the tape on the sides of the flaps then gently held the sharp edge over the length of the box and began slicing it open.

He held his breath as the scissors moved. There was no way he could hurt these things; it would kill him. He pressed the blade precisely, measuring, making sure the it didn't drop into the box a millimeter deeper than it took to cut the tape.

When the flaps were released, he inhaled and set the scissors down. He spread the opening, his heart pounding, the temperature rising in his apartment.

There was a layer of brown paper. He pulled it back. A layer of bubble wrap—he could see red through the folded sheets of plastic bubbles.

His heart jumped into his throat. His fingers were shaking. He couldn't bear to believe what he was about to hold. It didn't matter at that point that he needed a working pair of headphones; what was in there was more important than that. It was a piece of rock history, and it was his. It was something more valuable than anything else in his apartment, and he was about to hold it.

Zach curled his fingers under the bubble wrapping and lifted his delivery, pushing aside the box. He felt around until he found the tape keeping his prize safe and unpeeled it. He gently folded back the layers until it was naked in front of him, a tool of a rock god. And it was his now.

There was little choice in what happened next. Zach had to try them out. Yes, they were a piece of history, a priceless item (for which he would never admit how much he had paid), and it was probably best to lock them up in a glass case where all anyone could do was drool over them from the outside, but he couldn't stop himself. He *had* to try them. He had to know what they sounded like to Andy Underwood's ears.

He carried them gingerly across his apartment, both hands cupped around the red plastic as if he was protecting a newborn child. He sat at his rig in the living room, the computer, small USB interface, and set of sound monitors he used when he wanted to play with an idea and didn't want to run to the studio to do it. He plugged the gold-plated jack into the computer's audio interface and queued up the song, the only one that was important at that moment: "Mad Hatter".

He slid them on his head and his finger hovered, trembling over the keyboard's space bar. He was about to do the unthinkable. He was wearing the very headphones Underwood had worn not only to compose this song but to record it. His heart was as fast as the song. He couldn't believe he was about to do this.

Something—he didn't think it was him, but he was grateful for the push, even as it terrified him—lowered his finger onto the key.

And it started.

A crunching mechanical rhythm, heavy and fast, took control of his mind. It was like the sound was jacked directly into his brain, bypassing his ears. He may have heard the song a thousand times in his life, but as it played at that moment, as it pumped into his thoughts, it was more like an alien entity than an old friend he knew inside and out. The rise and fall of distorted chords, the heavy lows and screeching highs that somehow fit discordantly and melodically at once, were like magic; they were powerful. They pumped his heart into overdrive and set his brain on fire with thoughts and memories, plans and reminiscence. He saw his future, songs he could write if he allowed the inspiration in, and he saw his past, years of playing, years of mixing, being one with music and loving every minute.

The drums, bass, and lead guitar all joined the song, and any control over his body and mind Zach may have thought he had was wiped away in an instant.

Zach was in his bedroom, a fourteen-year-old in 1991 sliding the new Zombie Goat cassette into his stereo. His mom and sister were in the kitchen screaming at each other as he hit play and waited. He cranked up the volume, hiss streaming from the speakers, as the song that would change his life crawled eagerly forward across the rollers and heads of his shitty stereo's tape deck.

The high hiss of tape leader switched to the low hiss of blank magnetic particles as a brief tease of what was to come.

The sound that erupted next drowned out not only the screaming in the kitchen but every other concern Zach had in his life. He was transported to a world where his deadbeat dad, who lived on the other side of the tracks and spent all of his waking hours drunk, wandered onto those tracks one night and rid the town of his presence; to a world where his mother yelled herself hoarse and while she was at the hospital for a cure was accidentally injected with a drug that wiped her mind and sent her home a dazed and loving person; to a world where his bitch of a sister went on her next date with a guy twenty years older than her and never came home. It was a place of true harmony.

And then the drums started.

He was in Denver with his best friend Tony, and they were punching and kicking in the middle of the pit. Metallica had warmed up the crowd, and Zombie Goat had the audience wanting blood. They were in Detroit and swinging their heads with the song. They were in Tony's garage, covering "Mad Hatter" with John on drums and Tim on bass, screaming with the song, rage in their words and grins on their lips.

They were other lives, other worlds, and he was in them. He was fourteen once again, sixteen, eighteen. He was alive in a way that made his now old-man life depressing and sorrowful, even more so than he had thought it was before. He was truly amazed at those other places—places he had lived and forgotten how wonderful they had been—and when the music stopped and he was back in his apartment, the home of a middle-aged man who had never fully reached his dreams, he was cold.

A shiver passed over him along with a wall of sadness.

Had he wasted his life? Had he taken the excitement of his youth and squandered it on nothing? How had he become this man nearing the age of fifty who had lost that excitement and joy—let it slip through his fingers over nothing but time?

He was ashamed. He wanted to go back to the past and relive that life. He thought of hitting play one more time and praying those memories would return, but inside his shame was a layer of fear. He was instantly worried that this crippling feeling might actually get worse if he went through that again.

His breath shuddered as he slid the headphones off. He set them on his desk and leaned back.

It had been so intense. It was like he was there, really there, like his mind had been picked up and transported to those better times in his life. He couldn't explain that. All he could do was glance at his watch. It was ten thirty, and he had to be back at the studio at one for his first session of the day, and he had interrupted his sleep to answer the door.

Maybe that experience was all a brief dream? Maybe it was his lack of sleep attacking him for not being in bed when he should have been. It was as good of an answer as any, if he could make himself believe it.

Zach went back to bed and stared at the ceiling for an hour and a half until his alarm went off. After he ate breakfast, he was compelled to bring the headphones with him to work. They weren't done with him yet.

Four

Zach left the headphones in his office while he worked. He craved them during the hours they were out of his sight. He craved the feeling from that morning, the sense of invigoration and excitement that was missing from his life these days. He made do with one of the various pairs of 7506s from the control room cabinet, and he cringed, his fingers flexing on the console over and over again as he worked.

He recorded a guitar session for a local guy who did remote fly-ins for various jazz bands in New York and Los Angeles. He recorded a few chapters for an author trying his hand at reading his own books to sell online. His last session of the day, a radio spot, got canceled when the pastor of the client's church went missing. Zach had never been so happy for a client to cancel.

He sat in the office, his attention pulled between ordering lunch over the phone and heading back into the control room to record the rhythm track that hadn't worked out the night before—and getting to use his new headphones. He decided to do both.

Instead of using a delivery app, Zach called Milt's Diner, a short-order place on the corner of 6th Avenue and Hudson who knew his studio well, delivered there often enough that Ryan, the delivery boy, knew to come quietly back to the control room if he wanted a nice tip. With just a couple of words, "the usual," he was off the phone and headed into the studio, red headphones in hand and his heart rate elevated.

He set his tape on the reel-to-reel and threaded it through the rollers and heads onto the take-up reel on the other side, and as he did so, his fingers tingled. He was feeling a strange mix of emotions, and that tingle only complicated things. He hadn't shaken the sadness, the feeling that life had passed him by, but at the same time, at each glimpse of his new headphones there was a rush of expectations like he wasn't done yet, even if he had failed so far. Those headphones told him to slide them on, that he might just be on the verge of something monumental if he let it happen, that something he could never expect would change things, and that idea made his stomach feel tight and his palms sweat.

He armed track seventeen and recalled the settings on the mixing board. He plugged his pedal into the preamp and his guitar into the pedal. He set his instrument on his thigh and slid the headphones over his ears.

A chill ran over his flesh.

He didn't know if he was ready for this, what exactly was going to happen, or if he would be able to handle it. But there he was, his blood getting hotter and a grin growing on his lips.

It was time to fucking rock 'n' roll.

He didn't check the levels or test the sound. He didn't bother with any of his normal setup other than the essentials. He hit record and let the reels spin.

Jesse's bass drum thumped through the red headphones, and it was like Zach was no longer in the same world. The sound waves gripped his ears and musical energy rushed inside his brain. It wasn't just a drum track setting the tempo and leading him in; it was the start of a revolution, the birth of a new muse that drew him into an ethereal space between sonic greatness and reality.

His fingers jumped onto the frets, but not where he had written them to be. His digits had other plans, other notes that were destined to be heard, and he didn't have the will or the strength to dissuade them.

His pick set down on a vein of tightly strung nickel, and his passion exploded into life. He may have thought he was alive before, may have thought he knew what the world consisted of, but that previous reality had been nothing but black-and-white crayon on loose-leaf paper. This new world of sound was an odyssey of color and starbursts. It was an infinite void being filled with the power of a supernova, energy and light and spectrums of color beyond his imagination.

The rhythm rose and fell. The melody was heavenly yet dark and demented. It was fast and brutal. It was bone rattling. It was a song that would last through ages, and it was coming from his mind, through his fingers like the birth of a soul into an empty realm.

There was a beauty in the music he was making and confusion as to how such an amazing thing could come from the pitiful likes of him.

An instant later, the song was over. His fingers stopped, and the low hiss of the tape was all that came through his headphones.

He was shaking as he slid them off and hit stop. He disarmed the track—the thought that he could accidentally record over what he had just done was a split-second of terror. He set the 'phones on the cabinet beside the reel-to-reel, his guitar in its stand, and leaned back in his chair.

Hands over his face, he went limp. Had that really just happened? Had he really recorded a song from his mind alone, all the way through in one play, and had it sounded as magnificent as it did in his mind?

No. He was getting old, and he had had a stroke or something. There was no way he just laid down a track as heavy and as beautiful as that seemed. It was beyond his ability. He thought he was good, but he had stopped deluding himself into thinking he could become one of the greats a long time ago—and that song was truly great. Dare he even think it?—it had been "Mad Hatter"-level great.

No. It just couldn't have been.

He hit rewind. His stomach jittered as the tape flew in reverse. The counter approached zero, and he readied his finger. The digit was nearly numb as he pressed down and stopped the reels.

He had to brace himself as he hit play. It was going to be dogshit, he knew it. He just wasn't that capable, and in a moment he would prove it to himself that he had suffered a breakdown or hallucination.

The sound that erupted from the studio's monitors was like the work of a fallen angel. It was divine, and it was loud, and it shook the walls of his soul like the darkest of metal. It made him grip the armrests of his chair and hold on for dear life, because he felt like he was suspended between Heaven and Hell and only his fingers were keeping him on this mortal plain.

He stayed like that until the music stopped and that familiar tape hiss reminded him he was not in some mystical realm but inside his control room.

He had done it. The music had been real, and he couldn't put into words what that meant.

His elation leveled off, his fingers fumbled for the stop button, and that was all he could move until he heard someone clearing their throat from behind his chair.

Zach spun around, and as much as he was shocked by the unexpected noise of someone standing behind him, he was stunned by the beauty of the woman in his control room.

Her hair was dark, and her lips were bright. She had the kind of eyes that shined like gems as they pierced through your soul and ripped your attention in her direction. Her long hair draped over her shoulders and pulled Zach's eyes down her perfect chest, down along her arms, to her tight waist and his headphones in her hands, cord dangling past her knees.

"What—" Zach could barely speak as she lowered herself into the black leather love seat on the rear wall of the control room. He watched her descend, his eyes unable to pull away from the slit in her blouse where her perfect cleavage seemed to call his name. "Who are you?"

"That's quite a song you have there." She winked and smiled at him.

He felt a shiver. It cooled off the heat rising in his loins, but not by much.

She held the headphones in her lap and tapped them with her finger. "I don't think I've heard riffs like that in quite a while. Not since I met Andy Underwood."

Andy-Fucking-Underwood. Hearing that name in his studio after recording that song... Everything seemed to fit together in a way that should have made sense if he only had a single still-elusive piece, something that would tie this new, amazing sound he had created with the rock god he had loved since his youth.

"He was special," the woman said. She didn't move or speak in a particularly sensual way, but the longer Zach watched her, the more her voice slipped through his eardrums, the more he was enthralled by her. "Like you." She gestured at Zach.

There was a pause where neither of them said a word. He thought she would continue, but she didn't.

"Like me?" It was hard to fathom. Zach never saw himself as being on a level with Underwood—well, maybe some of Underwood's early stuff, or his sophomore work that didn't sell as well, but definitely not up there with "Mad Hatter".

She grinned. "Yes, you. Like him, I think you just needed a little push—a little help from your muse."

The headphones's cord swayed between her legs. The golden plug tapped the top of her tightly clinging boots.

"My muse," he repeated, and the shiny red surface of the headphones caught his glance. "Those things..."

"Yes, these things."

Everything seemed to click into place, the missing piece discovered. There was something... maybe... magical about those headphones, something that made him hear more, made him more inspired.

He reached toward them.

She raised them and set them coiled in her lap like a tired pet snake.

He stopped. He could take them. He felt the urge to grab her head by the hair and smash her into the wall. Then her fingers wouldn't be in the way. But they were sexy fingers, the way they stroked the cord.

"Zach, I'm not here to take them from you." Did she see it on his face? "Far from it. I want you to use them."

"You do?"

Her grin grew wider. "Of course." Her other hand twirled through the hair hanging over her breasts. "I just have to do my job first."

"Your job?"

"Tell you the deal."

He cocked his head to the side. "There's a deal?"

"An unspoken one, kind of *a silence is consent* type of thing."

He said nothing, taking it all in. He still felt the urge to rip the things from her lap, still wanted to punish her for keeping them from him, but that was behind his curiosity, at least for the moment.

"They're yours to use for one album. The best album of your career, of your life. At that point, they will be... repossessed. There will be no discussion on the matter, no extensions, no bargaining. When the last song is in the can, that's it.

"But it will be your ticket to immortality."

She was crazy. The whole thing was crazy. Yes, he had experienced some weird shit since the things were delivered, but she talked like it was a deal with the devil.

He found himself staring at the reel-to-reel. There was tape on that thing with the best song he had ever recorded, ever heard, let alone made himself. Regardless of what the woman said, he couldn't deny that. Could he possibly not try it?

He turned back, ready to say yes, he would take the deal. But she wasn't there.

The headphones sat on the love seat, their blood-red plastic shining in the studio light.

Five

Zach instantly pulled Jesse and Kyle on board for the changes in the song. They made him play the track five times and drilled him for a half hour, demanding to know where this song had been the last five years while they had been trying to record something groundbreaking.

"It's a new path, like from a moment of clarity," Zach explained. He wasn't going to admit he came into the possession of a pair of magic headphones.

"An epiphany," Jesse inhaled from his joint and passed it to Kyle. "You're saying you had an epiphany?"

"That's why you write the lyrics, man." Zach smirked. He toggled the transport controls on the mixing console, and the reel-to-reel whispered from the other side of the room. "So? You guys in? Totally new album, starting now. We ride this wave and record a fucking monster."

Jesse nodded. "Fuck yeah. Let's do it."

Kyle blew a cloud of smoke across the gap between them. "You want to trash all the songs we've been working on? That's like twenty songs. I like the new one, but that seems drastic."

"Thirty-four songs." Zach held up his notebook and tapped the stop button on the transport controls. "And we don't have to trash them, just... set 'em aside for now. There's some serious shit on the horizon, and I need you guys to trust me."

Jesse and Kyle shared a glance. Jesse nodded. "You heard that song."

Kyle nodded back. "Fuck it, I guess. What do we got to lose?"

"Hell yeah." Zach armed the tracks on the tape machine. They finished the joint, and he got Jesse and Kyle set up on the drums and bass, Jesse in the big room and Kyle and his amp in the isolation booth.

They had no song planned, only Zach's instructions to treat the next ten minutes of recording like a Phish-inspired heavy metal jam session and to follow his lead. He would play the rhythm and jump over with lead melodies—they always planned on getting another rhythm guitarist one day once they were ready to tour. He would guide Jesse and Kyle from inside the control room, and they would keep up. He was convinced they were about to create another diamond to stud this master creation.

He slid on the headphones and felt the world shift. There wasn't even any music playing yet, but this was going to bend reality in a way none of them were ready for—he could feel it.

He picked up his guitar and hit record, saying into the control room mic, "Set it up."

Jesse smashed his sticks on the snare drum twice. That was all it took to set them off.

Zach saw it all. The music played inside his head, flowed from his fingers, and as his reel-to-reel imprinted tape with a sound that would last the ages, he saw Andy Underwood.

Andy had gotten buy-in from the rest of Zombie Goat—of course he did after playing them the song on his four-track. He had gotten the label to splurge on the big studio, not the little one they had planned on being stuffed inside. He had talked his way into everything they needed to make the album the best damn thrash album ever heard. They had recorded ten songs—killer, phenomenal songs—and he just knew the best was yet to come.

He felt the final track stirring inside his brain, digging around back there, the tune that would be the pinnacle of his entire existence. It was driving him mad, and he liked it.

It was close to midnight when everyone was finally at the studio. Lines of coke were shared around the room, and Andy set the tone by heading into the larger of the two booths, his pedal and amp cranked up to eleven. His bandmates' eyes were on him. The engineer watched with bated breath for what he knew was going to be an album credit he would cherish.

Andy let his thoughts settle as he blocked them all out, headphones on his ears, fingers on frets, clutching his pick.

"Roll tape." It was the only thing he would say for the next seven minutes.

He heard the drums in his head, knew how they would be before they were laid down. The notes came to mind, and his fingers moved with a speed and dexterity he didn't know he possessed.

His eyes were closed, but as the heavy thrum of the beat drove him, he saw through his lids, through the open studio beyond the booth, into the control room. He saw his bandmates nodding and loving it. The engineer was grinning as his eyes darted back and forth from the tape meters to the console, desperate to know he was getting it down like the Grammy-winning recording he thought it would be.

None of the control room's onlookers saw the blood.

It pumped from their eyes without them even knowing. It was like tears at first, then it was heavier, running down their faces in streams. It leaked from their noses and their ears; it ran from their mouths in gushing waves. It slapped on the floor and ran over the console, spread across the equipment with each move of the engineer's hands as he tweaked the preamps and nudged the levels. It pooled on the floor below their feet, and they all watched the glass wall that sealed Andy into the iso booth with gaping jaws and stares of amazement.

Andy's grip was stone on his pick. His hands felt heat from his instrument, and it spurred them on. He didn't mind the blood in the other room or the reddening light. He heard his axe crunch even better as his fingertips bled down the strings and their vibrations spattered it onto the walls.

He could feel the magnificence from his amp. It shook the room and welcomed the pit that opened in the middle of the floor. Andy guided the gusts of heat that rose, the fire that spread, the calls of song from deep below as he saw the notes rise and fall, the melody shift, and the world beyond set to fire with the cackle of his own laughter driving the flames.

And then he stopped. He let his strings ring out to the distorted perfection in his headphones. He saw them all looking on, thumbs up and smiles.

The blood was gone, for now, but they still had a lot of recording to do before this thing was sealed up.

That was when the name of the song appeared in his mind: "Mad Hatter".

Zach struck the last note and heard Jesse's symbols crash. All three of them went silent, catching their breaths, and then Kyle screamed, "Yeah!" from the booth. They all laughed.

They gathered in the control room and played back the tape. Each of them listened in awe, not a single word spoken until it ended. Their eyes were wide and their mouths were open, none of them believing that the masterpiece they were listening to was a product of their own creation.

"That's a fucking hit," Jesse finally said.

"Fuck," was all Kyle could say.

It needed vocals. It needed doubling on the rhythm elements and laying another track to reinforce the lead, but those were just process at that point. Zach could see the finish line once it was all smoothed out and fine-tuned.

This album would put them on the map. It would make them stars and fill their pockets with all the money they would ever need.

He glanced at the headphones. It was all because of them. He had no delusions that he could have been capable of making such amazing music without them. They were *magic*. It was true.

The woman came to mind, the drop-dead hottie. She had said they were good for one album, but maybe that was just, like, a negotiation tactic. There was no way he was giving those things up after one record.

No. Fucking. Way.

He had regained his hope, his desire to live and thrive. It was possible for him to succeed where he had been failing for all these years. Sure, he had a studio that was *getting by*, but he hadn't gained an inch of traction with his music. That was all about to change. He had a future as long as he had those headphones.

The red light still flashed on the reel-to-reel, still in record mode. He thought of the scene he had witnessed—no, imagined, that was it. The blood, that demonic shit.

He shook his head. That stuff didn't matter. It was just his stupid mind running away with itself as he focused on playing—only, he wasn't really focused. He didn't remember a note of what he had played until he heard the tape.

It didn't matter. He had the headphones. He had recorded a mega-hit. He was going to be the next rock god.

Six

Zach could barely remember the blur that was the next three weeks recording his album. He unlocked the doors to the studio, his heart racing, knowing today would be the final day, the last song, and though he looked forward to the fame and the accolades he was sure were coming, he was also a little sad for it to be over. This had been history in the making—his recordings, his music going down for posterity—and after tonight, it would only be the mixing and the finishing touches.

They had written and recorded the words to all the other songs. They had added the extra tracks to weigh down the rhythm, sharpen the leads, and punch up the drums. The entire thing had come together like clockwork, like it was meant to be, and all they had to do was play their parts. Each successive song had been a thriving beast, now ready to be mixed, mastered, and delivered to what Zach was sure would be a ravenous audience.

They were almost finished. Tonight was the last one. Tonight would be his real signature piece.

All the rest had been amazing tracks, tracks that would stun the world, but he felt it in his bones that tonight would be the cherry on top, the song that would cement them into the Hall of Fame as the greatest metal band of all time.

He opened the door to the lobby, and the scents of molding trash and stale coffee hit his nose. Once they had decided as a band to focus full-time on the album until it was complete, he had stopped letting clients in. He had stopped cleaning and setting the place up nicely for customers, focusing only on the work. It occurred to him at one point that if this record didn't sell, he would likely lose the place. No clients in the room meant no income and no ability to pay the rent. But he had time, time to sell the album and make a hefty advance—that would keep things going and then some.

He started a new pot of coffee and thought about the only day they had actually taken off from recording in what seemed like forever.

They had run out of tape. That wouldn't have been a problem in a bigger city, but in Custer Falls, Montana, most of his supplies had to be shipped in. He couldn't just run around the corner to Guitar Center for extra reels. He could have slapped himself when he figured it out. He put in an order with the fastest shipping available, but still, it forced them to take a day off as they waited.

It felt so strange sitting at home after he woke up that day. He felt the call of the headphones but couldn't do anything about it. Then he got a text from Jesse, inviting him and Kyle over for a barbecue and some drinks.

What else was he going to do?

The three of them sat on Jesse's back deck and drank whiskey as the sun set and the grill heated. Zach began to wonder when the last time was that he had visited Jesse's place. Jesse was a family man who worked at a hardware store, and with a full-time job and two kids, his life and

Zach's didn't usually match up when it came to aligning their free time. The strange thing was, that day, Jesse's wife and kids didn't seem to be anywhere around. They were three drinks in when Zach realized this.

His eyes on the backyard playset, Zach asked, "Where's Melody and the kids? Soccer game or something?" As soon as he said it, he saw how dumb that was. It was nine o'clock at night; there weren't any kids' games this late, were there?

Late or not, it reminded him of his last visit to Jesse's. Jesse Jr. and little Ashley shot rubber darts at each other from opposite sides of the yard. Ashley climbed into the fort and fired from the window, while JJ ducked and shot back using the swings for cover. They giggled, and Melody worried about them shooting each other in the eyes.

Zach remembered there was joy on Jesse's face that night. He had been a proud dad and husband, and Zach had envied that.

Jesse seemed to ponder Zach's question for a moment, then lit a cigarette and leaned back in his chair. He sipped his whiskey and stared somewhere between the backyard and the sunset. "They're off at Melody's mother's. We made a deal to give me some space while we recorded the album."

"Shit." Kyle shook his head. "I wish I'd thought of that. Samantha broke up with me last week. Said I wasn't *around* enough. Maybe I should have planned better—you know, warned her or something." He ran a finger over the scrape on his cheek and then the fading black eye.

"Oh, she'll come running back once this record starts selling." Zach raised his glass and sipped. He had never been a fan of Sam. She only seemed to be interested in whatever Kyle was doing if Kyle was the one footing the bill.

"Yeah, I don't know." Kyle wrung his hands together, flexed his fists, and rubbed the cuts around his wrists. "I think it's pretty much dead."

"To the next phase, then." Zach raised his glass again, and this time, the other two joined him.

"To the next phase," Jessee repeated, and sipped.

"Hell yeah," Kyle agreed. He stared at the grill. "Are we going to get the meat going or what? I'm building up an appetite looking at this thing."

"Sure." Jesse rose and headed into the house. He slid the door open and closed quickly as if he was trying to keep an escape artist pet inside.

A rotten smell hit Zach's nose, and he decided that must have been why Jesse had them walk around the house to the backyard instead of bringing them through the inside. He must have had a sewer backup or something.

He brushed away the thought as he watched the sun dim, and Jesse returned with a plate of steaks for the grill. The thought of that smell seemed to linger as the studio coffee pot hissed and filled.

"What was making that smell?" he whispered to himself.

There was an electric ding as Jesse and Kyle opened the lobby door and walked in. They both wore grins like kids on Christmas morning. Today was the day, and they knew it. After today, it was all easy street. They would start firing off samples to A&R contacts and enjoying the bidding war to come. It was the end of their old lives and the start of something entirely new.

Jesse paused in the nook with the coffee maker and nodded at Zach. "You ready to make your last pot? After this, it's going to be servants and roadies doing everything."

"Hell yeah." Zach poured his cup and led the way to the control room. He eyed the greats on the framed posters as they walked. Hendrix. Sabbath. Zombie Goat. Megadeth. Exodus. Metallica. Slayer. Overkill. Anthrax. Testament. Soon he would be on posters. He would be lining the walls of fans and musicians everywhere.

When he walked into the control room, his eyes went straight to his headphones. Their red plastic shells shone like blood. They shone like jewels. The goat-shaped graphic watched him. The set waited for him at the edge of the console, knowing he was coming to pick them up and hold them close. They knew this was the highlight of a lifetime.

Zach ran his fingers over the smooth red shell, lifted them, and took his seat. They were warm in his hands. The feeling traveled up his arms and gave him tingles all over.

He took in the room: his bandmates ready and willing; the console which he spent thousands of hours in front of, honing his craft; the tape machine which held their future between its reels; and the padded walls that heard every note and every conversation ever had in this room. It all led to this. Every piece around him added up to their future, and he loved it all.

"You ready to do this?" Zach asked his friends as he picked up his guitar. Minutes later, they were in position, instruments ready. Zach pulled the headphones over his ears and took a deep breath.

He felt the walls shift around them. The air grew thicker. There was a scream somewhere in the back of his mind, a voice calling to him, beckoning him as he reached for the transport controls and hit record.

A swell of warmth filled the room. He gritted his teeth. He grabbed his frets. He closed his eyes as his pick touched a string.

He opened them and saw what Andy Underwood saw.

Seven

Andy stripped off the headphones and charged through the control room. His sweaty skin gleamed red in the bloody light. He lifted the music stand and swung hard, slicing through the engineer's throat. Streams of red pumped over faders and knobs, his eyes never leaving the meters, his ears fixed on the sound coming from the monitors.

Andy grabbed the man by the ankles and dragged him to the double doors that sealed the room. He dragged him out, into the hall, and down to the large studio where the sound of percussion pounded his eardrums through the walls even before entering. He pried open the doors and left the engineer on the floor in front of the drum set, blood pooling beneath him.

Andy glanced back at the control room window. She was there. She nodded and smiled at him. He saw her pick up his headphones as her body lengthened into something taller than a human, stretchy and sleek, ridged yet wavering in her dark elasticity.

He smiled back at her and walked around behind Jimmy Palmer, his drummer. He slipped one of the drumsticks from Jimmy's hand, and the drummer kept moving like nothing had changed.

Andy wound back his arm and thrust it forward into Jimmy's face, the slender piece of wood jabbing through the eyeball, the cavity, and into Jimmy's brain. There was a wobbling spasm as his body ceased getting instructions, and the drummer toppled over onto the snare, dragging the symbols, hats, and the rest of the set to the floor with a crash.

When Jimmy stopped moving, Andy dragged him and laid him down beside the engineer.

He walked to the first isolation booth. Rhythm guitar notes leaked through the glass, and Andy watched Billy Meyers bob and rock out, his face distorting with effort and concentration. It was the best way for Billy to go, in that zone, in that moment of joy.

Andy opened the door and stepped inside. It was even hotter in there. It smelled like sweat and liquor and cigarettes.

Andy jerked the cord from the amp and shoved it into the guitarist's mouth—Billy kept playing. He fed it deeper, inches into feet until Billy started to gag—as he kept playing. Andy plucked the microphone from the stand next to the amplifier and swung it from the cord. Once, in a long, weighty circle, twice, and with all his weight, he heaved forward and down The mic crashed into the guitarist's skull with a crack, and finally, Billy stopped playing.

Leaving a trail of blood across the studio's hardwood floor, Andy dragged his friend. He left him beside the other two and headed for the last iso booth.

Kade Harris's head rose up and down like an oil derrick as he picked his bass's strings. Andy slid open the door and leaned down, picked up loose coils of microphone cable, and gripped them tightly between his fingers. He slid the loops of cord over Kade's head and jerked him to the floor. He grabbed the edge of the bass amp and yanked it forward until it slammed over on Kade's skull.

The bassist twitched under the cabinet's weight, but he wasn't dead. Andy had to raise his leg and bring his foot down hard until there was a crunch under the amp.

Andy felt pride, a satisfied look on his face as he dragged his last bandmate to the circle of bodies. The album was done. It would live on. He would live on.

He sat cross-legged on the floor in the middle of the circle and pulled his revolver from his pocket. He glanced at the woman in the control room. She nodded.

Zach's eyes shot open as the revolver blasted. He saw his fingers moving and listened to the song. It was something like the song he had had in his mind, but it was darker, twisted, and more than that, he could tell from the rising crescendo blazing through his pickups that it was nearly over.

That thought sent a shockwave down his spine.

The song was nearly over. The album was nearly over. That meant the headphones would be taken (by the thing in Andy Underwood's control room), that his masterpiece would be at an end, and his band... Images of the blood ran through his brain, images of Zombie Goat on the studio floor, eyes gashed, heads smashed, necks slit, and a hole from one side of the skull to the other, a crater in a rock god's head.

Zach had heard stories. He knew Zombie Goat had all died soon after their final record was done, but he never imagined this. The label had to have covered up the details.

And with his album nearly done, what did that mean for his band? For Jesse and Kyle? For himself?

He sensed a darkness folding over the room. He could smell the iron scent of the blood to come.

He couldn't let it happen. It wasn't right.

Memories swirled in his mind, things he had seen but for some reason hadn't registered. There were the cuts and bruises on Kyle's hands, the sudden absence of his girlfriend, the pink stains of blood not completely cleaned from his boots. He remembered the odor from Jesse's house, and he knew what it was. It was *not* a sewage leak or a dead thing in a crawl-space. It was the smell of human remains decomposing in the house, probably lying in their beds, leaking their odors and their remnants into the home.

How could he have missed it all?

He looked into the studio, and his eyes fell on Jesse. His drummer's eyes were rimmed in black. His skin was thin and sagging as if he hadn't eaten in weeks, but his sticks flew like the wind.

Kyle's eyes were bleeding from their corners. His fingers were red and raw, leaving crimson moisture on his bass guitar's strings. He looked like he was dead.

So did Jesse.

Zach hated to think what he would see if he looked into the mirror—a face as haggard and lifeless as his bandmates, he was sure.

Doubt crept through his mind as his fingers ripped into the final chorus. Was this what he really wanted? If he and his friends ended up like Zombie Goat, was it really worth it?

He saw the blood spraying at the end of "Mad Hatter", and fear tried to pause his fingers. He didn't want to die. He didn't want this to be the end. There was supposed to be stardom and fame, stadiums filled with fans. There was supposed to be money and women. Not just death. Not just rotting into nothingness. He searched for a loophole. Maybe they could use one of their old songs as the final track and they could get out of this.

But his fingers refused to halt. They cranked away at the crunching rhythm. They squealed as they bled onto his axe, focused on the job at hand in a dedication Zach himself had never known.

Fuck! Zach panicked. His heart ran faster. His legs clenched, and his teeth clamped hard.

He couldn't stop. The song, his fingers, it was all happening without his control whether he liked it or not. And as he listened to the beauty that was blaring from the headphones, he was in awe.

His guitar, Kyle's bass, Jesse's drums, they were making something legendary. Epic. It was a song the likes of which had never been heard on the planet. It seeped into his soul and tears flowed from his eyes—not from the sadness of his impending fate but from the godlike way his music was touching his soul.

He didn't know how it could be. He knew this song was the one, his own penultimate master work that would top everything else he had done, even above the magnitude of what they had recorded this month—this... this... it was beyond his wildest expectations, something truly soul shattering.

His tears ran.

He let himself lean into the song. He stopped fighting it. He became one with the dark beauty of the melody. He imagined a world out there embracing his music, soaking it in, and it didn't matter anymore if he was going to be there to see it. He was creating it. His fingers were inside the magic, and his blood was the fuel making it happen.

He saw red clouds over cities and cars pumping his tunes at their highest volumes. He saw radios in houses, TVs, sound bars, Bluetooth speakers, headphones, all playing his music on repeat as blood ran in the streets. Weapons swiped through the air. The ground opened up, and beasts of unimaginable horror ran through the world capturing souls.

And at the heart of it was his music. At the core of everyone's thoughts was his sound.

He wasn't a rock god. He was of a god.

Zach played the final note and let it ring out onto the tape. He set his guitar down, and then, lovingly, the headphones. He hit stop on the tape machine and picked up the gun in his cabinet's secret drawer.

Jesse and Kyle kept playing as he walked from the control room into the studio.

They were all gods now.

The Worst Best Man

by Eric Butler

NICK SQUINTED AGAINST THE setting sun reflecting off the water. Closing his eyes, he leaned against the rail. They would be docking soon, and he could only pray the bride and groom didn't find out he lost their rings. His stomach rolled. *Maybe I'll get lucky and Chris won't ever notice.*

"Fat chance," he mumbled to himself.

Someone slipped next to him. "Don't give up before we even get there. Ally's maid of honor just might sleep with you. I mean, there is booze on the island."

Nick glanced over and forced a smile. "I'm pretty sure your blushing bride has been telling Kate tall tales about me ever since you popped the question."

"Three days trapped on an island," Chris shrugged. "Stranger things have happened." He held out his hand, turning it until the fading light caught the thick gold band on his ring finger. "I swear something's different."

The color drained from Nick's face. He tried to respond, but his voice caught. He cleared his throat and tried again. "Yeah, it's called polish. I don't think it had been cleaned since your grandpa died."

"That's probably it," Chris said, reaching over to squeeze Nick's shoulder. "No matter what Ally says, I'm glad you were able to make it."

"Like you said, three days trapped with you and your wife's friends.

What could go wrong?"

The group stood in front of a large cabin. Ally glanced back and held a finger to her lips until they settled down.

A man with a large smile and a clipboard stood on the top step of the porch. "Howdy, folks," he said with a half wave. "Welcome to Roles Island. You guys will have the whole place to yourselves for the next three days. This is the main hall. Here you will find the kitchen, a game room, and the theater. Mr. Miller has sprung for five other cabins to be open. They're off the three paths behind us. Your luggage has been delivered to your rooms."

He motioned over his shoulder, and two people, a man and a woman, in matching white uniforms stepped forward. "This is James and Gail. They will provide you with meals and can handle any first-aid emergencies. If there are no questions, I'll leave you in their capable care. The boat will return Monday at noon, and I will see you then."

He passed the clipboard to James then hurried down the stairs toward the path that led back to the boat that brought everyone to the island.

Gail clapped her hands, pulling the group's attention back to the cabin. "It's gonna be a fun three days," Gail said with a wide smile. "We have a simple dinner set up in the main dining room tonight, your choice of sandwiches or salad. The bar is open twenty-four seven, and, of course, each of the sleeping cabins have complimentary bottles of wine."

James held up the clipboard. "So, it looks like we have the newlyweds in the Honeymoon Cabin, Nick in Cabin Two, Kate in Cabin Three, Sara in Cabin Four, and Missy and Freddy in Cabin Five."

"It's," Gail checked the watch on her wrist and continued, "five thirty-eight now. We'll keep the dining room open until ten thirty. The lights on every path and around the cabins are on timers, so it should be easy enough to find your way around. Each cabin has a phone. If you need anything from us, just dial zero-zero-one."

"I don't know about the rest of you," Ally said, slipping her hand into her husband's and interlocking their fingers, "but I'd like to check out the room and...freshen up before eating."

"Just follow either path around the main cabin, and then find the one marked with your cabin number."

Chris smiled and scooped his wife up off the ground. Ally's startled cry quickly turned to giggles as he carried her away.

Nick couldn't make eye contact with his reflection in the bathroom mirror. He was pretty sure he was going to get away with it, and it made his stomach ache. *Still better than telling them what happened.* He shook his head, unable to accept the truth himself. It was an almost unbeatable hand, a full house, jacks over kings.

His stomach did a flip at the memory of those cards in his hand. Everyone else seemed to sense it and bowed out, but not Tony. *Fucking Tony.* Nick went to raise the pot, to milk every last cent from that bastard's pockets, but he was out of chips. He patted his pockets and paused when his hand pressed against the bands through the cloth. He pulled them out and tossed them onto the table.

At first, Tony hemmed and hawed, but then, all a sudden, he nodded and pushed the rest of his chips in. Nick should have sensed it then, but there was blood in the water. *Yeah, you dumb bastard ... yours.* He closed his eyes, reliving each card as Tony flipped them over. When the third ten appeared, Nick thought lady luck was going to give Tony a lesser full house, but instead, she blessed that cocksucker with a fourth ten. *Fucking four of a kind.* Nick slammed his fist on the bathroom counter. He wanted to throw up as much now as he did when the ten of spades came into view.

"Goddamn it," he grumbled, turning on the sink and filling his hands with water. He leaned down and splashed the cool water against his face. He did it one more time before turning the faucet off and reaching over for a hand towel. *Just make it through the next three days.*

Nick rubbed the towel over his face, soaking up the water and enjoying the soft cotton against his skin. He tossed it onto the floor and, after taking a deep breath, glanced up. His lips curled into a smile. *That's it, keep it light and easy. Shit, it's not even the biggest secret you're keeping from Chris.*

Nick's smile melted from his face, and he hurried from the bathroom to the minibar. He grabbed a small bottle of vodka, twisted the top off, and held it up. "Gonna be the longest three days ever. Here's to being the worst best man," he mumbled to himself before draining the bottle in one gulp.

Kate glanced up when the door to the main hall opened. She didn't hide the disappointment on her face when she saw it was Nick. *Of course he's the first one back.* She knew she should have waited just to make sure. He offered her a nod and walked over to the bar.

"You want something?" he called out, reaching over the bar to grab two glasses and a bottle of Captain Morgan. "I make a mean rum and Coke."

"I'm not sure they stocked any soda," she said, watching him walk toward her.

He shrugged. "I also make a pretty good glass of rum, so we'll be okay."

Nick motioned to the chair across from her, and after a long moment, she nodded. He placed the glasses down with a clatter and pulled the chair out at an angle. Sitting with a grunt, he unscrewed the top and poured a few fingers in each glass.

He slid her drink across the table, then scooped his up and drained it in a few swallows. He ran the back of his hand across his lips and sighed in relief.

"Whoa," Kate said, unable to contain her laughter. "Slow down there, cowboy."

"Not a fan of weddings," he said, his head slightly tilting to the right, "or people, for that matter."

Kate sipped her drink, making a face as the liquor burned its way down to her tummy. "Ugh. I may need to find a Coke after all, and from what Ally said, you're more of a bachelor party kinda guy...as long as it's at a strip club."

"Ally doesn't know everything," he responded, pouring more into his glass. He took a sip this time then held up the glass and stared at the amber liquid.

The silence stretched out, making Kate grow more uncomfortable with each passing second. She took another sip and grew a bit more re-laxed. She focused on his face. *He's handsome*, she thought, even though he wasn't really her type. His dark hair was shaggy and grew over his ears and hung down to the collar of his shirt. He shifted his gaze, locking his brown eyes with hers. They were slightly darker than the Morgans they were drinking, and she thought she could see something in them. Something soulful.

"Beautiful," she whispered. Her cheeks flushed red, and she prayed the word hadn't been uttered loud enough for him to hear.

The corner of his lips curled up, but before he was able to acknowledge it, the door opened. Sara walked in, offering a wave as if she hadn't just seen them before heading off to her cabin. Missy and Fred followed behind her.

"Oh, are the newlyweds still not back?" Sara said. She stepped to the table and took Nick's glass. After taking a long drink, she gave him a wink before placing it back down. "Wonder *what* they're up to."

Kate's stomach flipped, and a sense of unease settled upon her. She stared at the woman, unsure what was happening. Sara offered her a smirk and reached over to rest her arm on Nick's shoulder. Kate's eyes widened. *Oh my god ... am I jealous?*

"Freddy, grab some more glasses, will ya?" Nick asked. He reached out and grabbed the bottle to refill his glass.

"Sure, who all needs one?" he asked, waiting for Sara and Missy to motion before reaching over and grabbing three more. He walked to the table and placed them down next to Nick's partially filled glass. "I just want half that."

"Me too," Missy said, sliding next to Fred and wrapping her arms around his.

Sara laughed. "Go ahead and fill mine up."

Kate stood. "I wonder if Gail or James are around. They might know if there's any soda here."

"I'm ready for some food too," Fred said.

"I can help with that," Gail called out, walking into the main room with a notebook in hand. "Looks like almost everyone is here, so let's get started. Who wants a Cobb salad, and who wants a turkey sub?"

Missy, Fred, and Kate all raised their hands at the mention of the salad, while Sara and Nick nodded when the sub was announced.

"James is still not back," Gail said, her smile slightly strained, "so give me a few minutes to get everything ready. Oh, and there are sodas in the main fridge in the kitchen."

"I can help with the food," Kate said, falling into step behind Gail. "I don't mind."

"That won't be necessary."

"You don't want to pass up a chance to work with a sandwich artist," Nick said.

Kate turned her head and glared at him, but before she could respond, Sara burst out laughing. "Stop being a dick. I'm pretty sure they don't hire five-star chefs at Subway."

Kate fought the urge to stick out her tongue and, instead, offered a nod of thanks in Sara's direction. "They don't, and just for that, Mr. Best Man, why don't you get those sodas and stock the bar fridge."

She hoped he heard it as the command she meant and not a question that he could ignore. She turned her attention to Gail's back and smiled when she heard his chair scoot back and his footsteps grow closer.

Ally's body shuddered as her orgasm sent waves of pleasure through her body. Her eyes closed, and she bit her bottom lip. Chris slumped forward, kissing the back of her neck and shoulder. His hands slid from her hips, moving up her sides until he wrapped them around her in a bear hug. Every nerve in her body seemed to be tingling, and she whimpered when his now-limp cock slipped out.

"Damn," he mumbled into her hair. "If I'd known actually putting a ring on your finger would awaken this ... well, shit, we would have married when we met."

Ally shifted, forcing Chris to lay on his side. He tightened his grip, and she snuggled closer, pressing her ass against his crotch. *He's right. Ever since I said I do, it's like everything is on fire.* She giggled at the thought. Heat flashed through her body, traveling from her chest down to her loins. She wiggled her butt, excited to feel him grow harder.

"Babe," he said, kissing the top of her head. "We've kept our guests waiting long enough. They're going to think something's going on."

She released a huff and turned her head so he could see the pout on her lips. "Fine, but we better take a shower first." He released his hold, and Ally squirmed out of his grasp. She padded across the room and stopped, leaning against the doorway and thrusting her hips back. "Of course, it might go quicker if we shower together."

She disappeared inside the bathroom and turned the shower on. While she waited for the water to heat up, she thought of another man's touch. Her left hand began to squeeze her breast and her right slid between her legs. Chris entered the bathroom, and they locked eyes through his reflection in the mirror. A large grin grew on his lips, and she knew their guests were going to have to wait a bit longer.

James knelt in the dirt just to the side of the large window that let him look into the Honeymoon Cabin. He held his head at an angle, just enough that he could see directly into the bathroom. The happily married couple was in the shower. He slowly rubbed his crotch, enjoying the feel of his cotton shorts against his hard dick. He was about to burst, especially after the couple's first show.

The bride had called the main desk almost immediately after everyone scattered to their designated cabins. She said there was an issue with a water leak by the back door. He thought it was weird that she told him not to knock when he got there and to just fix the leak. He assumed it was because they were planning on returning to the main building for dinner.

When James turned the corner to the back part of the cabin, he realized that wasn't the reason. The man stood with his back to the window, shirtless and his pants lying in a pile around his feet. The woman knelt before him, her head bobbing back and forth at a slow and steady pace. He slipped his fingers into her hair and tried to speed her up. She pulled back and looked up through her lashes.

"Don't get ahead of yourself," she said with a wicked smile on her lips.

The woman stood, pausing for a second to give James the full view of her body. His eyes roamed over her naked flesh, noting the lack of any tan lines. His gaze lingered on her large breasts, enjoying the way she twisted and squeezed her nipples until they were hard. He glanced up, and his face flushed when their eyes locked. She winked, running her hand down her stomach and pulling his gaze to her tightly trimmed mound of blonde hair.

Movement pulled him from the memory. The woman, wet from the shower, leaned forward, her arms stretched high above her so she could hold on to the top of the glass shower wall. Her back arched, and she pushed her ass toward the man. He squeezed her ass cheeks, kneading them like a cat before sliding his fingers lower and slipping one, then another, into her.

Her head flung back, and she once again locked eyes with James. Her lips parted, and her whole body quivered from each panting breath she took. The man removed his fingers, and she reached back to guide his hard cock into her eager opening.

"I want to feel you inside me," she mouthed to James, and he couldn't take it anymore. He pulled his dick out then licked his palm, running his hand up and down the shaft, mirroring the man's speed as he fucked the woman in the shower. She ran her tongue over her lips, and he closed his eyes, imagining her taking him into her mouth. A small moan slipped past his lips. He was close.

A loud scream pulled him from his fantasy, and he blinked in confusion. The woman stood just outside the shower, a towel covering her in a way that somehow made her sexier to James. She raised her hand, and the light caught the gold band on her ring finger, making it twinkle. She smiled that same wicked smile from earlier and rolled her fingers in an exaggerated wave.

Where's the gu-

"So, you like to watch?" a gruff voice said from behind.

James's dick went limp in his hand. "Um ... it's not what you think," he stammered out, unsure how it could be anything else. He started to put his dick away, but before he could, pain exploded in the side of his head. He swayed, his eyes refocusing on the reflection of the man holding a hammer high above his head. His mouth opened to protest, to beg, but before he could get a word out, the man swung the hammer and James's world went black.

Nick carried a case each of Coca-Cola and Diet Coke to the bar. He squatted and started to load the fridge. A phone rang three times before it was answered, and Nick heard Missy say hello. There was a brief pause, and then she called out his name.

He stood. "What?"

She smiled, and for a moment, he thought she knew—knew that he lost the rings and replaced them without a second thought. He forced a sickly smile on his face. *Bullshit*. His stomach tightened.

"Chris says he needs to talk to you," she said, waving the receiver. "Guess he needs the best man to show him how it's done." She punctuated the last word with a giggle.

He walked over and took the phone, staring at Missy until she took the hint and walked away. He pressed the receiver to his ear. "What's up?"

"I need you to come to the cabin," Chris said, his voice oddly cool. "I ... I'm not sure what happened. Just hurry."

Nick didn't want to say out loud what he was thinking and instead hung up the phone.

The door to the kitchen swung outward, and Gail appeared holding a platter with a large salad bowl and sandwiches. Kate followed with plates, bowls, and silverware. She glanced around, and a smile came naturally when she locked eyes with him. When he didn't return it, hers melted away.

"Nick, you're about to eat those words," Sara said, pointing toward the food as Gail set the platter down on the largest table.

"I'm sure you're right," he said, offering a shrug. He started toward the door. "Make sure to save some for me. I've got to go help Chris, and then we'll come back and see."

"What do you mean?" Kate asked, her face reflecting the confusion in her voice. She put everything down and stepped closer to him. "What could he possibly need help with?"

"He didn't say. I'm sure he's just taking advantage of me being the best man one last time."

Nick started toward the door. He hoped she wouldn't follow but knew that was probably wishful thinking. *What if he did something to Ally?* He fought the urge to shake his head. *I'm sure he did … something, but you don't want to think about that, remember?* The last thing he wanted was the image of Ally's naked flesh flashing through his head. *Her long, blonde hair, her perfect breasts, the way her nipples stood out when she got excited, and her long, shapely legs spreading just enough to show off the promised land.*

"Goddamn it," he grumbled, shifting his thoughts to how crummy he felt afterward.

The knot in his belly grew. He opened the door and glanced over his shoulder. Kate was a few steps behind him. His mouth opened, the beginning of an argument on the tip of his tongue, but the look on her face chased it away. Instead, his jaw shut with a clack, and he let her pass through the door before following.

As soon as the door closed behind him, she turned, and he could see the worry in her eyes. "You don't think …" Her question trailed off.

"What?" he responded, trying to make his voice sound incredulous. "God no. I'm sure it's some dumb prank or something. You'll see."

Nick prayed his face didn't betray his true thoughts. *Anything's possible with Chris.* He stepped past her, taking the stairs two at a time until he was walking on the path. She fell in step beside him, and he fought the sudden urge to reach out and take her hand. *Cool it*, he told himself. *Now's not the time.*

They circled around the building and walked to the path marked Honeymoon Cabin. Nick let out a relieved sigh.

Ally waved as she walked toward them. She was dressed in a new outfit, a dark-blue blouse with the top three buttons undone and a white skirt that ended just above her knees. She wore a pair of flat sandals the same color as her top, and he admired the shiny, red polish decorating her toenails.

His gaze traveled back up and caught her staring at him. Ally flashed him a knowing smile and turned her attention back to Kate. She stepped to her maid of honor and slipped an arm through Kate's, turning her back toward the main cabin.

"I'm starving," she said. "I hope the food's ready."

"It is," Kate replied, "but is everything okay?"

"Yes. Why?"

"Chris called and said he needed some help," Nick interjected.

"Oh, yeah," Ally said over her shoulder. "He needs help disposing of some trash."

Nick watched the two women until they disappeared around the corner of the cabin. *What the fuck?* He shook his head and started toward the Honeymoon Cabin, unable to avoid thinking about the last time he took a long walk.

Numb, Nick walked the streets after the game. The wedding was six hours away, and he wasn't sure what to do. He could show up empty-handed or just leave the city ... the state ... hell, maybe even the country. He shook his head. Can't do that to Chris. Besides, I've already done enough to ruin my longest friendship without adding to it. *The sun slowly rose, burning away the darkness.*

Daylight streamed over the buildings, and Nick raised his hand to shield his eyes. Goddamn, that's bright. *A spike of pain shot through his skull, and he paused on the sidewalk, slamming his eyes shut. Pressing his knuckles against the side of his head, he stepped closer to the buildings, peeking to make sure he didn't run into a wall. He leaned his shoulder against the cool brick and waited for the pain to subside.*

A bell rang, the kind that announced a door was opening. An older man stood in the doorway. He studied Nick for a moment before motioning him inside. "You look like hell," he said, his deep voice hoarse. "Come sit down. I have some tea already made."

Nick pushed off the wall and, though he swayed a bit, managed to keep his balance. Sunlight illuminated the business's front window, and he glanced at the words painted in bright orange and red letters. The Dickens Pawn Shop: Turning Man's Misfortune Into Miracles Daily. In the corner of the window, the sign still read closed. The old man didn't flip it and instead locked the door after Nick entered.

The old man led him to a table with two chairs near the back and motioned for him to sit.

"I'm sorry if I disturbed you," Nick mumbled through the pain, "but I really appreciate this."

The old man waved the statement off and disappeared into the back.

Nick leaned forward, pressing his palms against his eye sockets.

"Migraine?" the old man asked.

Nick winced when his slight nod sent another spike of pain through his head. "Long night. I should have got some sleep, but I screwed up bad."

"Nothing a spot of tea cannot fix," the old man said, setting a sterling-silver tea tray on the table. He poured two cups. "Sugar or milk?"

Nick sat up. "Two sugars, please." He opened his eyes. Next to the teapot on the platter was a pile of pastries. His stomach grumbled. The old man motioned toward the food, and Nick reached out to take a cheese Danish. "Thank you," he said, his voice catching between the words as a surge of emotions seemed to bubble up from his chest.

"You are welcome, but I should be thanking you. I usually do not have the pleasure of sharing breakfast with anyone before I open."

Nick drank some tea and noticed the pain in his head subsiding with each sip. When it was manageable, he took a bite of the Danish.

The old man studied him while they ate in silence.

As Nick pushed the last bite into his mouth, a wave of contentment washed over him and tears came to his eyes. "Please forgive me," he said, his voice thick with emotion. "You've been too kind."

The old man waved his hand in dismissal again. "Nonsense. Anyone with a soul would have done the same. Now, tell me how you think you have screwed up."

Nick took another sip of tea, swirling the slightly bitter liquid around his tongue before swallowing. With a sigh, he told the old man everything. He was shocked at how honest he was with the stranger, but with each word, a weight seemed to lift off his shoulders. When he came to the end, he released a shuddered breath and felt a single tear escape from the corner of his eye.

The old man stood and walked behind the display case in the far-left corner of his shop. He bent down, disappearing for a moment before letting out an exclamation and rising. He made his way back to the table and sat, holding out his fist. "This may be your lucky day, after all," the old man said, a wry grin on his lips. His fingers curled open revealing two rings on his palm.

Nick leaned closer and his eyes grew wide. They look almost identical to the ones Chris gave me to hold. He couldn't believe it. "How much?"

The old man tilted his hand until the two rings slid off into Nick's. "I'm sure we can figure something out."

Nick studied them, amazed how close they were to the two rings he lost. He laid them on the table and pulled out his wallet. He opened it, not surprised to see he only had two worn five-dollar bills and a punch card for Smiley's Ice Cream.

"Do we have a deal?" the old man asked, plucking the punch card from Nick's grasp.

"Oh, I can't do that," Nick stammered, unsure what to do but too

ashamed to only offer the last ten dollars to his name. He reached into his shirt and pulled out the gold cross he wore around his neck.

Grimacing, the old man waved his hand. "Put that away. I will not separate a man from his faith so flippantly. Where's the fun in that? Besides, these two have had a rough go of it. They have somehow found their way back to me twice, so I am hoping the third time is the charm. If it makes you feel better, I will take an IOU for later."

It didn't, but the longer Nick stared at the rings on the table, the more he grew convinced it was the only way to solve all his troubles. He slowly nodded. "Okay."

The old man reached out his hand. "After the wedding, if all goes well, you can come back and we will discuss if anything more is owed. If not, then see that the rings are returned and I will continue to try and find them the perfect match."

Nick grasped the offered hand and gave it a shake. "Deal."

"About fucking time," Chris barked out, pulling Nick from his reverie. "I hope you brought a change of shoes, cause it's gonna get messy."

Nick stopped on the path.

Chris stood at the right edge of the cabin. He appeared disheveled, with half his shirt tucked in and his hair sticking up. He motioned for Nick to hurry and disappeared toward the back.

Honestly, what the fuck? Nick took a deep breath and followed. "So, what is so important I had to come now to—" Nick froze, struggling to process what he was seeing.

Chris stood over a body—a body that Nick could only assume was

James. The head and face were caved in, a mashed mess of blood, skin, and bone.

"I know what you're thinking," Chris said, holding his arms up with his palms out. "But he had it coming."

Nick shook his head. "No ... that wasn't it. Please tell me this isn't James."

"Dude was a fucking perv," Chris continued, unfazed by the obvious panic in Nick's voice. "He was watching Ally and I together. Shit, he was jerking it when I came out."

"And?" Nick asked, his voice growing louder. "That doesn't give you license to kill him."

Chris shook his head. "Fuck that. He was eye fucking Ally. My wife. What kind of man would I be if I let that go? She's just lucky I knew where she was at the time."

"Lucky?" Nick whispered, a sense of unease settling over him. "Okay, but what's your plan?"

Chris flashed a big grin and walked to the back porch. He grabbed a bed sheet and brought it back to lay next to the body. "Speaking of, you won't believe our luck."

Nick mouthed the word *our* but stayed quiet, waiting for Chris to continue.

"There's a cliff that way," Chris said. He motioned for Nick to adjust the sheet so they could get it under the body. "So, we don't have to dig a hole."

Nick stared at his friend with unblinking eyes. "You want to throw the body off a cliff?"

"Well, into the ocean, really," he said, rolling the sheet over the body. Blood soaked into the cloth, making Nick think of the Shroud of Turin.

"Into the ocean?"

Chris looked up. "Did you fall on your head?"

"Fall on my head?"

Chris stood up. He walked over and gripped Nick by the shoulders. He stared into his friend's eyes, his own squinting in concern. Chris gave him a shake then released his grip and started back toward the body. "You don't seem to have a concussion, so how about you cut out the echoing bullshit and let's get this done."

Chris wadded up the sheet around the body's feet and motioned with his head for Nick to grab the opposite side. Nick blinked, shifting his gaze from Chris to the wrapped body. He walked over, unsure why he simply didn't turn tail and run back to the main cabin. *Cause he's your best friend.* He knew the thought should be a question but understood it had been a statement for years.

Nick gripped the wadded sheet by the body's head and tried to ignore the bloody image staring back up at him. Chris counted to three, and the two men lifted the body.

"The path is wide enough for us to walk side by side once we get on it," Chris said. "Until then, do you want to go backward or forward?"

Nick glanced over his shoulder, and once he was sure it was clear, he took a step backward. Chris called out warnings whenever he saw an issue, and soon the two men were walking down the path away from the cabins.

"You're sure this goes to the cliffs?" Nick asked. He shifted his grip and tried to ignore the ache growing in his arms and back.

"Well, Ally and I saw it on the website," Chris said. "Besides, we are on an island, and it feels like we're on an incline."

Nick couldn't argue, especially since the ache had moved to his legs. Up ahead, the path disappeared into the trees. "Jesus, how much further?"

"Can't be too much longer. I remember the map showed the Honeymoon Cabin pretty close to the back. I guess so it would feel isolated."

"Lucky for you," Nick replied. The trees thickened around them, casting the path in shadows. He glanced up and noted where the last light was placed. "Well, shit. Will we be able to see?"

Chris nodded. "Think so. Moon's almost full, and once we get through these trees, it should be all open to the edge."

They maneuvered through the last few yards and stepped out onto a strip of grass. Chris was correct. Even though shadows covered everything, there was still enough moonlight to see the edge. Nick dropped the body with a sigh and stepped closer to look over. He could see it was a long drop, twenty or so feet, but it wasn't straight into the water.

"Dude, there's a strip of beach below," Nick said. He looked around, noting there were stairs leading down to a dock. *A dock with a boat.* "This might work if you go down there and cut the boat loose. Make it look like he tried to take off."

Chris slapped his hand down on Nick's shoulder and pulled him close for a side hug. "That's the spirit. Nothing we can't do if we work together." He released Nick and pointed off to the right. "What's that?"

"No idea," Nick replied, staring at the dark, shadowy shapes. "A machine of some kind, I guess."

Chris walked over to it and spun around when he got within a few steps. "Holy shit, this is exactly what we need to make this go away. Drag that motherfucker over here."

Nick's cheeks blew out with an exaggerated sigh. *Guess we're doing this?* Whatever this was. He grabbed the end of the sheet and pulled the dead weight across the rough and uneven ground. When he thought he was close, he glanced over his shoulder.

Chris stood, back straight and with a long-handled ax resting on his shoulder.

"What—" before Nick could finish his question, Chris stepped to the side and motioned toward the upright machine. Nick stared at it, unsure what he was looking at. *Holy shit.* "Is that a woodchipper?"

"Yessir," Chris said with a whoop. "We're going to roll it to the edge and spray this pervert out into the big blue."

"Jesus Christ, what is wrong with you?"

Chris grew still. He stared at Nick, and a silence settled down on the two men. Nick broke out in a sweat, shivering as it trickled down his face and back. Chris took a step, closing the space between them. He shifted the ax from his shoulder and used it as a pointer, first jabbing it at Nick, then the body.

"What's wrong with me? What the fuck is wrong with you?" Chris said. His voice was quiet and icy. "This peeping piece of shit probably planned on raping my wife. He would have killed me to get to her. Is my best man okay with that?"

"Of course not," Nick said. "I'm just saying you don't know that. Not for sure."

"I didn't vow to protect Ally when it was easy," Chris barked, and held up his hand, waving it at Nick. Moonlight glinted off the thick wedding band. "When I slipped this on, everything changed. She's mine. Do you understand? MINE! And I will destroy anyone who threatens our life together."

Nick stared at his friend, taking in the disheveled hair, the flared nostrils, and the curling sneer on his lips. He was unrecognizable. Nick held up his hands, palms out. "Okay ... I get it now," he said, struggling to keep his voice light. "But all this?"

"Jesus, keep up," Chris said, his voice once again rising. "I can't protect her if I'm locked up for a misunderstanding."

Nick gave a slow nod. "Sure, that makes sense."

"Now let's get this done so we can get back to the weekend's festivities."

Nick dragged the body to the woodchipper and released the sheet, uncovering the upper part of the body. "So, how does this work? We just feed the whole thing in there?"

The ax whizzed by Nick, who released a surprised yelp as he jumped to the side. The ax head slammed into the shoulder joint and tore through the meat and bone until driving into the ground beneath.

"Naw, it needs to be in pieces," Chris said with a huff. He pulled the ax free and raised it above his head. "It's like making sausage, but this time there's no casing."

Chris thought he would be more nervous, or even a tad more anxious, but he was calmer than he had been in months. He glanced over at the best man, his best friend Nick. If Ally had her way, he wouldn't be either. Honestly, for a while, he questioned it himself, and more recently than he wanted to admit. That's all in the past, *he thought with a grimace.*

Nick locked eyes with him, his eyebrows raised in confusion. Probably thinks I'm having second thoughts. *He forced a smile to his lips and gave a slight shake of his head. He was more than ready to say I do.* No matter what happened, *a tiny voice whispered in the back of his head.*

Before Chris could dwell on it, the music started and the door swung open, revealing his beautiful bride-to-be. He watched his future fa-ther-in-law walk her up the aisle, pause to lift the veil, kiss her on the cheek. Then she was standing before him. They locked eyes, and though the preacher spoke, Chris didn't hear a word.

It grew quiet in the church, and after a moment, Chris realized they were waiting for him. He racked his brains trying to remember exactly what they did in rehearsal. He glanced at the preacher, who mouthed the word rings.

Nick held out his hand, the two rings seemingly glowing in his palm. Must have cleaned them up, *he thought, grateful his best man had thought to do so without prompting. He nodded his thanks and scooped them from Nick's hand.*

"The couple will now exchange rings as a symbol of the promise of marriage," the preacher said once Chris and Ally were back facing one another. "A ring has no beginning or end. Its path is endless and a symbol of your endless love and respect for each other."

Ally smiled, and her face lit up.

A flash of heat traveled through him, but for a second, he couldn't tell if it was excitement or anger. All his focus resided on the rings in his clenched fist. His jaw clenched.

"By placing these rings on each other's fingers, you are promising to not just love each other, but to honor each other. To be compassionate, patient, and understanding with each other as you build your future together."

Future? *Chris flinched at the thought.*

The preacher raised his hands and continued. "You can both feel the love in this room. These rings represent this love. Not just the love you have for each other, but for everyone here today. Let these rings be a reminder of that love ... of what you are feeling today. Now Chris, place the ring on Ally's finger and repeat after me."

Ally reached out, and Chris took her hand, reminding himself to be gentle. He slipped the ring on her ring finger and said the words the preacher just completed. "I give you this ring as a symbol of my love with the pledge to love and support you today, tomorrow, always, and forever."

Ally took his ring, and Chris took a deep breath and released it slowly, feeling the tension slip out between his lips. Ally grabbed his hand, her delicate fingers rubbing softly across his fingers. A hunger shined in her eyes, a hunger that sent a shiver down his back. She jammed the ring onto his finger.

Chris went ridged, his eyes wide while Ally repeated the preacher's words. "I give you this ring as a symbol of my love with the pledge to love and support you today, tomorrow, always, and forever."

Forever, she says, *a voice hissed in his head.* You can't trust her. You can't trust any of them bitches … you'll see.

Chris stared blankly at Ally while the voice raged in his head.

The preacher stopped talking, and Nick nudged him in the back. "You heard the man. You're now husband and wife. Fucking kiss her already."

Nick rolled the machine to the edge of the cliff. He flinched each time the ax drove into James's body. His face scrunched up in disgust, and he tried to ignore the grunts from Chris as he pulled the ax free.

He fished out his phone and turned on the flashlight app to shine on the woodchipper. *How do you start this thing?* "Maybe this?" he mumbled, reaching over to fully open the choke and then press the speed lever from the turtle symbol to the rabbit. He gripped the starter and pulled. The machine grumbled then fired up.

"Hell, yeah," Chris hollered out. "Let's get the party started."

Before Nick could move, Chris scooped up a leg and rushed over to the running machine. He tossed it in, letting loose a wordless howl of excitement. The machine growled, shaking as it worked to grind up flesh and bone. Bloody chunks of meat shot from the discharge chute out over the cliff's edge.

The wind shifted and sprayed Nick with a cloudy mist of blood. "Goddamn it," he shouted, stumbling back. His heel slipped from the edge, and he felt his balance shift away from the steady earth. "Oh shit." His arms began to windmill, and he could feel gravity pulling him backward.

Chris rushed forward and swung the ax toward Nick, the head barely missing him as it whooshed through the air. "Grab it, dumb ass," Chris barked.

Time seemed to slow, and Nick struggled to process everything before him. He could see his best friend standing a few feet away, holding the ax out between them. His gaze darted down, and he noted the ax head was an inch or so away from his chest. Any moment he would be over the edge of the cliff. *Grab it, dumb ass*, repeated in his head. He snatched at the ax handle, wrapping his fingers around the tool's shoulder.

Nick shifted a hair, his feet sliding until both of his heels dangled over open air and he leaned back at an almost forty-five-degree angle. "Dude, pull."

Chris didn't move. He studied Nick's face, his own stone. "Did you fuck her?"

An icy wave washed over Nick. He tried to speak, but his mouth was suddenly dry. He swallowed and managed to croak out, "What?"

"You heard me. Did. You. Fuck. Her?"

Nick glanced over his shoulder. He could see the rocky shoreline below and the dark waves gently lapping against it. He wondered if he could make it to the water and, more importantly, would it be deep enough. Turning his gaze back to his best friend, he asked, "What are you talking about? Did I fuck your wife? No. No I didn't."

Sweat ran down his forehead and into his eyes. He blinked through the burn, desperate to keep his eyes on the man holding the other end of the ax. He could feel his grip slipping as his palms also became sweaty. He tried to slide them up the handle, hoping to pull himself upright and away from the edge. Chris took one step forward and, instead, sent Nick back a bit more.

"But did you fuck my fianceé?" Chris asked, his tone as cold as the ball of ice forming in Nick's belly.

His insides squirmed, and images of Ally's naked body wriggling beneath him flashed before him. He tried to drive them out by shaking his head, but that only seemed to encourage his memory to make more until all he saw was strobe light-like flashes of their last fuck.

"Of course not," he cried out.

"I was all ready to let it go, but when she slid this ring on my finger ... something changed," Chris said, before taking another step closer. "I can't let that go. That betrayal."

"STOP," Nick hollered, his legs beginning to shake like Jello. "Jesus, we're best friends. I wouldn't do that."

"I might have believed you," Chris said, his voice just loud enough to be heard over the machine's roar. "But then she told me. After I killed the pervert. Said you were so rough you made her bleed. Did you?"

"She's lying," Nick whimpered, fully aware just how rough he had been that last time. She had begged him for it, whining that Chris was too safe, too boring, demanded he do all the things his best friend refused to even try.

"She said if I loved her, I'd return the favor," Chris said. He pulled the ax toward him, jerking Nick from the edge and sending him sprawling onto the hard ground with a grunt. He stomped his foot down onto Nick's back and drove the air from his lungs. "The question is where did you make her bleed from?"

Nick struggled to catch his breath. He thrashed around on the ground, unable to wriggle out from under Chris's weight. A screech sounded, followed by a loud pop, and Chris tumbled to the ground with a thud, half his body sprawled over Nick. *Jesus, that was close.*

He squirmed out from under his friend and rolled over onto his back. Staring at the moon, he took deep breaths until he could find the strength to sit up. Chris lay still a foot or so away. Nick stared at his back but couldn't tell if it was rising or falling. *Is he dead?* His stomach twisted at the thought. He struggled to his feet, but his legs were still shaky.

He leaned forward, resting his hands on his thighs while he studied his friend's body. A small pool of blood formed around Chris's head, and he realized there was a jagged gash across Chris's forehead. He shifted his gaze and searched the ground around his best friend. *Holy shit.* He stared at the thick knot of bone lying a few feet from the body.

He glanced down one more time at Chris, resisting the urge to kick him in the ribs. *He's not breathing.* His vision blurred, and a single tear slipped down his cheek. He needed to get Chris help.

Another screech from the machine pulled his attention up, and Nick noted the smoke billowing from the woodchipper. It shuddered then grew quiet. He could see the bloody gore smeared all over the feeder.

"How do you explain this?" he mumbled to himself, shifting his attention from the machine to the mutilated body lying a few feet from it.

Nick pulled out his phone. Zero bars. "Fuck," he growled, remembering Ally's nonstop complaints about no cellphone service after Chris found the place.

He stood still for a moment, trying to decide what to do. Fuck it. He threw all the pieces of the body onto the sheet and dragged it back to the edge of the cliff.

"Sorry, dude," he said before tossing it all over the edge.

He put his foot on the back of the woodchipper and pushed. It tumbled over. He flinched each time it caught the cliff's side and waited until it gave one final crash at the bottom. He would figure out a way to get it into the water later. Now he needed to get some help. *If it's not too late.*

Ally stabbed her fork into the salad. She stared at the bowl but didn't really see it before her. Instead, she was replaying Chris's attack on the peeping tom. *The peeping tom I requested.* Her lips curled into a wicked smile at the thought. *Oh well.* In the end, she hadn't needed him. Chris had been surprisingly virile since they got to the island. Heat washed over her, and her heart beat faster.

Chris gripped her hips, thrusting into her from behind. His back blocked most of the shower's water, and she was getting cold. She opened her mouth, but instead of telling him to switch positions, she locked eyes with the man outside and ran her tongue over her lips. Chris grunted, but when he pulled out instead of coming, she knew something was wrong.

"What's a matter, baby?" she asked, making sure he heard the pout in her voice. "I was so close."

He reached back and turned off the water. "Who the fuck is that?"

She straightened and stared where his finger pointed toward. "Oh my god. Is he watching us?" she whimpered and grabbed at one of the towels lying close by.

He stepped out, marching through the cabin until he disappeared from sight. She listened to him rustling around what she assumed was the kitchen, then heard the door open and close. He wasn't trying to be quiet or sneaky, and it turned her on even more.

She stepped from the shower and wrapped the towel around herself.

The man outside was sliding his hand up and down faster.

She screamed.

James's eyes fluttered open, confusion plain on his face.

Chris appeared behind him and held a hammer high above his head.

Smiling, Ally raised her hand and waved. Bye, bye. Her skin flushed at the thought, and she moaned when the hammer slammed into his head. She slipped her hand under the towel, pressing and sliding her fingers against her sex. Her eyes locked on the hammer, watching it rise and fall, the head smashing into poor James's face until there was nothing left but a bloody, soupy mess.

Fingers wrapped around her arm. "What are you doing?" Kate hissed into her ear.

Ally blinked, pulled from her thoughts. She still held the fork in the salad bowl, but her other hand was resting against her crotch. Looking down, she was surprised to find her skirt had ridden up to expose her panties. She pulled her fingers away, wiping the moisture on the table-cloth. She looked around, but no one else seemed to have noticed. She shifted her skirt, pulling it down just enough then leaned over to Kate, brushing her lips against her ear before whispering. "Chris just has me so horny."

Kate laughed, shifting so they could be eye to eye. "Well, save it for when y'all get back to your room. I mean, if it's this bad, why did you leave in the first place?"

James's shattered face flashed before her, but Ally ignored it and shrugged. "We didn't want to be rude."

"Speaking of," Kate said, glancing at her watch, "where do you think the groom and the best man are right now?"

Ally shook her head. "I'm sure they'll be here any minute, and then we can get this party started."

Nick ran through the woods. If he remembered correctly, Freddy was an EMT and Missy was a nurse, or she dressed up like one on stage. He really should have paid attention during introductions. He threw up his arms, using them to break through the low-hanging branches and protect his face. He let out a loud cry of frustration and tried to ignore the pain as the tree limbs ripped across his skin.

A shimmer of light drew his attention, and his cry shifted to one of exaltation. He burst from the trees and stumbled when his feet met the smooth path. After a few steps, he regained his balance. *Almost there.* The Honeymoon Cabin came into view, and he sped up.

Nick slid to a stop and rushed up the steps to the porch. He slammed into the door and fumbled around trying to open it, his hands slipping over the knob. He could see the sweat and blood smearing over the brass orb. *Shit.* He grabbed the bottom of his shirt and wrapped it around the doorknob, took a deep breath, and turned it.

The door swung open, and he hurried inside. He just needed to find the phone and he could get help out to Chris. *If it's not too late.* He shook his head, trying to get the image of his best friend lying so still on the hard ground. He looked around, trying to remember where the phone might be located. *The kitchen?*

Nick rushed through the cabin and found the phone sitting on the counter by the fridge. He picked up the receiver and sighed in relief when he heard the steady note of the dial tone. There was a sticker on the counter by the phone which listed what to dial for each building on the island. He pressed his finger at the top of the list and started to slide it down, looking for the Main Cabin. His finger stopped. *There it is … 001.*

Before he could move to dial for help, a loud whoosh sounded from behind. He glanced back and caught the light flashing off the head of the ax as it sliced through the air toward him. His mouth popped open, the beginning of the word *stop* forming on his tongue. It shifted to a wordless howl when the ax's bit cut through his wrist and drove into the countertop.

He jerked his arm back, and blood spurted from the mangled wound. He held it against his chest, watching the blood gush out and run down his arm and soak into his shirt. He tore his gaze from the wound and found Chris struggling to free the ax from the counter.

"You think you can just fuck her and get away with it?" he screamed, the last word becoming a cry of frustration as he was forced to leave the ax buried in the wood. He spun around and lunged toward Nick. "You're going to pay for what you did."

Nick darted past him, whimpering with each jarring movement.

Chris howled in anger and swung back around.

The blood no longer gurgled from Nick's severed flesh, but he was still losing it at an alarming rate. He felt woozy, and for a moment, wondered if he might pass out. He pressed the stub against his shoulder, hoping to slow the bleeding with pressure and his shirt.

"I didn't do anything," Nick said, his voice high and whiny. "You have to believe me."

"I can smell her on you," Chris hissed. "You stink of her." He shifted his feet to attack again.

Nick grabbed the phone base and threw it at Chris, catching him on the chin. Chris stumbled, tripped on his own feet, and slammed his head against the edge of the counter and then again against the hardwood floor.

Nick stared at the severed phone line. *Goddamn it.* He grabbed a kitchen towel and wrapped it around his bloody stub. He held it tightly against his chest and rushed out of the cabin.

He shuffled down the path. If he was lucky, he would get to the main cabin before he bled out. If he was really lucky, someone there might actually be an EMT.

Kate was worried, and not just about how Ally had been acting since the wedding but also about whatever mysterious chore was taking Nick and Chris so long to finish. *Taking out the trash should have been a few minutes top.* She glanced at the clock on the wall. *It's been over an hour.* Laughter pulled her attention over to the bar.

Ally stood in front of Fred, her hand resting on his chest for some reason. Beside them, Missy stood on the balls of her feet and leaned over the bar, struggling to reach something Kate couldn't see. Fred's eyes darted to the side, his gaze glued to her backside. Ally pulled her hand off his chest and slapped it against Missy's wiggling ass. She let loose a squeal of delight and leaned farther, pushing her ass up higher.

Missy's legs quivered, and Kate could see she now stood on her tiptoes. Her legs looked even more defined, and her ass pressed tightly against the back of her jeans.

Ally slapped Missy again, making sure her hand landed on the oppo-site cheek. She let her touch linger, pulling her hand slowly across Missy's backside. About halfway, she pressed her fingertips against the seam and followed it down until her fingers were between Missy's legs.

"I'm not sure where that is going," Sara whispered, her face suddenly just over Kate's shoulder, "but someone might need to go find Chris before something happens Ally can't sweet talk her way out of."

Kate jumped and let out a gasp of surprise. "Jesus Christ, Sara. You scared the shit out of me." Her hand went to her chest and pressed against her pounding heart. "Nick and Chris are supposedly on their way. Any minute now from what I was told earlier."

Sara slipped into the chair next to her and patted Kate on the knee. "I hope so, for her sake."

Kate tore her gaze from the three at the bar and stared at the hand now resting on her knee. Before she could respond, the front door swung open.

"Is there a doctor in the house?" Nick called out, his voice thick and a bit strained.

Kate rolled her eyes, sure there was something asinine about to follow his question.

Sara's hand slipped from her leg, and she stood.

Kate's breath caught once Nick stepped into the light.

"Oh my god," Sara said, her hand covering her mouth in shock.

Blood splashes decorated Nick's face, and his shirt was soaked through with the red gore. Something was obviously wrong with his hand, but she couldn't see what exactly since he had a towel wrapped around it.

"I think I need—"

Light glinted off the ax's head as it sliced into the room and drove into Nick's head, splitting his skull in twain.

Sara's scream cut short as chunks of half-digested sandwich sprayed out between her fingers. She bent over, more vomit heaving from her belly, splashing down on the floor.

The ax jerked free, sending blood and brain matter into the air. Each side of Nick's head flopped over to rest on his shoulders, and his body swayed back and forth.

"What the fuck?" Fred cried out.

Something shoved into Nick's back, and his body tumbled forward with a thud. Chris stepped into the cabin and pointed the ax toward the three at the bar. "That's exactly what I'm wondering. What the FUCK is going on?"

Ally pulled her hands away from the two and turned to face her husband. Missy slid down from the bar and stared at Chris with wide eyes. Fred tried to step in front of the two women, but Ally threw out her arm to stop him.

"About time your dumb ass showed up," she said, glaring at Chris. Ally walked toward him, and Kate noted there was a bit more sway in her step than usual.

Ally's approach pulled Kate's attention to Nick's body, and a lump formed in her throat. *He never got to taste my salad.* Anger washed the thought away when Ally simply stepped over it and continued to her husband. *What is she doing?*

She stopped a few feet from Chris and, standing straight, threw her head back in defiance. "What's the meaning of this? Are you trying to ruin our wedding celebration?"

Chris stared at her, his body quivering with each huffed breath.

Fred stepped closer, motioning for Missy to stay put. "Dude, whatever you think is happening isn't," he said, trying to keep his voice light. "Just take it easy."

Sara nodded and wiped at her mouth with a napkin she took from the table. She stepped away from the pile of vomit and moved to stand behind Kate's chair.

Kate stood.

But nothing pulled Chris's attention from Ally's face. "It's pretty hard to take it easy when you've married a WHORE," Chris screamed, spittle flying from his mouth on the last word.

"And what are you going to do?" Ally asked, laughing before he could answer.

Kate flinched. Usually Ally's laughter sounded like bells, but not this time. This time it was darker, harsher in tone, and filled with nothing but mocking cruelty.

Chris's face scrunched up in fury as Ally continued to laugh. He swung the ax back, letting it hover over his right shoulder a moment before driving it toward his wife. The ax sliced through Ally's neck, cutting off the laughter just before removing her head completely.

Screams filled the room, and Fred rushed forward.

Ally's head tumbled from her shoulders and rolled across the room toward Sara's pile of vomit. Blood gushed from the wound, splashing down onto the hardwood floor.

Chris jammed the eye of the ax into the chest of Ally's headless corpse, knocking it to the ground.

Kate watched in wide-eyed horror as the blood continued to pump out in waves of gore.

Fred's foot came down into a fresh pool of sticky hot blood. It shot out from under him and sent him to the ground with a thud. The air whooshed from his lungs, and he lay there struggling to breathe.

"You stink of her too," Chris snarled before driving the ax down into Fred's back. He wrenched the weapon free, raised it higher, and slammed it back down. Blood sprayed out, splattering across Chris's face.

Missy howled and rushed toward her lover. Chris lunged over the body and dipped low enough to drive his shoulder into her chest. A loud crunch echoed through the room, and Missy flew backward, landing in a heap. Chris lifted his foot and drove it down, smashing his heel onto her skull. It burst like a watermelon falling from a rooftop, her bloody, mashed brains oozing out of the split.

Sara whimpered. The noise grabbed Chris's attention, and his head swung toward her and Kate. His lip pulled back into a sneer. "Some maid of honor."

Before Kate could respond, she felt Sara's hands pressed against her back. The air rushed from her lungs, and she stumbled forward. She threw her arms out, desperate to regain her balance, but her foot kicked into Ally's head and she tumbled to the ground. Movement in her peripheral let her know Sara was trying to run toward the door.

Kate pushed up, the mix of blood and chunky vomit squishing between her fingers.

Chris roared and threw the ax toward the fleeing woman. It spun through the air, and the head drove into Sara's back with a wet, meaty thunk. She flopped to the ground, and her body slid across the floor.

Kate struggled to her feet, and after taking a few steps to steady herself, sprang toward the kitchen doors.

"Where are you going?" Chris said between heaving breaths.

Heavy footsteps sounded behind her, but Kate refused to look back. She slammed her shoulder into the door that led to the kitchen, letting it swing all the way in. She darted out of the way knowing it would swing back in place and hoping it would meet Chris when he tried to follow. A loud crunch told her she had timed it perfectly.

"Goddamn BITCH," he roared, though the words sounded garbled.

Kate rushed to the sink and snatched up the kitchen knife she had used to cut the sandwiches.

The door slammed inward, smacking hard against the wall. Chris stomped in. Blood ran freely from his nose, and when his eyes fell on her, he offered her a bloody grin. "You did this to her," he said, jabbing his finger toward her at each word. "Now you're going to pay."

Chris lunged toward her and wrapped his meaty hands around her throat. He used his weight to drive her to the floor and slammed the back of her head against the tile. Stars bloomed before her, and darkness began to creep in. She struggled to focus. Something heavy sat in her hand. *Oh, the knife.*

Kate gripped the handle and drove it into his side. He blinked, but his grip only seemed to tighten. Blood dripped from his nose and splashed down onto her cheek. She stabbed him again and again, until her hand was slick with his blood. Her eyes fluttered, and for a brief second, she thought she could see a face staring at her through the tiny window of the walk-in freezer. She slipped the knife in once more but left it there, no longer able to will her body to do anything. *So cold*. She welcomed the hot gush of his blood on her stomach.

The light began to fade from Chris's eyes, and a look of confusion settled on his face. "What ..." He slumped forward and, after a shuddered breath, grew still.

The old man looked up when the bell announced someone was opening the front door. A woman started to come in but stopped to glance over her shoulder.

"May I help you?"

"Yeah, I got your card from ... an acquaintance. You buy jewelry and stuff?"

"Of course, my dear," he said with a smile. He motioned for her to come closer. "You look a bit frazzled. How about a cup of tea while we discuss what you've brought me."

She stared at him and, just when he thought she might decline, gave a slight nod.

His smile widened, and he clapped his hands together. "Splendid. Now, how do you like your tea, Ms. ...?"

"Uhh, just some sugar please," she said with a sigh. "And it's just Gail."

"A pleasure," he said, stepping from the room a moment to return with the tea tray. He motioned to a small table and two chairs. After they sat, he poured two cups. "Let's see what you have."

She looked around once more then dug into her purse to produce a cloth bag, cinched at the top. The old man took it and loosened the opening. She sipped her tea, and he was glad to see the tension begin to leave her face.

He turned the bag over and emptied it of its contents. "Interesting," he whispered, taking in the collection of watches, earrings, and rings. He used the eraser end of a pencil to make three separate piles. "Oh, I guess I'll be cashing in that IOU sooner than I thought."

Gail glanced at the piles and then back at the man. He tried to keep the smile on his face, but it melted away. "What?"

He waved her concern off. "Oh, there is a set of rings here that I was sure I wouldn't see again, but I guess the third time wasn't quite as charmed as I had hoped. What would you like for this pile of treasure?"

"Money, I guess."

"Then money you shall get," the old man said. He moved to the cash register. "Now, would you prefer cash or a check?"

"Is there a difference?"

"I can offer a little more with the check, but I'm not sure it's worth your trouble. How about four hundred for the lot?"

Gail looked down at the items one last time. "Okay."

"So, it's a deal?" he asked, stepping back to the table.

"It's a deal," she said, her voice catching. "Thank you, Mr. Dickens."

"Oh, that was the name of the previous owner. My given name is Oscar Lawrence Scratch, but you can call me Ol' Scratch for short."

Inked.

M Ennenbach.

"I LEARNED A FEW things in my life, kept a mental list of do's and don'ts to keep myself on the straight and narrow. There ain't no manual to this ever maddening, incrementally increasing journey into entropic dismay in which we call life, just a particular set of poisons in which we gladly ingest until something fails, and believe me, inevitably, something is gonna give out. It's slow at first. Barely noticeable. Suddenly, the gradual decline becomes an oil slick on a gradually melting iceberg in the gently warming, rising oceans congested with plastic. The do's and don'ts begin to trickle, one by one, like childhood dreams into the ravenous maw of eternity. A woman may suddenly appear with regrettable bangs, or a new beau approximately half her age. A man will likely substitute the bangs for a sports car in the hopes of attracting the attention of a new lover, still in the half-the-age bracket. Others take solace in food or drinks, get hopped up on prescriptions, or gradually drift toward whichever path of self medication makes it all tolerable.

"I was an early bloomer. The bulk of my twenties are a drunken blur. My thirties were spent in mental breakdown. And my forties, where the cold grip of death slowly unravels all fiction toward virility, instead darkly illuminating the rickety basement stairs into obscurity, I find myself feeling every single one of a lifetime of mistakes as I fall apart. The thought of three days to recover from an overly expensive night of half-remembered bravado held zero appeal. Eating an assortment of debilitating pills in an effort to balance out my brain chemistry while forgoing small things such as sex and the ability to feel anything except numb at the cost of the liver my abstinence was saving seemed flawed. And while I quite enjoyed mushrooms and acid, it is a thin line between self-betterment and destruction of self, so those were limited. I didn't make enough to buy a Lamborghini. I was worse off than most of my contemporaries. Listless. Bored.

"I chose one of the only paths left open to someone in my position of limited options. I am not proud of what I was forced to do. Save your pity, your shameful glances. I know exactly what I did, who life forced me to become.

"This is harder than I expected. Gimme a second.

"My name is Wolfe, and I write poetry.

"The two questions I am asked, nearly universally, can be answered as such.

"Yes, with an E at the end. My father quite liked Jack London, my mother quite liked morphine, and the nurse simply wanted her paperwork complete before the end of the shift. It is not, to the best of my half-assed research, a family name. And to be as open and honest as possible, the first picture of me, a yellowed Polaroid at approximately an hour old, was in the arms of my father. I will not say he had been drinking. He was, however, wearing a lime-green shirt and maroon bell bottoms. My mother can be seen staring quite intently at the bright lights. Make of it what you will.

"The second question, one usually asked with a near-breathless apprehension, as if I will suddenly begin to expound upon the brilliance of Robert Frost (his syphilitic verses are all quite repulsive), is actually quite simple. One day I wrote an atrocious poem. Sophomoric trash. But there was something in the act of writing I found unique. The next day, I wrote an even worse attempt. Before long, I found myself writing poetry all the time." I paused, thinking about the next poem.

The cars on the overpass looked like rows of ants slowly making the long trek back to the hive.

"'Did you ever get better?' a voice said, startling me from my reverie as I stared at the phone in my hand.

"Better at what?" I asked, confused. Who was this? I must have been rambling again. I do that.

"'Writing poetry,' the voice answered. 'Did you ever get better at writing?'

I frowned. "No. Not in the slightest. It's all a pyramid scheme. I get you to read my book. You get your friends to read my book. Maybe they get their friends to read my book."

"'That sounds like you're at the top of the pyramid, though.'

I barked a derisive laugh. "Sure, on a granular level. But I am on the layer right above you, and the only difference between us is I have written a book while you haven't. At least not yet. And while I am not sure how many levels are above me, likely thousands, they still all end with one solitary block smack dab at the top.

"Me? I'll be lucky to make enough to buy a paperback copy for my shelf. If I manage to ever to write one thing worth a billionth of a fuck, I have the possibility of one day inspiring someone who has the same useless passion for a dead art I did into writing the next great, ignored work, which may or may not only enable this cycle of insanity."

"'I had no idea,' the voice answered, actually sounding interested.

I had no idea who I was talking to. That happens. I get all manic and lost, lose time, get high to feel normal. Rinse. Repeat.

That, or my liver and ability to feel, that is.

I decided to ask the question out loud. "I'm sorry, but why did you call me again?"

There was a long pause. Not uncomfortable, but awkward. 'You called me. About the typewriter? The one my *aunt* left when she passed away?' the voice finally answered, just as confused as me," I said, finally stopping to take a drink of water.

"Tell me you didn't," Rob begged, his head bowed over his beer.

"I most certainly did!" I exclaimed.

"Did what?" Corey asked as she sat her Coke on the table.

Rob shook his head in disgust. "This pretentious fuck ..."

"I got a typewriter! It's turquoise and came with its own case!" I answered happily.

Corey nodded. "You know how they say the Sahara was once a great sea?"

I nodded, eager to tell them about the former owner of the typewriter.

"My vagina just experienced the same phenomena. Total evaporation. Instantly," Corey said as my eagerness shattered.

"It's turquoise," I tried.

"Might want to get some Chapstick. Seems like your nether region is going to experience a continued drought," Derek mumbled. He was really quite funny, but soft spoken.

Whoever said do what you love was an asshole who was clearly just doing as they were told.

The typewriter sat in my backseat for three weeks. I was taking Dani to the store when she asked me what the big black case was. I didn't say when I finally remembered; I didn't want a rehash of the great Saharan vagina. Last I heard, Billy and Pat had started calling Corey Sarah, Corey Sahara at the bar.

Always seek the silver lining. Or better friends.

It made it indoors and took up space on the table. I quickly realized I had been in love with the *idea* of owning a typewriter. Bukowski and Plath. A cigar, a few empty bottles of wine, Wagner on the radio, and the clickety-clack of keys as the next mediocre lines were written.

Mostly, I got high on the couch and scribbled whatever before getting out the laptop. It worked.

I decided to finally bite the bullet. Went to the store and got a couple packs of paper, three new ribbons, and a box of pencils. I didn't know what I was planning, but something about being around all the supplies kicked the busy bee from grade school into action. I wanted to create something new, maybe finally try and write that novel I had been toying with. Something with an old-school-beat aesthetic, channel the spirits of Kerouac and Bukowski at their drunken best. Raw and unfiltered. I would X my mistakes and demand they be left in the manuscript like well-earned scars.

I lived alone in most aspects. No roommate. Not a lot of contact with my friends, except our monthly meet up. My dad died when I was little and had left me enough of an inheritance to live as a hermit with enough to get by.

My entire life I had always been off. Eccentric and moody. I just thought everyone was like that, until my early thirties when I started to see I was usually the cause of all my misfortune. That was when I found out I was bipolar. It explained so much. Why I was different. How I was different. And I learned I had to navigate this duality, which had always seemed so normal, in a new way. How do you know you're crazy when crazy was all you had ever known? Sure as fuck goes from crazy to normal to crazy how normal being crazy can be. I didn't like being alone, but in moments of clarity, it was probably best for everyone.

The bipolar led to the desperate need for the mechanical paperweight. It also led to having no practical interest in it once I scratched the itch. And now it was my stubbornness which had me loading up on supplies instead of just admitting my lack of self-control won yet again.

Rob calling to make fun of me didn't help. I could only imagine what he would say if he knew the fucking thing hadn't even been used. I figured it was nearly time for the meet up and that having a couple typed poems might shut him up. Was I aware of how deep in denial I was as I sat there opening the pack of paper and feeling absolutely zero inspiration to write a single line of poetry? Probably. It still didn't stop me from rolling the sheet in. I set my fingers on the keys like they had taught in school and stared at my hands intensely.

I had no clue how to type.

I shook my head. It was fine. This was fine. Everything was fine. I was sure Bukowski didn't know shit about shit when it came to typing. Hunter did, I knew that from documentaries. I couldn't imagine Sylvia hunting and pecking. Honestly, Bukowski was probably a pretty solid typist. The more I thought about it, I was likely one of maybe a handful, excluding isolated tribes, who couldn't type on a keyboard.

I glared at the typewriter in sullen anger, a $150 turquoise example of my own undying idiocy.

I knew buying it that I would need to learn to type correctly. I didn't look at the ukulele, guitar, harmonica, or easel sitting forlorn in the corner, each one bought under the same regurgitated lie.

This time would be different, I told myself, the lie sounding hollow in my own head.

I rolled my neck, and a series of satisfying pops rang out. I could do this. I cleared my mind. I could feel the words beginning to sing, almost as if forks of lightning danced across my nervous system. The first word began to form, and instinctually, my forefinger began to press down on the key.

And then I let out a surprised shout of pain and glared at the typewriter and the drop of bright crimson blossoming on the tip of my finger. I bent my head down and stared at the keys to find the source of my wound. I found a sewing needle next to the T key and pulled it out. The sucker was really wedged in.

I held up the offending implement of phalange torture and sighed. "Must have fallen in and, in all the commotion, gotten stuck at the perfect angle to stick me."

This was, after all, pretty par for the course when it came to my luck.

I got up and grabbed a paper towel when I realized the blood was dripping onto my brand-new, worthless, fucking typewriter. I cleaned it up as well as I could and decided to tear it down over the weekend and give it a thorough cleaning before attempting it again and closed the lid.

To add insult to injury, as I went to bed that night, I could feel the first inklings of getting sick. It was warm outside, yet I couldn't manage to stay warm. I debated calling and canceling on the get-together but decided to give it a night's sleep and see how I was doing.

Two weeks later and not only had I not thoroughly cleaned the type-writer, I hadn't even touched it. It was impossible to forget about the thing as it took up a place at the dinner table. But I did my best to keep myself preoccupied with the lingering malaise I had been dealing with. I wasn't sick, just exhausted. Rob and Pat said it sounded like the most pathetic case of middle-aged mono to ever exist. I would have laughed if I wasn't so uncertain. I couldn't stay awake. I sleepwalked through work. By the time I got home, it was all I could do to force down a sandwich and fall asleep on the couch before eventually finding my way to bed.

I was just settling down on the couch when a loud knock on the door nearly made me pee, and I was pretty sure one more urine stain and the couch would be refused by Goodwill. I sat up and bellowed, "What?"

The door opened, and Corey stood glaring at me. "Aren't you too old for mono by like twenty years?"

I glared back. "Did you come over at this ungodly hour just to ridicule a sick man?"

She snorted. "It isn't even six. For fuck's sake, at least watch the opening to Matlock before giving up. You need a fruit cup?"

I wanted to pretend to be angry, but my stomach rumbled loudly and I ended up laughing instead.

She looked at me for a second, really looked at me. "You do look like shit, though. You taking vitamins? Sounds like you're not eating. Get up, put on a clean shirt, and we can go get a pizza. My treat."

I wanted to sigh, to refuse the obvious pity pizza. I got up and grabbed a shirt from the basket and changed.

She nodded. "Good. Go splash some water on your face."

I wasn't sure how to handle this nicer version of Corey. Maybe feeling like hammered shit had its perks. I splashed some water on my face in the bathroom and took a look a myself. I avoided mirrors typically. I had no real need for one. I shaved my head and wore a hat. I tended to shave and then grew fresh beard until I got tired of playing with it and started the cycle all over again. I didn't even know my eyes weren't brown until I was in my thirties.

Corey was right. I looked about as good as I felt. I looked sleep deprived, which made no sense since all I did was work and sleep. Guess I just expected this new hell was yet another in the gradual decline. No amount of water splashing was going to erase this, so I gave up and toweled off.

She shrugged at me, and we left without a word. By virtue of parking behind me, she got to chauffer us the four blocks to Sam's. We ordered—onion, pepperoni, extra cheese—and grabbed a booth in the back of the tiny pizzeria.

"Have you had an AIDS test?" Corey asked, sipping her coke.

I nearly choked on mine. "Are you being fucking serious?"

She shrugged. "As likely as mono."

I nodded. "Fair. I am pretty sure it isn't mono. Or AIDS. Probably a bad down cycle. I had a decent run manic a month or two back. Always comes time to pay. Can we pretend the pity pizza isn't heavy on the pity?"

She frowned. "I don't think you're supposed to acknowledge pity pizza."

"How did you pull the short straw?" I asked.

Corey rolled her eyes. "First, there isn't a short straw checking on a friend. It's offensive to even suggest that. And secondly …"

I slapped my forehead. "Dart season just started up."

There wasn't a ton to do in Illinois that didn't in some way lead to a bar. If you go to a bar every single night and drink yourself into a stupor, people begin to think you have a problem. Join a dart league, of which there were several spread out around the year, and go to a bar and drink yourself into a stupor *while playing or practicing* darts? That's just dedication.

Corey nodded. "Without you there to mock them with me, the dumb fucks begin to take it serious. It's fucking embarrassing."

I shivered. "Gross."

The pizza arrived. We mostly gossiped about how after thirty years weight and hairlines seemed to be the only thing which truly changed. There was a comfort in that I couldn't explain, the type of thing so easily taken for granted as sure as the sun would rise tomorrow. We weren't misfits. We just never really settled down. We may have slowed down, due to necessity as much as anything, sure, but at our core, we were who we always had been. It was quiet moments in a pizza shop with the only friend not using darts as an excuse to drink that made me appreciate the times laughing as the jukebox was up too loud and Billy missed another triple.

I began to feel a little better, even if it was just a placebo.

"I saw the typewriter," Corey said around a huge bite of pizza.

There was that wave of cold reality I had missed.

"Uh huh," I said noncommittally.

"It sure is turquoise," she replied, equally non-committal.

After being made fun of, having the moment of clarity which allowed me to accept I deserved to be made fun of, the failed lone attempt to use it, and my then getting sick and not writing anything at all, I'm not sure I was mentally prepared for the beating I rightfully deserved. But I had also forgotten to tell anyone the one possible saving grace of the entire purchase.

"It once belonged to Candace Pfeiffer," I said, less confidently than life allowed me to feel, which was super fucking sad.

Corey blinked at me slowly. "Candace Pfeiffer. As in The Candace Pfeiffer?"

I nodded. "The Cock Slasher."

Corey just stared at me for a long moment, as if she was rebooting. When she finally blinked, she said two words. "Bull. Shit."

I smiled. "Nope. I found it online. I didn't believe it, either. Then I talked to her niece in Providence."

Corey whistled. "Way to fucking bury the lead on that one."

I frowned. "I tried. And you turned the conversation into one about the billowing sands in your vagina."

She stared at me for a minute and then smirked. "Wait until those fuckwads hear about this newest wrinkle. They've been having a field day with this for weeks."

I smiled knowing how relentless they could be.

She looked away from me. "I have a confession."

I was confused at the sudden shift. "Okay."

She blushed and looked down at the table. "I may have glanced at what you're working on now."

I didn't have a clue what she meant.

Something about my confusion must have seemed angry, and she quickly held up her hands. "It's fucking amazing. I didn't mean to peek. I know you prefer for us to wait until you're done. But I couldn't help myself. It was hypnotic."

"Corey, I don't know what the fuck you're talking about," I said, not getting the joke. Was it her way of making fun of how much of a waste the damned thing was?

Now she looked confused. "The stack of papers? The fucking one loaded in the typewriter half typed? What do you mean?"

I shook my head. "I haven't used the typewriter. I tried to and pricked my finger. I was manic and it sounded cool and I have poor impulse control. You know how I am."

She nodded but didn't seem to believe me. "The guitar phase."

I nodded.

"Wolfe, if you didn't write what I read, who did? I was like fifteen pages. Dark. Darker than your normal stuff, I should say. Don't be mad at me for sneaking a look. It's amazing," Corey said with a reassuring smile.

I wanted to argue more but didn't. I didn't see the humor in this one, so I chose to ignore it. Not every prank lands, and this one was a harmless dud.

"I didn't know you read any of my stuff," I said, grabbing a corner piece.

Corey smiled, her real smile, the one I always melted over. I saw it less and less often nowadays, and it made me happy to see it sneak out. She looked away again. "Don't be stupid. I read all of it. I love it. But it's already pretentious enough writing poetry. Can't let you get a big head as well."

I bit my lip and looked away. I wasn't good with compliments or praise, and that was her doing her best to keep me comfortable. "I'm no Robert Frost," I said with a shrug.

Corey laughed and passed me her vape pen. "No button. Just suck."

I raised an eyebrow at her.

She rolled her eyes. "Indica heavy hybrid. Think it was called Blue Moon or Blood Lake. You know I wouldn't give you a sativa."

"Blue Moon over Blood Lake?" I said with a cough and cloud of vapor. "And you think poetry is pretentious?"

She laughed. "I was saying *your* poetry is pretentious."

I shrugged. "Fair enough."

We got high and ate a little more. I couldn't remember the last time she and I had hung out without everyone else. Years. I knew why, could never forget. It was no secret I had a crush on her all the way back in high school. We were destined to always fly by one another, but life found a way to keep us apart.

It was a night of firsts and lasts. I got annihilated on Apple Pie shots and bong rips with the guys to celebrate Pat's second wedding. Corey had just come back to town after three years in Vegas. I took it as a sign and drunkenly confessed my feelings.

She had just left a bad relationship. The last thing she needed was me dropping this nuke on her. She didn't say a word, just glared at me and walked away.

I wondered if she knew how many of those poems she had read were about her. I never imagined her reading any of it.

"Gentle comes the tide, erasing all traces of life, as if god shook her etch-a-sketch in petulant sorrow. I yearn for this cleansing to take the crescent moon of her smile, allowing me to breathe once again without briars in my side. I cannot fathom the joke where the punchline is knowing heaven exists yet always lies out of reach," Corey said softly, tracing her finger on the edge of the pizza pan.

I knew the words and felt their weight as I longed to take her hand. I smiled instead. "Definitely no Robert Frost. "

Corey nodded and finally looked at me with that smile. "Thank god."

We sat and talked until Vinnie came over with a to-go box and a patient smile that meant he wanted to go home. I didn't want to break the spell of such a nice night spent with her.

That was the thing about the sweetest dreams; the alarm always sounds in the morning. But for an evening, I didn't feel anything but content.

The next evening she brought soup.

"You made this?" I asked, savoring the tender gnocchi.

She cocked her head at me. "We are middle aged. Of course I can cook. This worries me about how you've managed to survive this long without basic skills."

I pursed my lips and considered her words, then shrugged. "I got an air fryer."

Corey sighed. "I guess that's a start. You're kind of a mess, aren't you."

I nodded and tried to smile, but it felt sad. "I have a few set skills I excel at. The rest is a kerfuffle of discombobulation at the best of times."

"A kerfuffle," she said, then took a long hit from one of the vape pens on the coffee table, "of discombobulation. Sounds like something from *Alice in Wonderland*."

As she passed me the pen, I noticed the Band-Aids, minus dinosaurs, on her fingers. "You didn't get those making this soup, did you?"

Corey looked at her hand and shook her head. "No, Wolfe, I didn't cut my fingers making the soup. Happened at work. I was the unfortunate victim of a half-folded staple. Damn thing got me as was entering paperwork into the computer. Now, are you going to quote more *Wonderland* or get high with me?"

Despite my exhaustion, there was no other place I wanted to be than on the couch with her. We talked for a bit, and she put some show on

Netflix. I was full, sleepy, and next to Corey. I yawned loudly and looked at her, worried she would take it as a hint to go. Instead, she patted her lap, and I laid my head on her thighs. If this was a dream, I didn't want to wake up.

"Psst, Wolfe. Hey, sleepy head," a voice whispered into the void.

I opened one eye and glared up. Corey was standing over me. I smiled, confused, and said, "Hi. Sorry. I must have crashed hard."

She looked at me funny. "Yeah. For like an hour."

I looked around and realized I was in bed. I looked at her. "Did you put me to bed?"

"Ha-ha, very funny," she said. Then she stared at me. "Wait. Are you being serious?"

"We ate. Smoked. Talked. And then I laid my head on your," I could feel the blush blooming, "on your lap. Then about two minutes ago."

Now she looked concerned. "Wolfe, you fell asleep for like an hour. Then you woke up. Are you telling me you don't remember waking up?"

I shook my head. "Nope. I don't even remember getting up to pee."

She sat down on the edge of the bed. "You slept an hour or so. I don't know, episode and some change of the show for sure. Then you woke up and smiled at me. You told me you had to write. None of this is ringing a bell?"

I reached over and grabbed my notebook off of the bedside table, flipping to the last page. I frowned and showed her. "I haven't written anything in two weeks. Did you fall asleep too?"

Corey pushed the notebook away. "No. You went into the kitchen and wrote. On the typewriter. I must have fallen asleep on the couch. I woke up and you were in here. I didn't want to just sneak out."

"I haven't used the typewriter. Once. One letter," I said, and held up my finger to show her the fresh pink where the needle hole had healed, "and when my finger got poked with a needle, I decided to call it quits."

I paused and remembered her saying something about reading what I was working on. It got lost in the conversation. Conversations.

I sat up and flung off the covers.

Corey turned bright red and turned away, informing me that I had, as always, gone to bed nude. She stood up quickly. "You get some clothes on. I'll be right back."

I didn't know what was happening. I did. I had apparently slept, written, and then just showed Corey my penis. I was conflicted which one bothered me more as I pulled on basketball shorts. As I put on a Melvins shirt, Corey came back into the room. The moment I looked at her, she blushed again. Seemed the both of us were embarrassed by my penis. Great.

Then she held out a stack of paper, at least fifty sheets, toward me. "This is what you were working on."

I took the pages from her and began to read. It was good, dark, but really altogether good so far. It seemed to be about a woman who had found the key immortality, and her struggle with the cost. I sped through it, disappointed when I got to the last sheet.

I looked at Corey. "This is pretty good."

She nodded. "I told you it was coming along great."

I looked back at the sheets of paper. "I didn't write this. It isn't my style at all. The word choices, the descriptions, I don't recognize a line of it."

"Wolfe, I watched you typing it out last night. Is this some kind of joke?" she asked, her eyes tightening.

I shook my head and spread my hands. "I know my voice. This isn't it. I can't even type. This would have taken me weeks to write."

"You were typing like a professional last night," she said, the anger growing.

I took a deep breath. I didn't like this, her getting mad at me over a story I had no recollection of writing. The idea I was up all night writing a book made no fucking sense. But it did. I felt like I had been getting maybe three hours sleep a night, no matter how late I got up. What if I was up most of the night writing this book? But how?

I laughed and pointed at her. "Holy shit. I almost fell for it."

She frowned. "Fell for what?"

I held up the pages. "This is almost diabolical. What happened? I fell sleep and you let Rob or Pat in? While I was asleep, they copied some book so you could pull this elaborate trick? Then what? You convince me I'm sleep-writing the novel of the century? I'm impressed."

Corey shook her head. "That's fucking insane."

I laughed. "And sleep-writing isn't?"

"Wolfe, I don't know what's happening right now. Either you're fucking with me and being a total asshole about it ..." Corey snapped, then trailed off as she stared at the pages on the bed.

I took a deep breath. "Fine. Let's say I am sleep-typing. Why doesn't any of it feel familiar?"

She shrugged. "You've said before that you don't always remember the words you write."

I nodded. "And it's true. But I can recognize they're my words when I hear or read them." I pointed at the sheets of paper. "This is reading someone else."

"Then how do you explain it?" she asked. "I watched you write for a while before laying back on the couch. It was you."

I couldn't. It made zero sense. To hear her, I was a typing virtuoso when I knew for a fact I could barely hunt and peck my way through mediocrity.

I smiled at her. "Thanks for the soup. And for staying last night. I really appreciate it."

She smiled, but the tension around her eyes remained. "Don't change the subject, Wolfe. But you're welcome. I don't like you being sick."

I smiled bigger. "And dart season is so fucking boring."

She rolled her eyes. "So fucking boring." She looked at the clock, and her eyes got big. "Shit. I need to go. I have to be at work in twenty minutes."

I yawned. "Okay. I need a shower before I go in as well."

She started to leave but stopped in the doorway and pointed at the manuscript. "What are you going to do about that?"

"No idea," I said, still uncertain about it all.

She nodded and smiled. "Talk soon."

I smiled at her and hoped so. I listened as she walked downstairs and shut her front door behind her. Flipping through the pages again, I tried to find a connection to the words. There was nothing. I had no insights into the characters, no understanding of motivation. The language was flowery, more descriptive of things I never focus on. None of my tendencies came through. This was filled with long paragraphs and the dialogue felt stilted, whereas I preferred shorter chunks and punchier dialogue.

It was good, though. Just not me. At least I didn't think it was. It made a strange kind of sense when I thought about the exhaustion. Writing takes it out of you mentally; compound that with a lack of sleep and you had a recipe for perpetual exhaustion. I've never had a history of sleepwalking, and despite being single for long stretches, I had a few long-term relationships where we slept together for long periods. If I was up practicing my typing all night, one of them would likely have mentioned it.

I felt a cold sliver of dread poking around inside of me.

Corey came over again that night. This time she brought Rob with, to my disappointment.

"You have the Cock Slasher's typewriter?" Rob exclaimed the minute he entered. "I take back three bad things I said about you."

I sighed. "Only three? That doesn't even include the ride over here."

Rob laughed. "It barely covers walking up the steps. Where is it?"

I nodded toward the kitchen. "On the table."

He rushed to the kitchen, and Corey smiled apologetically at me. "He asked how you were, and I told him about the typewriter. He had to see it for himself."

"What did you tell him about it?" I asked, worried about how far out of hand this was going to go.

She looked at me seriously. "Just who owned it. Nothing about your nocturnal writing."

I nodded and smiled slightly. That was a relief.

"And he only stopped by on his way to practice," she added

I smiled even bigger at that. Then I felt a shiver of discomfort when the clacking sound of keys being struck filled the room.

"Ouch! Fuck!" Rob yelled suddenly.

Corey and I looked at each other in confusion and went to the kitchen to see Rob holding his bleeding finger. I grabbed a paper towel and handed it to him, asking, "What the hell? How'd you manage to do that?"

Rob pointed at the typewriter, sending a droplet of red splashing on the piece of paper he had been typing on. "Something fucking stabbed me as I was playing with the Cock Slasher's typewriter!"

Corey laughed as I inspected the keys. I froze when I saw another needle propped up, next to the space bar this time. I grabbed a pair of pliers from the drawer and carefully extracted it.

Rob glared at it. "A fucking sewing needle? How many times have you used the typewriter? Not many if there was a needle poking up you managed to miss. Or did you do it on purpose?"

"Stop being a little bitch, Robert," Corey snapped. "It's just a poke, for fuck's sake. I saw him typing like crazy last night on it, and he never got poked once. Probably got dislodged from you hammering away."

"I got jabbed too," I said, and showed Rob my finger. "I thought I checked for more. Must have missed it. Let me get you a Band-Aid."

I had looked, even shined a flashlight to make sure there wasn't one lying hidden. I grabbed the iodine and a dinosaur bandage I had forgotten about.

Rob glared at the red stegosaurus for a second. "Better not fuck with my throwing tonight."

"Probably make you better. You've been the worst in the league for the last ten years running," Corey said.

"Hey! Only nine of the last ten years!" Rob exclaimed, then pointed at me. "There was the year Wolfe played. He was way worse than me."

"That was why I quit," I said with a shrug.

"Some people are capable of learning and moving on," Corey said with a sweet smile at Rob.

Rob gave me an arched eyebrow. "Giving up and moving on are two different things."

I blushed, knowing exactly what he was intimating about my feelings for Corey. He wasn't wrong. An asshole? No question. But not wrong.

Rob looked at me and smiled, probably realizing he went too far. "I'll admit that owning the typewriter of a famous serial killer is pretty fucking cool, though. I went when they finally caught her. It was in the photo on the front page. You guys remember that?"

We both nodded. It was a big deal, around here at least. Candace Nola, the book reviewer and author who was known for her sharp tongue and scathing reviews of both books and the authors themselves, also happened to be quite a prolific serial killer on the side. When they finally realized it was her and went to take her in, she greeted the officers with a smile and a loaded shotgun. She chose suicide by police over whatever extended stay in prison would have come her way. The photo on the front page was black and white and showed police officers and FBI agents in her home. The typewriter had sat prominently on the desk.

"How did you manage to get it?" Rob asked, snapping me back to the present.

"I saw a post about it. Was up manic in the middle of the night and caught it as it went up. I jumped on it before anyone else had a chance. All of her stuff was seized by the cops. A couple months ago, someone realized they still had it all and contacted her only surviving family member, Megan, in Tennessee, a second-cousin or something. She barely knew who her distant relative was, and once she found out, she didn't want the stuff any longer," I answered with a hint of regret.

Rob whistled. "She could have made a fortune off of that crap. People love serial-killer memorabilia."

I nodded. "After I secured the typewriter, I told her that. She knocked a bit off of the price for the tip. She was coming up for work and agreed to meet me halfway. Said she had offers in the five figures for some of the stuff."

"When Corey canceled on darts practice, we were all curious what had stolen her attention. Pfeiffer's typewriter is definitely a good excuse. Even if it bites," Rob said. He looked at Corey. "You sure you don't want to come?"

Corey smiled. "I'm sure. Wolfe has Netflix. And beer. And I don't have to hear excuses on why no one can hit the bullseye."

Rob glared at her, then at me when I laughed, before walking toward the door. "Fuck both of you. I nail Pat's bullseye every evening."

"Like parking a smart car in an airplane hangar," I said as he walked out the door.

His laughter trailed as he yelled, "At least I'm getting some!"

Corey grabbed a beer from the fridge and looked at me. "You want one?"

I raised an eyebrow. "You just using me for me for my serial-killer typewriter and Netflix?"

She walked over and leaned against me. I was positive she knew exactly how that would affect me. She said coyly, "Don't forget the beer."

"I'll get more after work tomorrow," I said quickly.

She laughed and remained leaned against me. I didn't want to break the spell and was disappointed when she pulled away and made for the living room. She looked back with a smile. "The Netflix is in here."

We cuddled on the couch and got high. Neither of us brought up the late-night typing. She didn't stay, but it was clear she wanted to. That was enough for both of us.

I snapped the typewriter case closed and put it on the top shelf of the hallway closet before going to bed that night. I didn't know what was happening with it. Or with Corey. I felt all over the place, which didn't help with the constant malaise that seemed to swirl around me as I sleepwalked through the day.

Someone said things look darkest before the dawn. That was valid. I also learned things seem brightest before the night falls. The universe, the insipid, ever-expanding cunt, loves nothing quite as much as balance.

I woke to my alarm and felt better than I had in weeks. I thought about the typewriter and chuckled to myself. Putting it in the closet was probably just a placebo—ineffective in the grand scheme of the universe, but infinitely valuable for my mental health. I made coffee and wrote poetry as the sun shimmered lazily through the curtains. I really did feel free, and as I sipped my coffee, I wondered if I had fallen into a down phase and Corey hanging out hid it. It was highly possible.

And it did nothing to explain the sleep-typing. What else did I sleep-do? The world may never have known.

I sighed, just relieved to feel better. The idea of an electrified jellyfish piloting a meat rocket into its inevitable demise was tricky at the best of times. I was ready for some better times. I grabbed my stuff and walked outside with, not a smile, less of a grimace.

It became a full-on grimace when I saw Rob sitting in my drive way. Not that I minded him stopping by. Maybe a little; I wasn't the type for random pop-ins. He was sitting in his truck staring off into space and didn't even notice as I walked up to the window. He nearly jumped out of his skin when making faces and flipping him off didn't get his attention and I finally tapped the glass.

"Hey, buddy, whatcha doing?" I asked as he rolled down his window.

"Wolfe? Fuck, man, I must have been on cruise control and just came this way. That's weird as hell. I could have sworn I was on my way to work," Rob said with a look of pure confusion.

"That is weird. I know you've always thought I was cute, but you're not my type. I'm not saying in a pinch, but this isn't a pinch," I said with a wink.

He scowled at me. "Don't go getting a big head, you sack of shit. Now, if you'll excuse me, I'm running late for work."

I looked at my watch. "Well, that makes two of us. Try not to accidentally drive to the wrong place, Colonel Buttplug."

He muttered something about me being a butt plug as he backed out.

"Oh shit, Rob!" I yelled as he was about to pull away.

"What?" he yelled back.

"You're the butt plug, Colonel Buttplug!" I yelled back, and got into my car so I didn't have to hear his reply. He honked twice, but I simply held my middle finger up and put the car in reverse.

The day was starting off pretty well, indeed.

I felt so much better that I called Corey and invited her to dinner. Small towns tend to hide secrets, and one of the most magical was the dirty grill at a dive bar for the single-best burger you've ever had. I didn't know if it was the absolute lack of hygiene or some conglomeration of congealed fat burned down to some purest level of permanent grill coating that imbued each and every patty with an ever-intensifying culinary blessing. Both may have been at play; it was impossible to tell. But one bite of the Italian sausage burger with grilled onions caramelized in that intoxicating fugue, as the gentle heat warms your mouth, an explosion of flavor rendered even the most sophisticated person into a snarling, salivating fiend.

As was in evidence across the table from me at that exact moment. I found it adorable. I hated myself for it.

"What?" she managed to mostly articulate around a half-masticated chunk.

I frowned. "What *what*?"

She eventually managed to swallow the frankly monstrous bite and gestured at me. "Why are you grinning as this delicacy fucks my taste buds?"

"I wasn't aware I was," I said as a blush erupted across my cheeks.

Her eyes sparkled at me, but she just nodded. "Okay."

"I'm not going to take the bait," I said confidently as I reached for a fried pickle.

She snatched the pickle from my fingers and popped it into her mouth with a grin.

I opened and quickly shut my mouth and grabbed another. Her eyes focused on it, and I saw her tense up. Then her phone buzzed, and she took her eyes off the prize long enough for me to eat it. She casually flipped me off, which seemed harsh but fair.

"Billy and Pat are asking us to swing by the bar tonight," she said as she read the text. "Rob's a no show for darts and they need you to sub."

I sighed loudly. "That sounds terrible."

Corey nodded and reached out and squeezed my hand. "They're aware, but you're the only option."

I looked at her, confused. "I mean playing darts sounds terrible."

She smiled sweetly and nodded again. Her hand was still resting on mine, and as much as I wanted to call her out for being an ass, I didn't want her to move.

I frowned. "I saw Rob today. He did seem a little off." I told her about the strange interaction. "Being under the weather would explain it, I guess."

"He was born a little off. No sickness required," Corey said with a smirk. "Is that a yes for darts? If so, we need to get moving."

She moved her hand, causing me to sigh and nod. "I guess so."

Two things were brought to my attention, repeatedly, throughout the evening. Throwing darts was not the same as riding a bicycle, and my barely adequate skills had suffered from a disgusting amount of atrophy, apparently, was the first. The second was I always played better when I was just drunk enough to not think about what I was doing. I also discovered that finding the right spot of inebriation to correctly hit a triple nineteen and the place where everything was slightly spinning was a matter of a shot or two.

It was sometime after the fifth or fiftieth reminder that I decided a shot was better than more grief. No one mentioned how Corey seemed to always be near me or the incidental contact she made. Not out loud. Instead, they must have thought pantomiming shock was the more subtle path to acknowledgement, which in turn had me do more shots to try to balance the joy and forced awkwardness.

Ultimately, it led to Corey taking me home. We stoically ignored the cat calls as I staggered to her car, where I gracefully poured myself into the passenger seat. The best part of small towns was everything was relatively close. Likely the worst part, as well. Nature craved balance.

"You can spend the night, but no funny business," I said, staring out the window and feeling a slight case of the spins.

"Oh yeah?" Corey asked. "And what if the only reason I offered to bring you back was for funny business?"

I turned to look at her, a bit too quickly, and had to close one eye to focus. "I am a *gentleman*."

I could only assume her laughter was born of the deepest respect for my virtue. I felt her hand on my thigh, and I placed mine on hers as I set my head against the wonderfully cool window. Everything felt so ni—

"Wolfe, hey, we made it," Corey said, gently nudging me.

I lifted my head, unaware I had dozed off, and looked around in confusion. The confusion only intensified when I saw lights on inside my house. I never left the lights on. "That's weird," I muttered as I focused more.

"What's weird?" Corey asked, concerned.

"I don't remember leaving a light on before I left," I answered as I got out of the car.

I felt Corey's hand grip my arm. "You think someone broke in?"

I shook my head. There was crime in little towns, sure, but everyone knew everyone, which meant everyone knew I was a broke writer with little to my name. "I think it has more to do with the number of shots than any potential burglary," I said as I fumbled for my keys. I walked through the house, but everything was in the same state of chaos I had left it in. When I returned to the living room, I shrugged. "Must have just forgotten to turn it off. My dad's probably rolling in his grave about needing to light the entire neighborhood."

Corey smiled at me then pressed herself against me with her head on my chest. "Not only a gentleman, but fiscally astute as well."

I wrapped my arms around her, breathing in the scent of her hair, which felt as intoxicating as the too-many shots. I didn't want to move, to do anything to shatter this moment I had dreamed of for too long. I looked into her brown eyes and felt the pull of eternity in the fathomless depths which I had only glanced at from my periphery in scenes written for someone else. Her lips slightly parted, and I leaned in for the kiss every atom of my existence craved.

Queue the universe.

Ding.

We both halted the forward momentum of our lips.

Clack. Clackclackclackclackclackclackclack.

An instant infusion of frozen fear flushed through my veins.

"Is that the typewriter?" Corey asked quietly.

I nodded. A cacophony of keys sounded out a metallic storm. I unhappily disengaged my arms from around her. A cold sheen of sweat seemed to materialize across my back.

"I thought you said there was no one else here," she said, a quaver in her voice.

"There wasn't," I said as I grabbed a chunk of wood from next to the fireplace.

"Didn't you say you put the typewriter in the closet?" she asked, her hand shaking on my shoulder.

"I did," I said as I stared down the hallway at the kitchen light burning, trying to remember if I saw it on my drunken circuit through the house.

We shuffled together down the hallway, her hand on my shoulder and the wood clenched so tight in my fist I could feel splinters pressing beneath my fingernails. I took a deep breath at the doorway and jumped into the room with what I hoped was a ferocious scream. The kitchen was empty.

Ding.

Corey screamed, and I nearly shit myself as I spun erratically around the room. There was nothing. No one.

Clackclackclackclackclackclackclack...

I felt the laughter well up in my chest and nearly bent in two as it wheezed out.

"Wolfe!" Corey yelled at me. "What in the fuck is so goddamned funny?"

I managed to catch my breath from the near-hysterical fit of laughter and wiped tears from my eyes. "I bet the damned thing fell just over. Wouldn't be the first time I slammed a door and knocked something on the shelf over. Once, it was big-ass bag of flour, and when I opened the pantry door, it rained down on me. I looked like Tony Montana."

She frowned. "Who?"

I sighed then scrunched up my face and did an appropriately terrible Pacino impression. "Say hello to my little friend."

She shook her head. "You said no sex. Your little friend isn't saying hi to anyone."

I punched the bridge of my nose and sighed. "It's from the movie *Scarface*."

That's when I saw the way her eyes were crinkling at the corners and realized she was making fun of me.

Ding!

The witty retort froze on my tongue. The bell shouldn't ring unless the carriage hit the stop. The sound of the carriage ratcheting back made the contents of my stomach go oily and sour. There was no way it simply tipped over.

Clackclackclackclackclackclackclack

I took a deep breath then pulled the hallway door open. The fucking typewriter was still in its case on the top shelf. I approached it like it was a rattlesnake, not wanting to touch it. I closed my eyes, grabbed the handle of the black case, and yanked it down. I forgot to compensate for the weight and was nearly pulled off of my already wobbly feet. I set it gingerly on the table.

Corey and I stared at it, waiting for the top to open and some monster to leap out at us. No noise emanated from the hard-plastic shell. It didn't jerk or shudder. It just sat on the table.

"It's like it didn't want to be in closet," Corey whispered.

"It's a fucking typewriter," I countered, even though part of me agreed.

She gave me a quick side-eye. "Then open it if it's just a *fucking* typewriter."

I worked through any and every way to possibly weasel my way out of this one. Not a single one of them seemed to work in a way that possibly one night she would say hello to my little friend if I didn't man up and snap the two latches. So I did.

I didn't know what I expected—blood dripping from the lid, a portal to hell with Satan himself ready to pull me through.

"What in the fuck?" Corey muttered next to me as we read the words typed on the sheet of paper.

Letmeout.Letmeout.Letmeout.Letmeout.Letmeout.

The paper had wound around the cylinder, and the words had been typed enough in some places they were just blurs.

"This is fucking insanity," I said.

I snapped the case shut, picked up the goddamned thing, and took it outside and placed it next to the garbage can.

When I walked back in, Corey was sitting at the table rolling a joint. I sat down at the table and watched her practiced ease as she did. I had no ability to roll one. I didn't mind a joint, but I had always preferred my bowl, until the vape pens arrived. She didn't say a word, but her hand shook as she raised the joint to her mouth. I grabbed the lighter and lit it for her.

She passed it to me and let out a cloud of smoke.

I took a deep drag and passed it back.

Corey looked at me before taking a hit. "Do you think that type-writer—"

I waited for her to finish, but she just shook her head and took another hit. "I don't know what to think. And I don't care. Tomorrow, the fucking thing will be in the back of the garbage truck, on the way to the dump," I said, reaching over and squeezing her hand.

"Should we call a priest?" she asked after a few rotations.

I almost laughed. Almost. What the fuck was happening? It was just a typewriter, a stupid impulse buy when I was manic. One which had proven to be a mistake from the very first mention.

"I don't know what I was thinking. I wasn't. There was no reason to buy a typewriter. I was fine writing on my phone. A matter of convenience for me, really. I could write anywhere the inspiration hit," I said softly. "It seemed like it was meant to be, you know? I had been thinking about one for a few weeks, and you know how my brain works; a simple idea becomes a driving force becomes an obsession. Then I saw the post. It seemed to be fate intervening."

Corey didn't say anything, but I saw her flinch a little when I said obsession. Did she think I had been obsessed with her as well? Was that why she never gave us a chance? Did she worry my brain told me I felt something for her the same way I needed the typewriter? Another desperate plug in the leaking hull, doing little to stem the tide slowly bringing my vessel lower and lower into the inky brine?

Was she right to feel that way, assuming she did? If so, why were we growing closer now?

I didn't speak any of this out loud. I was well aware I would eventually ruin this dream. It was sort of my superpower. I could ruin anything simply by falling into my patterns. Time and time again this was proven true. It was why I had loved her from afar, all the pain focused internally so I didn't hurt her. Fuck. This was one of the thoughts I refused to ever verbalize, the reality I never wished to create.

Corey squeezed my hand. "It is just a fucking typewriter, Wolfe. That's all. Pull yourself out of the spiral I can see spinning in your eyes."

I didn't speak; the ice-cold ball of roiling anxiety forcing its way up my esophagus prevented that. I nodded and took the joint.

"Now, would you look at that?" Corey said with an arched eyebrow.

I looked around the room, startled and expecting some fresh hell but saw nothing. I frowned. "What am I looking at?"

Corey smiled and nodded toward the red display on the stove. "It's after midnight."

I squinted, and the numbers came into focus—*12:03* flashed dimly. I looked at her, still confused. "It is. Thinking tomorrow is going to be a sick day."

Corey shook her head. "It is tomorrow. You know what that means?"

"We stayed up too fucking late?" I asked.

She laughed, and I felt a smile crack my dour face. "Nope."

I was truly confused at that point. "Then what does it mean, Corey?"

She leaned forward and kissed me. Softly. Then nibbled my bottom lip as she pulled back, smiling the half smile I had seen in my dreams so many fucking times I knew it better than my own face.

I didn't know what to do. I didn't want to move or speak or breath and break the spell. I didn't have to.

She leaned again and kissed me once more.

This time I wasn't surprised by it and joined in with intensity. I could taste the lingering smoke on her breath, the hint of oak-aged whiskey on her tongue, and the faint cherry of her lip balm. Her hand slipped onto my thigh as mine snaked around her, into her long, brown hair.

I stopped her as she reached higher, toward the eager bulge pressing tightly against my checkered pants, and breathlessly whispered into her ear, "I'm a gentleman, Corey. Remember?"

She grabbed my hand and placed it on her breast. I squeezed, feeling her hard nipple through the T-shirt. She moaned and kissed me harder. Somehow my hand got under her shirt, my callused fingers ran along her ribs to cup her breast again, taking her hard nipple between my thumb and forefinger and squeezing until she moaned into my mouth, pulling me closer. Her fingers rubbed the shape of my cock, sending shivers though me as she slowly traced the outline of the head.

I tried once again to stop her, half whining and half growling. "I said no sex."

She smiled at me and nodded. "Yes, you did." Then she pulled her shirt off and set both my hands on her breasts. "But that was yesterday. And you did such a good job being a gentleman you deserve a reward."

"And what do I get as my reward?" I asked. Before she could answer, I licked a lazy circle around her erect nipple, eliciting a deep, happy moan.

Corey stood up in front of me, and I shifted my hands to her hips, kissing her stomach. "Anything you want."

"Anything?" I asked as I unbuttoned her jeans and tugged them down her sexy legs.

"Everything," she whispered.

"Wolfe, hey, sweetie, time to wake up," I heard Corey calling to me.

I smiled without opening my eyes. "Ten more minutes."

The open-handed slap erased all feeling of being tired, compounded by my jerking back and finding my arms were bound around the wrists. I opened my eyes to see Corey standing over me, fully nude and glaring at me. I was in bed, naked as a jay bird, a length of rope around both wrists and run through the headboard of the bed. There was enough rope to allow some movement but not enough slack to let me reach either wrist to free myself.

I was confused and more than a little hungover. "I don't mind a little bit of roleplaying, Corey, but it's only right to get consent first. Hell, I haven't done anything like this before. Not that I mind, per se, I just wasn't expecting it."

She smiled. "Moving a little fast for you?"

"Maybe a little. And I have to pee," I said.

I heard noises in another room and frowned at her. "What's happening, Corey? I don't think I like this anymore."

She sat down on the side of the bed and patted my thigh. "Wolfe, I don't know how to tell you this without seeming like a bitch, so I'm just going to say it."

I cocked my head and waited for her to continue.

Ding.

"All you had to do was write, Wolfe. Hell, besides eating pussy, five-star performance by the way, it's your only talent. It was a perfect match, honestly," she began.

"My ability at cunnilingus and my writing?" I asked, confused.

Corey stared at me for a second and shook her head. "No, Wolfe. The cunnilingus was just a bonus. I meant your writing ability *and* the typewriter. A match made in, well, I guess hell. So much went into this perfect alignment coming to pass. But you stopped writing. And now you want to send the typewriter, *her* typewriter, to the dump. You understand she simply *cannot* allow that, don't you?"

I just stared at her. None of this made any sense.

"Now, she doesn't know if it's your being crazy letting you fight back or what. But she didn't like being put in the closet. Not one bit," Corey continued.

"Corey, baby, I don't know who you're talking about. What the fuck's going on?" I asked, close to begging.

She stared at me. "I mean Candace, the owner of that typewriter."

I laughed, but it froze in my throat as I saw her serious expression. "The Cock Slasher is dead, Corey. When the police stormed her cabin, all they found was her corpse."

She smiled and shook her head. "That wasn't all they found, now was it, Wolfe?"

Ding.

I didn't understand. I figured I must have been in one of those deep dreams where you can't differentiate from reality. None of this made any fucking sense. It had to be a nightmare. I thrashed against my restraints, but all it did was rub my wrists raw and make the headboard creak.

"Corey, this is crazy. Untie me. I don't understand the game you're playing at all, and it's beginning to piss me off. Please. We can have coffee and talk it over. I don't mind role playing, I just need a bit to get into it," I said, slightly out of breath.

Corey shook her head and patted my cheek. "Unfortunately for you, Wolfe, she needs you to finish the story. Neither of us have the talent she requires."

"Neither of us? Who else is part of this fucking madness?" I asked, nearly screaming. "This isn't fucking funny any longer, Corey. Let me loose."

She sighed. "Soon enough, Wolfe. But first, you have some writing to do."

"You shouldn't have fought her. She didn't like being ignored," Rob said from the doorway.

I stared at him. "Rob! Untie me! I don't know what this is, but it isn't fucking funny in the slightest."

"On that you're absolutely correct," Corey said. "This is no fucking joke."

Something slammed into the side of my head. At least twice. Then darkness took control.

"Wakey wakey, eggs and bakey, Wolfe," Corey whispered into my ear, stirring me from the onyx depths. Not fast enough, apparently, as she backhanded me quickly after.

The act of raising my head took far more out of me than I expected, and as the room came into focus, I discovered I was in the kitchen, chained and bound with duct tape and rope to a chair in front of that goddamned typewriter. After a bit of frantic struggles, I eventually relaxed and glared at Corey and Rob.

Corey smiled. "It has come to our attention that this entire situation was well under control before this one interfered. This all could have been so much easier. Faster. Efficient."

"What the fuck are you talking about?" I asked.

"You were already ours. It was nearly done," Rob said, frowning slightly. "The transfer was progressing."

"Shut the fuck up, Rob," I spat. "I was talking to Corey."

This time Rob backhanded me. I began raging against the restraints, petulantly and ineffectively.

"Finish the story, Wolfe. Don't fight it. We need you to finish what you began," Corey said sweetly.

"Write it your-fucking-self," I said angrily.

"They cannot," a voice whispered.

I looked at Corey and Rob, startled. "Who in the fuck was that? Who else do you have roped up in this little scheme of yours?"

Corey and Rob smiled, eerily at the exact same time, and their lips mouthed silently as the voice whispered once more. "Hello, Wolfe. Nice to finally introduce myself. My name is Candace, Candace Pfeiffer."

"Oh, for fuck's sake!" I shouted. "Is this some kind of fucking prank? Huh? Is it? You decide it was time to fuck with a stoned nutjob? Find the right moment to swoop in when I'm rundown with a cold and pretend to care about me? Was that the goal? Well, fuck both of you and this stupid little joke. Untie me and get the fuck out of here. I never want to see either of you again!"

Neither of them so much as flinched at my outburst, which irrationally pissed me off even more. I jerked so hard trying to free myself that I knocked the chair over. Something popped in my shoulder, and I let out a sharp cry of pain, then a second as Rob pulled the chair, and me, back up to its legs.

"Write!" the voice howled from within my skull, and simultaneously from Corey and Rob.

"Fuck off!" I yelled back.

"There was an easy way and a hard way we could have gone about doing this, Wolfe. You seem intent on doing it the hard way, don't you?" the voice asked.

"And what the fuck are you going to do about it? If you aren't the worst fucking prank ever, you're still just a voice whispering. I've had enough of this shit, you hear me? I have had enough!"

"I am already inside of you," the voice hissed.

I sighed and let my agony-filled skull hang for a second. "I don't even know who in the hell you're supposed to be."

"I already told you who I am, Wolfe," it whispered again.

I barked out a harsh approximation of a laugh. "The disembodied voice of the Cock Slasher? Oooh, scary."

My entire body went rigid against my restraints, as if supercharged by a bolt of lightning arcing from head to toe. I didn't know how long it lasted; it felt somewhere between forever and an eternity. I felt pain like I had never imagined possible. My mouth flooded with a metallic liquid, and I was sure I had bitten off the tip of my tongue. Between spasms, I could see Corey and Rob staring at me, expressionless as mannequins in a store window. Then, mercifully, there was only dark.

When I opened my eyes again, I was still tied up but no longer to my own kitchen chair. Instead, I was manacled to a wall somewhere I had never been before. I fought against the restraints and only succeeded in tearing up the skin around my wrists and ankles. Once the initial panic wore off, replaced with my original initial panic, I took stock of my surroundings. All there was around me was darkness and the scent of rusted metal. The wall I found myself bound too felt damp and flexed with my movements in a pliable yet unyielding way. The pain in my mouth throbbed as I let the bloody spit roll down my lip and into my beard. My stomach was filled with sour booze and too much blood to ever hope to calm.

The wall behind me went rigid suddenly, and I braced myself for whatever fresh hell was coming. There was a booming click, and I felt a gust of wind before I was sent flopping as a gigantic metal object, possibly a piston-driven sledgehammer, slammed into the wall fifteen feet to my right. I let out a scream of fright as I reverberated with the strike only to bounce once or twice. There was a slight ticking noise, and the entire wall shifted a few inches to the right. There was another thunderous metallic click, and the metal sledge slammed into the wall closer to my new position. Despite the insanity, it seemed familiar somehow.

"Hello, Wolfe," Candace Pfeiffer said, stepping out of the shadows to stand in front of me.

For a dead woman who seemed to be haunting my mind, she looked awfully real. I knew it was her the moment I saw her; hell, I imagine most people my age would have. She had been on the cover of every magazine, her face shown on every news channel.

"Ms. Cock Slasher," I said with a sarcastic nod.

Candace laughed and shook her head. "It's funny, getting a nickname like that from the press, as if that was all I had done. They focused on the bastards and their precious little, and most of them were nearly microscopic, dicks. You know why I mutilated their genitals?"

I nodded. "I do. They were rapists. You took away their weapon, their sense of self-worth. But you have to admit, The Sexual Assault Solver doesn't have the same ring to it, does it?"

She laughed again. "I guess it doesn't flow off of the tongue as well. But do you really think that's why they called me the Cock Slasher?" She paused, a look of savage fury passing over her face. "They called me that because it was demeaning. They sought to take away the message I so carefully tried to impart."

"Don't fuck with the mentally unstable?" I asked flippantly.

"Don't fuck with women," she answered coldly.

I laughed. "Lady, near as I can tell from my perch up here, plus taking into account the bullshit of the last few weeks, it's a tomato fucking potato situation. How about we skip the misunderstood serial killer act and go right to the crazy bitch who possessed not only a typewriter but the woman I have loved for a decade or three and one of my best friends? Or you could just let me go from this fucked up hellscape to continue being a bipolar asshole who writes shitty poetry on the side."

Candace sighed. "This wasn't supposed to happen. None of it was according to plan. For that, at least, I'm sorry."

I nodded as if any of this bullshit made sense. I shifted over to the left slightly. Click. The metal sledge struck again. I realized at that moment exactly where I was.

"Am I in the fucking typewriter?" I asked. "Look, I don't have the slightest fucking clue what's happening. I've never sexually assaulted anyone. Myself, maybe, after too many drinks and trying to tug one off, but I don't think I'm willing to press charges."

Candace smiled. "True. You're not my typical target. As much as I despise this, though, I knew I didn't have any choice in the matter. My work is far too important. Your friend, Robert, he and his dark side are more in line with my usual choice in prey."

"So why am I stuck to a fucking ribbon in hell's typewriter and not him?"

"Because he can't write, not the way you do. Not even close. And that's the key to this elaborate spell. It didn't have to be you, Wolfe. You're the tenth attempt to find someone with the necessary skills to complete the ritual," Candace explained.

"What ritual?" I asked as the next letter slammed into the ribbon. I remembered the Band-Aid on Corey's hand. "Is this why there are so many fucking needles?"

"Very good. Pretty obvious, but exactly right. I bled myself into the being of the typewriter with the help from an ancient tome I found on the internet. I knew my time was nearly up. I got sloppy, left too much evidence in my haste. I didn't know if it would work, but I was fucked either way. A lifetime in prison seemed like a waste. You can probably imagine my surprise when it did. You cannot, however, imagine my frustration at being trapped in this typewriter," she answered. "You will, though, soon enough."

"What the fuck is it you want from me?" I asked, furious and confused.

Candace laughed once more. "You're already doing it, Wolfe. The only thing you're good for. I just need you to write."

I jerked frantically, trying to free myself even slightly. "I won't do it! Fuck you, you crazy cunt!"

Candace reached up and patted my leg, and with a shake of her head, she whispered, "You already are, Wolfe, like I said. I just slowed things down so we could speak for a moment. To thank you for your sacrifice."

I glared at her. "Go fuck yourself."

Candace smiled. "I understand. Maybe we'll meet once more. Good-bye, Wolfe."

Candace, The Cock Slasher, vanished before I could spit at her. Then the ribbon began shaking and I heard the loud clicking speed up. The letters began to hammer against the ribbon, and the incremental sliding to the left became a smooth movement. No matter how much I fought, the hammers kept crashing closer and closer, until it crashed right next to me. I closed my eyes, afraid to witness the speeding metal, to acknowledge my own impending demise.

Ding.

Blue Caps
Will Suffer

To say Justin Cane knew where he was going would have been a gross misunderstanding of how Justin did anything. If there was a job to do, it had to be done in the correct mindset. Video games meant either weed or acid. Poker meant beer or pot. Music and movies could be either weed, acid, or shrooms, depending on the artist or flick. Going to get shrooms—that meant a handful of the fungi on the way, just to get started, and who knew how many freshies while on the search.

He parked at his usual spot, and man were the caps he'd swallowed on the ride kicking in at that point. He headed into the forest that lined the fields, and the tall, scrubby Florida pines swayed like giant brown stalks of rubber with fuzzy green hair on their limbs. They whistled at him as the breeze blew, and their long emerald locks begged to caress his head as he strolled below.

Later, he would remember reaching the edge of the field, the early morning sun shining a hazy, warm glow over the pastures that birthed those magic mushrooms and the glorious cow patties that hosted them. He would remember stepping into the tall grass, licking his lips, and knowing that the tripping gods were on his side as he spotted the first cap a few yards away.

Then he was in his car. It was almost night. And his basket was overflowing with the weirdest little treats he had ever left with.

Once at home, Justin dropped a quarter of his haul into a plastic storage container and the rest, save one, into his three food dehydrators. He plopped down on his couch, and windows shaded and the AC cranked, he raised the single mushroom cap in front of his face to examine it.

It was three inches across. and the top was solid blue. It was wide and thick like a blue ringer, and the bottom was bluish gray but with red at the base of its gills. It was the strangest-looking thing he had ever picked, and other than the three with bites missing from them, he would have never imagined trying the thing. There was a rule in mushroom picking: if you can't 100 percent identify it, you don't eat it. That was how people ended up dead from misidentified poisonous species. But the fact that he had three in his basket that he had obviously nibbled on, then collected more, and he had tripped his balls off so hard he couldn't remember the journey—and lived—meant there was something to these things.

But since he couldn't recall the trip, he couldn't describe it to people. And he was a salesman, after all, so he needed to be able to describe the high if he was going to unload them. He would have to remedy that failure.

Justin bent the cap until it ripped in half. The inner meat was purple, and dark-red liquid seeped from the break. He ripped one of the halves in two and popped the quarter cap into his mouth. He needed to feel this one slow and on its own, with no cross-contamination from other species, and at a low dose so he didn't blackout again.

He set the rest of the cap on the table as he chewed. There was a mild iron taste. It had a little grit, but not much, and after a few seconds, there was a sweetness to it. Based on the taste alone, he was pretty sure he could sell these, no problem.

It was only a few minutes later—way faster than he anticipated—when the walls began to melt.

While the walls of Justin's apartment were something of a dull gray, a color he was unable to paint over without his landlord's unattainable approval, the way the paint melted made them look more like a light blue—an almost glowing blue.

Lines of iridescence, like bright, shining liquid metal ran from the ceiling to the floor. They leaked from behind the window frames and seeped from the sides of the door jambs. The TV, which Justin had thought was off, showed a blue-tinted black-and-white video of a place Justin thought he recognized, but it took a minute for him to be sure.

He did know that place. He couldn't say why he didn't recognize it immediately other than the color and the fact that he hadn't been there in ten years.

It was the front yard of his childhood home in Fort Jeffrees, Florida, thirty minutes north of where he lived now. It was a hell on Earth he was just lucky enough to have escaped from, and why it was on his television he couldn't understand, other than... he was tripping.

He wanted to look away. He didn't want anything to do with memories from that place. They were all bad. They were the things of unending nightmares and therapy, not good trips. But he couldn't turn. He could only focus on the front door as it came closer and closer, as the broad wooden surface opened. He was thrust inside, the smells of his mother's potpourri and his father's overpowering aftershave flooding his senses.

Then the door slammed.

He spun, taking in the living room. He was there. He was somehow inside his memory, no longer in his own apartment, and he was short—the size of a child. He was actually inside the blued, muted version of his childhood home, and with no explanation for how this had happened, his fingers trembled. What if he was stuck there?

Justin was immediately flooded with a sense of shame. He had done something wrong, probably more like a thousand things wrong, and he was about to be held accountable for them all. He had done so much since he moved out—and so much before that he could never admit to—and his parents would have killed him for any of it if they could. There would be blame, and there would be fear. Then there would be punishment.

"No, no, no, no, no." He went to the door and tried the knob. He knew it wouldn't work, and he was right. The knob was as stiff as a statue, refusing to turn. Just like his days of terror as a child, as the impending doom of his parents' wrath was inevitable then, it was again.

"Justin, is that you?" Mom called from the kitchen.

"Get in here." It was Dad, and he sounded pissed.

The kitchen was ahead, through the dining room and to the left. Justin's room, where he wanted to escape to, was on the right. But they would find him there; they always did. They would drag him into the kitchen, and he would be punished.

"They know what I did," he whispered. The waves of guilt rolled over his body, guilt he had avoided in all but his darkest thoughts over the past ten years. It was a creeping thing, a slimy blackness that left irrevocable traces on everything it touched. He had tried to bury it in his mind, forget that the event ever happened, but there was no running from yourself. The darkness always catches up. The memories could live forever. And back then, there was no running from Mom and Dad.

But this wasn't *really* then, was it?

"Just-in!" Dad called. "I said get in here."

His legs went to jelly. His stomach was a boiling bowl of slime waiting to erupt through his mouth.

He couldn't face Dad. He just couldn't.

He took off to the right, toward his room. He felt his rear end warm, knowing the beating he had in store. He felt his insides hollow and melt the way they did when Mom had her turn, tearing him apart with words, with blame, with stories of how he was the root of all his parents' problems, from money to her failing health.

He reached the door to his room and grabbed the knob. It wouldn't turn. It was just like the front, frozen in place and impassable.

"Justin! I called you!" Dad was even louder. The floor shook with his footsteps, and they were coming nearer.

"Over here," Myra whispered.

Justin spun. His little sister stood inside her bedroom door, only exposing her face and using the slab of wood like a shield.

"Come on." Her eyes darted up the hall, looking for Dad. "He's coming."

Of course he was. The man was lazy, never rising from his chair even to look for a job, but if a chance to punish one of his kids came along, he would find the motivation to move. He could pull all the energy out of the ether he would need to conquer a small nation if it meant he had a chance to *teach his boy a lesson.*

Myra stepped back, and Justin darted through the door. She hurried to her window and unhooked the latch as Justin closed the bedroom door quickly and quietly.

"Go on." She had the window up.

The sight of the outside world flooded Justin with hope. If he could make it through, plant his feet on grass, he could run. He would run back to his apartment and never come near this place again, like he had done ten years ago.

He took the windowsill in both hands, preparing to lift himself up.

Myra stood there watching, her small face tense.

Dad pounded on the door. "I know you're in there, Justin. Hiding behind your little sister? That's disgusting."

Myra was wringing her hands. She was going to get spanked for this—maybe worse. Justin might escape his father's terror, but it would only be at the expense of letting the man loose on her.

"Come on," he told her. "You're coming with me."

The door shook in its frame as Dad beat on the slab of hollow wood.

"But they'd be mad," Myra said.

"They can't punish you anymore. Come on." He held out his hand.

She glanced at the door as a crack shot down the trim to the right.

"Now!" Justin took her hand and pulled. She followed his direction up and through the window. He lifted himself and put one leg through as the door burst in.

Dad was bigger than Justin remembered. He was bulging and bald, his chest heaving as they locked eyes with each other. Dad rushed at the window, and Justin dove outside.

He felt the heat of Dad's hands as the man's enormous fingers swiped at his arm.

Justin reached the ground with a thump and scurried to his feet. He took Myra's hand and led her. They ran into the street, and Justin could feel the anger in Dad's voice as he yelled for them to come back.

Never. He never would. Not willingly, anyway.

It was the next morning when Justin's alarm sounded from his phone on the coffee table that he realized he had blacked out again.

He understood a few things then: the table only held a crumb of that mushroom—he had eaten the rest during the night; he was still alive, meaning it really wasn't poisonous; and he was hungrier than he could remember being in his entire life.

With a groggy head, Justin wandered to the kitchen, started a cup of coffee, and checked the fridge for anything breakfast-like. There was a single half of a stale English muffin and enough jelly if he scraped at the jar for a solid minute.

It would have to work. He was too slow to do anything other than that this morning, not if he was going to be on time for his job.

Coffee and the half muffin in hand, he sat at his dining room table and tried to figure out what happened last night. He remembered the walls melting and the TV turning blue, and then it was a blank. Again. Those were definitely some strong caps.

He decided to eat a few bites and see how it did at work. He was just running drive-thru, after all, so it wasn't that hard. And he didn't really need the job, it was more of a front to make his drug money look legitimate, so no worries if he got fired.

This time he used a butter knife and sliced a cap in half, sticking the other half and a couple whole tops into a plastic baggie and stuffing it in his pocket for later.

By the time he reached the door, the paint was coming off the walls in metallic blue streams. He reached for the knob and jumped back as he saw who was standing beside him.

"Myra?" She looked the same at three feet tall as the last time he had seen her. Her face was light blue, reminding him of a fact he couldn't grasp that slipped further away the harder he tried to pin it down. When *was* the last time he had seen her? "What are you doing here?"

"I'm going with you to work today, remember?"

He did. She sometimes went to work with him and played in the Kidz Zone while he was working. You would have thought it might cause a commotion, a little blue girl playing in the ball pit and using the slide, but no one had ever said a word about her.

"Yeah." He nodded. It was good to see her. He had missed her.

Justin parked at the far end of the Rockin' Rodeo's parking lot, where all the employees were supposed to park. Myra immediately jumped out of the passenger seat and raced across the lot, yanking the door open and rushing into the Kidz Zone.

The way her long black hair bounced as she ran made Justin smile. He didn't know why. Thinking about his kid sister always did that, as if she was made of nothing but joy and that was what radiated whenever she was around. Ever since they were young it was that way. He guessed her attitude was why no one cared that she hung out there. In some ways, it was like no one even noticed she was around but him.

He was glad to step inside. It always felt too bright outdoors when he was tripping, and he was really feeling the blue caps.

Roger, the assistant manager, stared at Justin as he crossed the store and made his way behind the counter. The guy glared at his watch as if some magic would make whatever it said imprint into Justin's brain.

At the fries and bagging station, Scott was scooping up a large onion rings. He nodded at Justin and tapped his nose. He wanted something.

Justin ignored the lengthening tip of Scott's nose, which looked like it could fall off and drip into the onion ring carton. He nodded back and continued to the drive-thru window, where he waited for Nat to pass an order to a customer so he could clock in.

When she turned and saw him, she smirked, her hip shifting to the left. It was subtle, but Justin knew it was for him. Ever since a month ago when they closed the store together and had sex on the prep table, her flirting game had accelerated.

He smirked back. He liked her, really liked her, not enough to accept her as a girlfriend, though. It wasn't her that was holding up his decision; it was that his independence was more important than the idea of settling down, even if the root of his resistance was from fear of both constraint and rejection. Nonetheless, she was warming her way into his heart, changing his mind, bit by bit.

"You are fucked up," she said, leaning on the counter and blocking his access to the register.

He didn't feel that fucked up. Sure, the walls were quivering and her eyes bulged a bit from her face as she spoke, the sounds of the fryer, the fans, and the sizzling on the grill all made it feel like he was in a dryer, getting tossed in circles as they had their conversation, but that was like so many other days. It wasn't special other than the blue tinges on the corners of every surface and the teal hue that lay over the world.

He felt the baggie of blue caps in his pocket and the urge to pop another bite into his mouth. "I'm fine. Just another day."

She rolled her eyes. "Your pupils are huge. Do not look Roger in the eye."

He chuckled. She shook her head and backed away from the register.

Justin stepped up to the touchscreen POS system. The display looked like an electronic mouth with a gray border and a wide, curved area for him to tap. He moved his fingers quickly, a worry in the back of his mind that it may bite if he tempted it with his flesh for too long.

He entered his employee number and his passcode, tapped Clock In, and was ready to take the reins from Natalie.

She looked at him doubtfully. "So, you got this?"

Roger watched them from the front counter.

Scott read the monitor at the fry station and started bagging the next order.

"Don't I always?"

She turned and headed to the front, taking the register beside Roger. A car pulled up outside, its order taken by the AI program at the drive-up menu. Justin read the total from his screen and opened the sliding window.

Humid air hit Justin in the face. "That'll be twenty-three fifty-eight."

The guy in the driver's seat was twice as wide as Justin, and the large mustache on his lip looked like a big fat caterpillar squirming around and brushing up against his nose. Someone was in the passenger seat, but Justin couldn't see more than their legs. What made him pause in place as the man handed his card over was what he saw in the back seat.

He had to wonder if there was a new trend with kids, because the small face he saw looking up at him was as blue as his sister's. While he hadn't asked Myra why she was so blue, he had assumed it was something she had chosen. People didn't just turn blue for no reason, after all, and she acted perfectly fine. It had to be a choice.

He accepted the card, though it was hard to take his eyes off the kid. The little guy stared at Justin like he had a giant booger hanging from his face or something. And those eyes, they were glowing, even in the daylight. How did a kid get eyes like that?

He swiped the card and made two drinks, handing back the card and the cups. A minute later, Scott was there with their food, a pair of burgers and a pair of fries.

Nothing for the kid? Whatever.

He handed the big man the bag and watched the kid as they drove away. The little guy's face seemed to melt in streaks of cold blue as the car pulled into traffic.

"What the fuck," Justin whispered to himself. He had seen some weird, even gross, shit on shrooms before, but there was something about that kid, the way it stared at him, that made him feel hollow, somehow frozen inside.

"How 'bout it?" Scott asked.

Justin spun and found his coworker an inch away. "What the fuck, man?"

"Well?"

"Well, what?" Had they been talking?

"Do you have anything on you? I can tell you're tripping balls."

Was he? He didn't even eat a full cap. He didn't think he was that far out of it.

Sweat ran down the side of Scott's face. It glistened in the bright lights. His lips seemed to wobble as he waited for an answer, and there was a twitch in his ear that Justin didn't think he had ever noticed before.

He felt the plastic baggie in his pocket without even moving. Yes, he had some, and he decided it was probably a good idea to get a second opinion on them before he started selling them.

Over the following forty-five minutes, Justin took the half-cap left over from home and slipped it to Scott, Scott flipped it into his mouth and gobbled it down, and the tint of the entire restaurant gradually became deeper and deeper blue.

As far as the blue went, it was no longer just the shine of beads of water or the walls' continuous lines of sweat. It was everything. All of the walls, the soda fountain, the register, the counter, the ceiling. It was like something had taken the world (well, most of it) and covered it with one of those gels that they put on light bulbs in the theater. The exception was the people. They actually seemed pinker and more flushed, other than Myra, who he peeked in on every once in a while over in the play area. She was still a Smurf, just like that weird kid in the car.

As far as Scott went... yeah, that guy was definitely tripping. He stared at the fries as they cooked, watching the bubbles encircle the individual potato slices. He salted them and leaned to the side as salt crystals tumbled, as if the secrets of the universe may reveal themselves within those tiny rocks. Justin even went over and tapped him on the shoulder when he started talking to the monitor that displayed the orders.

But Scott could get through it—at least Justin thought he could. It wasn't the first time Justin had *shared* at work. And Nat helped. When she needed something from Scott, she let him know, and it was working out.

Or Justin thought it was working out.

A gray Honda some-fucking-thing SUV came to his window. He read the total from his point-of-sale display and leaned out into the thick

Floridian humidity.

"Nine fifty-three," he told the driver.

The woman in the car stared at him like he had a second nose on his face or something, and all Justin could think was, *I'm not staring at you as weird as you look.*

Her skin was blue. Her eyes were blue—like, the entire things, not just the parts that were supposed to be colored. Her lips were blue, and blue puss dripped from the corners of her mouth.

Justin was sure now he didn't like this fad. It was creepy. Her eyelids were drooping from her sockets, and her mouth seemed to be splitting at the seams. He wasn't sure if it was from the make-up or whatever treatment people got to make themselves look that way, but it was just sickening. He would have to talk to Myra about it later on.

But then again, he thought, *maybe I'm just tripping.*

"Nine fifty-three, please," Justin repeated.

She raised her hand, and for a moment, Justin thought she was handing over a card or some cash, but it was empty. Her finger extended, and her strange eyes went even wider.

A scream followed. Then another from inside.

What the fuck? Justin spun around. He was definitely in an altered reality now, because what he saw couldn't have been real.

"I'll help you!" Scott screamed, one of his hands in the fryer. Steam rose around his wrist as it cooked, and vapor sizzled away from his flesh. He reached deeper, and his fingers sorted through the fries as if he was looking for something. "Hold on!"

Nat shrieked. She darted from the register and grabbed Scott's shoulders, pulling him away from the fryers.

"No! I have to save him!" Scott's hand was red and blistered, swollen, and dripping with oil. His nails hung from his fingertips, bloated, angled outward, and ready to fall away.

"Scott, stop it!" She pulled him to the counter, and his elbows went back, thudding into her ribs. She let loose and doubled over, and Scott raced back to the fryer.

He grabbed the basket and yanked it out, throwing half-cooked fries and searing oil onto Roger, who seemed almost as stunned as Justin as the sizzling wetness splashed his eyes and face. With both palms together like a diver, Scott leaned forward, shoving his hands, arms, and face into the open pool of hot, bubbling oil.

"No!" was all Justin could get out, and then he froze. He didn't understand what he saw next.

Scott actually disappeared into the oil.

The fryer only held like five gallons, but somehow, he vanished as if he had dove into the mouth of a skinny pool.

"Scott!" Nat screamed, and came to the edge of the fryer. She looked inside, covering her mouth, and her other hand reached out, trembling. She wanted to touch something with that hand but refused to, either from fear or disgust.

Tears ran down her cheeks. She turned to Justin.

Justin's mouth hung slack. He walked toward the fry station.

The woman in the drive-thru was howling, "Send an ambulance!"

Roger was sobbing, his hands hovering over his burning face, afraid to touch it.

When he reached the fryer, Justin looked inside.

He wasn't sure what he expected to see, but it wasn't this: there was a small blue child at the bottom of the fryer. Just lying there all alone. As if someone had laid it to rest and then started cooking on top of it. It may have been a boy, but he wasn't sure. The skin was peeling off and blue liquid was swirling from the body, mixing with the amber oils but not quite combining. Scott was nowhere to be seen.

Justin's mouth was shaking. His heart was on a rampage as he tried not to think of what the fryer could do to human flesh. He had to back away.

He put a hand on Nat and pulled her with him. She shouldn't see that, even if she already had.

Sirens rang in the distance. They were getting louder.

"Nat..." Before Justin could say another word, oil erupted from the fryer. A wave of hot golden fire splashed over the ground, the entire fry station, and nearly onto Justin.

The employees watched, the drive-thru watched, the customers at Nat's register watched, all in horror, as a person too red and bleeding and deformed from loose skin leaped from inside the fryer. He gurgled and rolled, landing on the floor with an audible splat. His skin split apart as his wet flesh shattered on the dark-red tile.

He didn't say another word. He made sizzling sounds and hissing noises, and Justin saw what was in his arms—the cooked blue child.

Roger wept. He looked at the horror on his floor and he shook, either with sadness or pain, Justin wasn't sure which.

Nat leaned forward and puked. It slapped the floor in the puddle of cast-off oil.

Customers everywhere yelled with disgust and fear.

The sirens were almost there.

Justin's heart may have been pounding, and his mind may have been fried, but he was aware enough to know what he had to do. He jumped over the counter and ran to the Kidz Zone, grabbing Myra by the hand and pulling her out the door.

She didn't argue. It was like she already knew. The cops would know. They'd know he was tripping, that Scott was tripping, and that he had given Scott the drugs. It didn't matter that none of the rest of what happened didn't make sense. The fact that there were drugs involved—Justin's drugs—would mean he went to jail for it.

As they sped away, Justin couldn't help but think about his parents' place. He knew that somehow this whole tragedy started there.

Justin felt soaked through with dread. The cops were coming. Scott was dead. Nat probably wouldn't talk to him again. The road ahead spread out like a vast white plain and shrank to a narrow path as the cars on either side of him seemed to skirt closer then farther in a game of bumper cars he didn't choose to play.

The events around him were dragging pieces of him away. They were tearing him apart and taking chunks of his soul with them. He feared there would be nothing left when it was done, nothing but the worthless center of hate and despair at his core, nothing but the shameless good-for-nothing person his parents had molded him into.

He was ten years old, and Myra was screaming. He burst from his room, across the hall, and stood frozen once he saw what was in hers.

Dad, the hulk of a man, sat on her bed. The waves of hate and frustration radiated from him, the anger over what he perceived his life should have been if he hadn't been saddled with his whore of a wife and these ungrateful kids. His hand was high, belt tight in his grip. Myra was lying over his knees, bare-bottom up in the air and red from the first of what would be too many strikes.

She howled, her face just as red, wet from tears, and her eyes sealed shut in terror.

There was nothing Justin could do.

He wished he was a hero, He-Man, The Dark Knight, anyone who could stop injustice. He was just a little kid, small for his age, with scars on his own rear from being in the same position his sister found herself in at that moment.

Helplessness. It ate into his gut as Myra screamed and the belt came down. He was worthless. He was nothing. What kind of a boy couldn't protect his little sister? The world was bad and unfair. His father was a monster. He was a weakling, an ant.

He couldn't watch, but he couldn't move.

His eyes found a shelf on the other side of the room. Tiny blue figurines stood frozen in dance, celebrating something Justin had never taken the time to understand, though Myra had watched the show a thousand times in the living room while singing along. Their faces were pure and bright. They had love, peace, and harmony between them. Justin wanted so much to be there, in the middle of that dance, where the black horrors of his father's rage and regret couldn't reach him.

He didn't hear his sister or his father shouting at him to go away. He only felt the sting when the belt snapped across his chest, knocking him back into the hall.

He ran away, like he was running now.

He fled from Dad, leaving her to wail through the walls—leaving Nat crying and Scott dead.

The sun blazed too hot through the windshield. Was he melting, as the world was around him?

He cranked the air conditioning and turned into Little Jimmy's apartment complex. He drove around the back, where his car couldn't be seen from the main road, and parked under the canopy of a large date palm. The shade was instantly soothing.

He glanced at Myra. She smiled up at him with an innocence that melted his heart.

"Come on. We'll be safe at Little Jimmy's."

Little Jimmy opened the door and looked down at Justin. At nearly six foot six, he was as tall as the doorway. At 250 pounds, he swallowed the opening with his body. While he may have held the nickname Little, it didn't come from his bulk—that was more of a high school thing after the giant was spotted in the showers and his... manhood... didn't quite seem to fit the girth of the rest of him. After the nickname was passed around school, followed by a series of bloody beatings administered by "Little" Jimmy, people stopped using it in front of him—but it didn't die. Instead, it lived on in the whispers.

His expression turned from a skeptical *who's at my door* to hopeful as he set eyes on Justin.

"Shit, just the man I wanted to see," Jimmy's voice bellowed into the parking lot. "Come on in."

Tina, Jimmy's girlfriend, was on the couch, and her face lit up as Justin and Myra entered. She set her phone on the coffee table and opened the drawer underneath it. "Welcome, Mr. Candyman." It was a name she had been trying to make stick for years, but it had never really caught on.

Justin simply smiled and sat on the end of the couch as she pulled out a pipe and packed it with florescent green buds.

Myra sat on the floor beside him.

Little Jimmy took the big recliner, leaned forward, and rubbed his hands together, watching Tina start on the bowl. "Did you get any?"

The flare of Tina's light was too bright, bathing the room in an orange glow. A second later, the beige apartment was back to dripping drops of blue oil from its popcorn nubs. Its pictures were coated in azure shine, and their subjects danced in their frames. A surfer rode a never-ending wave, and Justin could smell the sea. Snow came down on a distant mountain, and the clouds swirled around the peak.

It took Justin a second to realize Jimmy's question was aimed at him. "Any what?"

"Dude, you said you were going shrooming yesterday."

He did, didn't he? He said that and then he went. There were blue ones in his pocket. He pulled out the baggie and looked down at it.

"That's what I'm talking about!" Jimmy yelled and reached. "Can I see?"

Tina offered Justin the bowl.

"Yeah." Justin took it and glanced down at Myra. She was glued to the television. There was a show on the screen, frolicking blue people that reminded him of the Smurfs if they were all grown up and (dancing on her shelf) tall instead of mushroom sized.

Jimmy reached and took the baggie. Tina leaned in and looked too.

Justin flicked the lighter and hit the bowl. The walls crowded closer and the air thickened.

"Why are they blue?" Tina asked. "Are you sure these are safe?"

Were they safe? Justin had to think about that.

The blue people sang. It was a nice song. Myra hummed along.

"Look at him," Jimmy said. "He's on them, isn't he?"

"How much, Candyman?" Tina licked her lips.

Justin had heard that song before. Probably a thousand times in his living room or seeping through the walls of Myra's bedroom. He didn't hear himself say, "You can split one. It's cool." He didn't think about what had happened to Scott. As he hit the pipe, that previous horrible event felt like it had happened a decade ago.

Jimmy opened the bag and took out the largest one. He was a big guy, after all; he needed a bigger dose than other people. That was the same logic he used when he cut the thing and ate three-quarters of it, giving Tina the smallest chunk.

Justin wasn't sure what happened over the next hour. He heard things, but they didn't quite sink in. There were noises from the bedroom. The TV people continued to sing. Myra joined them at times. There was stomping and screaming. He hit the pipe again.

It was the streaming blue blood over the TV screen that caught his attention.

Justin was trembling. This wasn't right. None of it could be real. None of it. It didn't make sense.

But the room was how it was, and after watching for five minutes, after they kept doing it, the fear in his chest didn't drain. The beating of his racing heart didn't subside.

He glanced down at Myra. She smiled at the TV. None of it seemed to bother her.

Three blue children tore pieces from Little Jimmy's naked corpse. He was on the floor between the couch and the bedroom. The miniature monsters held them up curiously to their faces, sniffed each one, and tossed them across the floor as if they had yet to find the piece of gore they were looking for.

Tina sat with her back to the wall. She held a blue baby in her hands, chunks missing from its flesh, and her mouth was stuffed with blue meat. Her eyes were wide and her chest was still. Justin wasn't sure how it killed her, but it had happened before he noticed.

He reached down slowly, taking Myra by the hand. They stood and inched toward the door.

He was quiet and prayed Myra would be too. The things hadn't been interested in them so far, but he didn't know why or if that would change.

The slurping sound of their fingers in Little Jimmy's flesh was all he could hear. He felt the carpet sliding under his shoes. He felt the stifling air—the AC must have turned off. He felt his sweat running down his face and his heart slamming into his lungs, threatening to take up his entire chest and suffocate him if he didn't move faster, if he didn't save them now.

They reached the door, and he opened it slowly, quietly, the squeak of the hinges like daggers in his ears.

As soon as the crack was wide enough, he darted through, dragging Myra, racing to the car. The blue things were watching him. He felt them behind him, but whether it was three feet or thirty he wasn't sure.

He jerked open his door and hurried Myra in and across the seat. He slammed it behind him and cranked the engine. He backed up and sped from the complex without looking back.

There was only one safe place left that he could think of.

The sun was setting behind Justin. Orange light made his eyes twitch as he crossed town, heading east until he turned onto Nat's street.

Natalie lived in a neighborhood lined with duplexes and townhouses, the classier side of rentals in town, or so the owners tried to impart despite the fact that there were at least two visits from the cops each day to the neighborhood. Sometimes it was a domestic disturbance.

Sometimes it was a noise complaint. It was almost always drug or alcohol related.

The street made Justin think of his parents' place. They were the same style of fifties/sixties era homes with jalousie-slanted windows and a mix of brick and stucco exteriors. The queen palms that lined the roads were tall and tried to team up with the short, wide sagos around the houses to convince visitors of the neighborhood's classic Floridian charm. Justin thought it almost worked if you didn't look too long—if you didn't catch the bars on half the windows or that almost every car windshield blinked with its own alarm, if you weren't around for the pops at night that made you wonder doubtfully if it was from fireworks or gunshots.

He blinked, and the street was blue. He wasn't on Nat's road anymore; he was on his parents'.

"*No.*" He shook his head. He hit the brakes and jerked the wheel to turn around. It didn't stop the car. He was pulling up the driveway to his childhood home. He was out of the car and moving toward the front door, not walking, not willingly carrying himself, but almost floating in a smaller body, his childhood self.

The door opened, and he hovered inside.

"No." This time it was a whisper because he didn't dare call his father's attention down upon himself or let his mother know he was back.

He hovered across the entry, across the living room. The afternoon light was draining, and the farther he moved over the carpet, toward the room he may have feared the most, the darker the home became.

Dad was at the kitchen table reading the paper. Mom was at the stove, stirring something. The air smelled like Tuesday night, pork chops and green beans, but under a wet, moldy odor. Myra sat quietly, hands on her lap, watching Justin enter. Blue blood was splattered across the walls.

Something ran across the room. It was short and fast and disappeared into the darkness. It happened again, appearing as a blurry blue trail until it vanished under the table.

Justin froze in fear. What if it alerted his father?

Justin wasn't supposed to be there. He was supposed to be in school, but today he had slipped out of class, Myra on his mind. It was the day of her surgery, and he had to see her before it happened. He had to talk her out of doing it, regardless of what Mom and Dad said. It was going to go badly, and he knew it.

The newspaper shifted, its crinkling sound slicing through Justin's nerves and jolting his heart ever faster within his chest.

He reached toward his sister. Her hand went up, waving him off. He was being dumb and pressing his luck, and she was trying to warn him up until Dad's paper dropped and his eyes locked onto Justin.

His eyes were gleaming sapphires, shining in the dark room within his mashed-up face of ripped blue and dark, indigo blood running down the side of his head. (Justin had done that. He wasn't sure how, but he had done it.) Those sapphires locked onto Justin. His face stretched, dripping from his skull, and the wet crimson muscles below peeked through.

Dad growled.

Mom turned, the frying pan in her hand and the corner of her skull collapsed inward. She walked over to Myra. She pushed the top of Myra's head back and pulled the child's mouth open.

"Stop!" Justin saw it all happening in his head before a drop of oil left the pan. It crushed him.

The sizzling liquid ran from the edge of the skillet into Myra's mouth. She screamed, but she didn't move from beneath the waterfall of super-heated butter and pork drippings that boiled her lips and tongue and scorched the inside of her cheeks as it ran down her throat.

The scent in the room changed. Justin could smell her blood as he drifted closer. The searing butter was cooking it, and he was forced to breathe it in.

One pork chop tumbled from the pan, then another. They clogged the opening of Myra's small mouth, and two more toppled out. With the pan empty and the girl's face burning, Mom turned the skillet upward and used the handle to shove the meat into Myra's maw, down into her throat. She punched and stuffed and shouted as she did it. The depression in her head bulged and bled.

"You're not good enough." It was Mom's shrill voice, the one that only came out when it was time to hear the daily dissertation of how ungrateful and sloppy and lazy her children were. "When I was your age, I helped my mother from dawn to dusk. I took care of my father and my family. I got A's on all of my schoolwork. I knew how to be appreciative and do my chores without complaint."

Blood and grease spattered from Myra onto her mother. She gagged and shuddered.

Mom's blue skin slipped from her face and hung from strands of muscle. It came free and flopped onto the floor.

"You pieces of trash. You useless piles of garbage. You mistakes. You should have never been born."

Tires screeched, and Justin's car thumped. He was shaken up and down, and there was a loud thud as metal crunched and the car slammed into something solid.

The front of his vehicle was embedded in the corner of Nat's house. He had hopped the curb and ran across the grass.

"Fuck."

The gloomy world outside bled in lines of dark-blue blood. It dripped from the sky—was it raining?—and it covered swaths of the windshield.

"What the fuck?" His head was ringing. Had he hit it in the wreck? He glanced to see if Myra was okay. She wasn't there.

"Myra?" Where had she gone? Panic raced through his bloodstream.

He may have been hoping to elude the cops already, but this really put him on edge. His sister was everything. He didn't know what he would do if something happened to her.

Justin flung open the door and got out. Blue blood was all over the car, and as he looked around for his sister, he saw why.

Nat was on the roof. She was crumpled and twisted, her arm folded backward in the middle of her forearm, and her head was cracked open and hanging over the windshield. The thick blue was coming from there, streaming from the holes in her face and scalp.

She gasped and twitched.

Shivers ran over his skull, down his arms and legs. He had done this. *Fuck.* He had been driving all fucked up, and he had run right through her, tossing her up there.

Tears ran. He remembered her laughing and joking as they worked together. He saw the lines on her face as she smiled and felt the joy when her fingers ran over his cheek. He remembered holding her tight in the back of the store and wanting to take her home with him, wanting to make them official and have her around forever, but being afraid he would ruin it—because he would have.

He would have turned into his old man. She would have turned into his mother. They would have hated their kids for making them into prisoners of their own creations, and it would have become their own Hell.

He couldn't have done that to her. He wanted her so badly, but he wasn't safe.

And look what he had done.

There was a tugging on his arm. It was hard to pull his eyes away from the devastation, but he had to.

Myra pointed into the car. They had to go.

"No." His chest trembled. He wanted to sit down and die right there.

There was no reason for going on after this. He was destroying everything.

But there was Myra. There was her little blue face, and he had to get her out of there. He couldn't let the cops arrive and take her away.

Justin shook as he lifted Nat's now-stilled body from the car. Her blood had turned red, and it drenched his shirt. His tears left faint streaks on her face as they poured.

He set her by the side of the house.

Myra was in the passenger seat.

He climbed inside the car and raced away, not knowing where else there was to go.

Justin nibbled something. It was earthy and sweet.

He remembered sitting by Myra's bed. She didn't want to get up and play. It seemed all she wanted to do was sleep.

He nudged her, and she pushed him weakly. They laughed quietly. They lay there. They didn't say much.

The taste was heavy on his tongue.

There was sadness in her bed. There was a wish for hope and a dark despair that it would never come.

She was so tired. It was unlike her.

They played every day before then. They were the life of the house, even if they were mostly confined to either her room or his. There were stories and forts and games and laughter, and now there was only this, this sickness that seemed to consume more than just her body, but her entire being.

She wasn't her.

Myra wasn't this tired girl, too weak to move more than a few inches without her breath leaving and her heart spasming. She was a ball of energy who drove him toward joy through laughter and imagination. And even that seemed sick.

It seemed every few minutes she was napping. In the middle of the day, she was napping like a baby. In the middle of a conversation, she was dozing off, and the idea that could have bloomed into a joke or a long whimsical tale that kept them busy for hours with effervescent wonder on their lips died in the silence between her soft hungering breaths.

It wasn't right. It wasn't fair. She deserved so much better than he could do for her, what Mom and Dad could do for her. And his hands were tied.

There were streetlights. There was that taste again, grainy and damp and just a bit sweet. There was a sense that time was going so slowly, yet it was not on his side. There was never enough.

He was on the edge of her bed, and she was there. And then she wasn't. There should have been more for her. There should have been a lifetime of joy for them to share once they were older and out of the house, past the bonds of Mom and Dad, out from under the umbrella of their screams and rants and anger.

The headlights of passing cars were blinding, but he didn't stop. He wasn't sure what it meant, but he wouldn't stop. She was too tired, and she needed help. He was too scared he would get caught, and he was too scared to lose her.

The garage was right in front of his face, and he slammed on the brakes. The car skidded to a stop, and his head bashed into the steering wheel. Lightning burst from the bridge of his nose and hot wetness ran down his face. It tasted like blood.

Panic. *Is Myra okay?*

He spun to the passenger seat. She was gone! He searched the car. She wasn't there. She had just been there. *What happened?*

Movement outside the passenger window.

There she was. She was slow and wobbling toward the home's entrance. She needed his help.

Justin threw open his door and hurried around the car. He passed the edge of the garage and saw her by the front door. She was reaching for the knob, her hand moving slowly—had she been injured when he slammed on the brakes? Was this his fault? Again?

Her hand didn't reach the knob. It fell as her legs gave out and she drifted toward the ground. He ran, his arms outstretching. Her head was dropping toward the hard concrete and he rushed to intercept it.

Not again!

He scooped his arms under her body as her head slammed into the cement. There was a crack, and the sound sent shivers through his flesh. Blood leaked onto the ground, onto his arms, into the grass.

There was so much. It didn't make sense. It was running from her little blue head onto a world of muted darkness, and the red was blinding.

He needed help. He needed help now.

He lifted her up and took the last step toward the door. He didn't ring the bell or knock; he pushed through into the house and screamed, "Help her!"

He wasn't twenty, he was ten. He wasn't rushing to get her into the house, he was by her bed, pulling her covers back and sliding his arms below her body to pick her up.

She couldn't have been that heavy. She was so small.

He lifted and strained. She didn't make a sound other than a light groan. She clutched the blue figurine in her left hand. Her right held tight to her left.

Her breathing was so slow. Her heart was barely beating. Justin didn't care if Mom and Dad said the doctors couldn't do anything, if her condition was incurable, if they refused to call an ambulance to get her to the hospital for better medicine. Someone had to do something.

He turned toward the door.

If he could get her out of the house... If he could get her to the bus stop... He could get her to the hospital himself, and they would save her.

His arms burned as he crossed her room in the darkness. Only the soft blue light from her night light lit the gloom.

There was shuffling behind the toys. There was something moving in the darkness.

He didn't care. He would ignore it. He had to get her out of there.

He made it to the door and leaned through the opening. It was dark in the rest of the house. All he could see were the blue eyes at the end of the hall, a small blue child skittering away, hurrying out of his sight.

Justin felt her soft breath on his neck as he crept from the room. His fingers burned. His legs felt weak.

How was she so heavy? She was such a little thing.

He carried her down the hallway and peeked into the living room. Myra let out another moan. It made him clutch her tightly, praying she would be quiet long enough for him to do this.

The room was empty. The TV was on, and blue light covered the walls as it flickered from scene to scene.

He pulled her against his chest as he walked to the front door. He held her dearly, remembering every hug she had ever given him, the love in her eyes as she took her big brother into her grip and gave all that love to him, her squeeze as the messenger, telling him she would never let go.

But she was. She was letting go. Whether it was her choice or not, whether Mom and Dad were making her or the doctors were failing, it didn't matter. She was letting him go more and more every day, and he had to do something.

He took the knob in hand, balancing Myra over his shoulder.

She whimpered. Her left hand slipped out of her right, and her arms hung as he pulled the door open.

"Justin?" she whispered as they crossed the threshold into the outside world and the heavy humidity of night swallowed them whole.

"Gonna get you help," he whispered back.

"I love you." She didn't open her eyes.

He didn't know if she was awake or talking in her sleep. He only knew it mattered now more than ever that he got her help.

There was a shuffle in the bushes and another behind the sago. Blue eyes twinkled in the darkness, glowing, watching, too many pairs to count—more than last time.

Justin hated them. It meant he had failed.

There was a *clink* sound as the figurine slid from Myra's hand, crashed into the sidewalk, and shattered. Justin didn't notice it until his foot, still bare from his rush out of the house, stepped right on top of jagged ceramic shards.

Everything seemed to happen so fast. He had no control, his body and gravity doing what they wanted and him unable to do anything but watch.

His leg jerked back from the pain, a stream of blood gushing from his sole. Without balance, Myra in his arms, he twisted, she twisted, and they fell.

He was above her, watching the ground come closer. He saw the bright-white concrete step that led to their front door as they sank toward it, as she sank toward it, the back of her head just waiting.

He wanted to scream, but there was no time.

The rear of her small skull cracked into the hard corner. She didn't even whimper. He landed on top of her, and she shook, her bloody head rising and bashing down into it again, a sound that was almost like glass knocking and breaking.

The walkway flooded with red. The step, the path, the doormat. It streamed into the grass and the flowerbed, where the little blue children watched him, their faces melting, their eyes crystal-blue witnesses.

His breath hitched. He couldn't feel anything beyond the swell of sour, burning pain in his gut from an erupting sadness that he would not be able to contain.

It couldn't be. It just couldn't be.

The blue things crept closer.

He knew there was no help, but his arms worked to scoop her up again. This time, it was back into the house. Mom and Dad had to help. They had to.

She streamed blood over his arms and down his front as he carried her into their room and screamed, "Help!"

"Help!" he howled into the moldy room.

Mom and Dad weren't there. He could still see their corpses where they had lain the last time he was in this house after he cracked their heads open just as he did hers. Only now it was ten years later, and all that remained of his family was the pain.

Myra wasn't in his arms anymore. She was by his side, holding his hand. They looked into the empty, dust-covered bed where their parents had slept, where he had murdered them a week after they failed to help him save her.

They were both sorry, but it didn't matter.

The blue things crawled from under the bed and through the window. They came from inside the closet and the bathroom. They crawled from the vent in the ceiling, and they came for Justin.

He could have run, or he could have tried, but inside, he knew he would not have escaped.

Myra gave his hand a gentle tug, and he followed her down to the floor where, together, they sat cross-legged. She held his hand as the blue babies and children climbed into his lap and pried open his mouth. She squeezed his fingers as they ripped open his jaw and reached inside and tore out his tongue and scratched their way into his flesh, eating and crawling inside him.

He cried. For her now and her then. He cried for himself, because this never should have been, and they deserved so *so* much better.

"It's how it should be now," she whispered.

It's how it should be now.

He could taste the blood and their sweet earthy hands inside his mouth, but when he opened his eyes, he didn't see his parents' bedroom. He saw the shaded tree where he had parked by the pasture. The inside of the car melted in lines of shiny blue. In the seat beside him was a basket of blue-capped mushrooms. He had never tried blue-capped mushrooms before, or so he thought. The one on the top of the pile had a big bite mark in it.

A hand reached from the back seat and touched him on the shoulder.

He saw her in the rearview mirror, her face an adorable shade of blue.

Myra asked, "How was it?"

He started the car. "Pretty good."

It had been so long. He was so happy to see her.

Acknowledgements

Thank you to the indie horror community, the readers, reviewers, and authors who hold it all together.

Thank you, Heather Larson, for your superb job editing these stories.

Thank you, Matt Seff Barnes, for creating the amazing cover art.

Thank you, Patrick C. Harrison III, Micah Castle, Robert Essig, Jay Bower, Megan Stockton, Eric Butler, M Ennenbach, and Will Suffer, for allowing your words to make this book the crazy menagerie of horror it has become.

Thank you to the families and friends of each author for your support. Without you, none of us would be able to do any of this.

About the Authors

Patrick C. Harrison III

Patrick C. Harrison III (PC3, if you prefer) is an author of horror, splatterpunk, and all forms of speculative fiction, and his works include *100% Match*, *Grandpappy*, *A Savage Breed*, *5 Tales That Will Land You in Hell*, and *Cerberus Rising* (with Chris Miller and M. Ennenbach), along with other books; and his short stories can be found in numerous anthologies.

Micah Castle

Micah Castle is a weird fiction and horror writer. His stories have appeared in various magazines, websites, and anthologies. He's the author of *Reconstructing a Relationship*, and *The World He Once Knew*.

While away from the keyboard, he enjoys spending time with his wife, playing with his animals, spending time in the woods, and can typically be found reading a book somewhere in his Pennsylvania home.

You can find him at his website: www.micahcastle.com, or on other platforms: www.linktr.ee/micahcastle.

Robert Essig

Robert Essig is the author of *Baby Fights*, *Disco Rice*, *This Damned House* and many more. His novella, *Master of Bodies*, was nominated for a Splatterpunk Award. He has published over 100 short stories and edited three anthologies. He cites discipline and a healthy imagination for his prolific output. Robert lives with his family in east Tennessee.

Jay Bower

Jay Bower is a horror author living outside St. Louis, MO in the forest of Southern Illinois. He spends his time reading, writing, and convincing his wife the dark stories he writes do not involve her.

One time punk-rock skateboarder and heavy metal kid of the 80s, Jay approaches his work with the same indie attitude as those early punk bands.

Megan Stockton

Megan Stockton is an indie author who lives in Grimsley, Tennessee with her two children and her husband, who is an indie filmmaker. She writes in a variety of genres that all have dark/horror elements, and all of her work is character-driven and immersive. She is known for delivering works that are raw, thought-provoking, brutal, and cinematic. She has been writing since she was a child and was always obsessed with horror and the macabre. When she isn't writing (or working her day job) she likes to work with the animals on their farm, read, play video games, and watch movies.

D.W. Hitz

D.W. Hitz is the author of all things Custer Falls, including *Bloodtooth*, *Garrets Lodge*, and *Black Creek Mystic*, as well as other tales like *Food Court of the Damned*. He is a Splatterpunk Award winner for Best Anthology 2023. He loves the outdoors and enjoys making it a background character in his work. He devours stories in all mediums and enjoys writing in the genres of Horror, Supernatural/Paranormal Thriller, and Science Fiction/Fantasy. He aspires to tell stories that thrill the heart and stimulate the imagination.

When not writing, D.W. enjoys spending time with his family, hiking, camping, and playing with the dogs. Stay up to date with D.W. by becoming a member at patreon.com/dwhitz

Eric Butler

Eric Butler does the daily bidding of three huskies, but somehow finds time to write horror fiction. With a twenty-year marriage and a grown son by his side, he won't be running out of material any time soon. His works include The Pope Lick Massacre, The Rest Stop, and The Shadow Within, and his stories can be found in countless anthologies. Eric and his family call North Richland Hills, Texas, their home.

M Ennenbach

M Ennenbach is a poet in Texas. Author of *Cuckoo*, *Hunger on the Chisholm Trail*, and *dreamwhispers*. Co-author of *Bishop 2* with Candace Nola. Member of Cerberus and The Four Horsemen of Texas.

Will Suffer

Will Suffer is a fiend for the dark, disturbing, and mean. He hopes to bring his nightmares into yours with his written words. He has no off time, only existing in front of his writing tools, so he cannot tell you about his life. And you're better off that way.

Find more work by Will Suffer at willsuffer.com

Camp Slasher Lake: Volume Two

A tribute to the glorious slasher movies of the 1980s, Volume 2. Featuring stories from: Jay Bower, Justin Cawthorne, Kay Hanifen, D.W. Hitz, Brett Mitchell Kent, Aaron E. Lee, Kevin McHugh, Carl R. Moore, Daniel R. Robichaud, Darren Todd, & Mark Wheaton.

Camp Slasher Lake: Volume Three

A tribute to the glorious slasher movies of the 1980s, Volume 3.

Featuring stories from: Jonathan Maberry, Will Suffer, MJ Mars, Brian G. Berry, Megan Stockton, Jay Bower, Eric Butler, M Ennenbach, RJ Roles, Angel Van Atta, and D.W. Hitz.

Cody Was Here and Other Stories by D.W. Hitz

Cody Was Here and Other Stories is a chilling collection of works. They range from tales within Hitz's town of Custer Falls, known well from his novels and novellas, to stories of Sci-Fi Horror, Folk Horror, and even a ghost story.

The World He One Knew by Micah Castle

Jay has been uploaded into a new body to investigate why the transporter ship Candlemass went dark fourteen days ago. After the ship's owner gives him the rundown of the assignment, he's quickly ushered on board.

In the halls of the derelict vessel, Jay discovers black sludge coating the inner hull, leading him to a container in the Cargo Bay.

If only he could have stopped there.

The World He Once Knew is a transcendental, sci-fi horror novel set in the distant future. Here, the deceased's consciousness can be bought and uploaded and forced into labor. They can't quit, even if their new lives make them wish they were dead again.

Black Creek Mystic by D.W. Hitz

Nikka's nightmares could spell her end if she doesn't find a cure. The cure could spell her end if she doesn't follow the rules.

Nikka was a pretty normal high school girl until she saw something horrific through her bedroom window. They told her it was a delusion. But whether real or not, the event was stuck in her brain. Now, after years of unrelenting nightmares, Nikka learns of one last hope, a mystic on the outskirts of Custer Falls who might be able to save her from the terrors that are bleeding into her waking life and driving her to self-destruction.

For the promise of a cure, Nikka makes a deal with the witch: one month of work to end her nightmares. But can she stomach doing the witch's tasks? Or are her bad dreams destined to destroy her?

Thank You for Reading